Gardening in the Dark

I0636508

Jennifer Syrkiewicz

chipmunkapublishing
the mental health publisher

Jennifer Syrkiewicz

Published by
Chipmunkapublishing
PO Box 6872
Brentwood
Essex CM13 1ZT
United Kingdom

http://www.chipmunkapublishing.com

Chipmunkapublishing gratefully acknowledge the support of Arts Council England.

Gardening in the Dark

Foreword

I was born in Sheffield, in 1976. I grew up in the countryside in Derbyshire, before venturing to Sussex to attend the university. I was diagnosed with Bipolar Affective Disorder in 2007.

Having a mental illness is a shocking experience. From wondering periodically why I was thought of as 'quirky' or 'different', because of my endless energy, creative ambitions and penchant for trying every new hobby which I could think of, I suddenly became 'mad'. There is a dividing line between the 'sane' and the 'not sane', and I was alarmed to have crossed it.

Over time, I have come to embrace Bipolar Affective Disorder as a part of my life. It does not define me, any more than an epileptic is defined by their seizures. I have learned that it is possible to have Bipolar, without life grinding to a halt. Life is essentially beautiful and kind, for those of us who choose to see it! There are very few challenges which can't be overcome, if we stay positive and lean on the amazing people we all have around us.

These days, I use the upswings of the illness to create, write, study and work. I am a writer, I run a communications business, and work part time as a Counsellor and Hypnotherapist. I have a great marriage, and am happy much more often than I am not.

I wrote 'Gardening in the Dark' because it was a story that needed to be told, before I could get down to the business of pure fiction. In many ways, it is an autobiography, but in equal measure it is the story of all of us, who hold our experiences and our stability in precarious balance.

I would like people to know that it is possible to be fulfilled, happy and strong, regardless of what label they are given, and how their mind chooses to operate. Mental illness affects one in four people on the planet. Perhaps it is time that we started to think of it as being part of 'us', rather than 'them'. This is what I have learned; this is my story.

There's no point trying to identify the characters in 'Gardening', as each person within the book is a purely fictional creation, made up of the traits of some of the wonderful people I am lucky enough to share my life with.

Thank you so much for choosing this novel, and sharing my experiences. I hope it gives you as much pleasure to read as it did me, to write.

Jennifer Syrkiewicz x

Gardening in the Dark

This novel is dedicated to six very important people

To Lydia Dyer, for being so patient and kind, creative and
supportive throughout the writing process.

To John Cooper, with eternal thanks.

To Jeremy Youngman, for his amazing proofreading power, and his
patience.

To my parents, Chris and Terry Marshall, for being the most
beautiful people I have ever met.

To Paul, simply for being perfect, and for the way he keeps the
shadows at bay.

Cover design by Kevin Smith.

Jennifer Syrkiewicz

Gardening in the Dark

'Because an only life can take so long to climb clear of its wrong beginnings.'

Philip Larkin

'Our greatest glory is not in never falling, but in rising every time we fall.'

Confucius

Jennifer Syrkiewicz

Gardening in the Dark

Chapter One

Albert Camus wrote that the only real question a human being has to ask of themselves is: 'Should I live, or should I die?' Before this question is answered, we are unable to progress with life, unable to seize the grass and the smiles and the sunlight, because we are still pondering. Alex was considering this thought in an alcoholic, stumbling sort of way, as she walked down the garden path, after having shut the dog inside, locked the door carefully, and turned off the lights.

She turned away from the gate and looked back at the house, a semi-detached cottage in a Yorkshire village. It looked…nice. Nice in that it had a hanging basket swaying in the evening breeze. Nice, in that whoever lived there obviously took some pride in its upkeep. The windows, protected by Trust regulations, were uneven but clean. Double-glazed carefully to retain the original features. It had been painted recently, and looked proud and orderly, if one could move one's gaze away from the coffee jar overflowing with cigarette butts, or the piles of dog shit concealed by darkness in sludgy clumps in a corner of the lawn. A nice respectable cottage, in a nice respectable village.

Alex turned back to the gate and breathed in slowly. The night air was too crisp, and it hurt her lungs. So. Where was she? Ah, yes, whether or not one should live, or one should die. She squared her shoulders as best she could, heavy as they were with cheap whisky straight from the bottle, and squinted her eyes. What rationality should she apply to this situation? On the plus side, she was thirty-one, attractive, intelligent and well-read. On the negative, life was clawing at her insides begging to be set free, under an overwhelmingly illogical weight of sadness. Recurring sadness. And yet, she could still appreciate the taste of a strongly brewed deep-rust cup of tea, or the smiling heads of large sunflowers, impulse purchases from the flower stall at the railway station. But the sadness, illogical and all-consuming, ate away at her and made her lose her curves; it turned her from being an outgoing, vivacious and eccentric young woman into a bag of sighs.

How does one weigh it up? she wondered voicelessly. She didn't want to cry any more. She didn't want to feel. She didn't want to be continually failing, continually drinking more and more alcohol. She especially didn't want to be inconsiderate any more, hurting her friends and family, begging for an answer for which she couldn't frame a question. And, of course, there was the permanence of this sadness. It wasn't a constant ache, like cold or hunger that went on and on until it was remedied. It was a slow slide which took her by surprise periodically, for no reason.

And, this time, there really was no reason for it. That made it hurt more, seem more overwhelming and all-consuming. There was such sadness in her eyes each morning when she opened them and surveyed herself in the mirror. A sadness which was cloaking, coating, sticky and useless. The *pointlessness* of the sorrow was the problem. The unadulterated oddness of it. She had, essentially speaking, nothing to be sad about. Which meant only that she was destined to be sad, and therefore needed to do something to stop it altogether.

The gate, wooden and jaded, lay beneath her cold hands like a full stop. She moved away from it in order to pull it open. She stood on the other side, taking that step into the world, away from the nice house with the hanging basket and dog turds. She was on the wrong side now. Away from warmth, into uncertainty and the unknown. She looked up at her car, a sleek Jeep which needed washing. It was also a killing machine, designed specifically to bring her relief, a way out. She had collected the materials needed to end her life; it was just a question now of taking the time out to do it in the most considerate way possible. She felt lighter when she thought about the possibilities, lighter since she had made this decision.

The benefits were only visible if one held them up and scrutinised them, like a scientist searching for molecular change in some illuminated Petri dish. Death meant nothing, and nothing was infinitely preferable to the perpetual sadness that she felt. It was becoming a gradual, gnawing, nagging thing which needed to be stopped. Like drinking, or taking drugs, or smoking, it needed to be finished, or conceded to. One or the other.

Gardening in the Dark

Alex chewed her finger thoughtfully. She was outside the gate. The pavement, blurred in darkness, brought to mind the Robert Frost poem, 'The Road not Taken'. But which path was the right one to take? What options were there for someone so sad? She had called the Samaritans that afternoon, getting initial relief from hearing and speaking to a voice which couldn't censor her. But the relief soon gave way to a feeling of guilt and shame at putting another human being, who had evidently made the decision to live, through such a self-absorbed diatribe of misery. She had hung up after pretending that they had solved the problem, rather than ruining their long evening by thinking they had lost someone else to the sadness. Alex shook her head, picturing the woman whom she had spoken to sitting in some office somewhere (which for some reason resembled a classroom in her confused mind), putting the telephone receiver down and feeling pleased with herself for saving another life.

Alex had used up the traditional options. She had trawled the Internet seeking out polite and discrete ways to end one's own life, and had been offered the following: God (she had tried that, it didn't help before and wouldn't now); a link to some other religion which encouraged it; and finally a rather compelling site which stated that if one really wanted to die, one should just do it, stop thinking about it and get on with it, because the world was already overpopulated and for fuck's sake why would you stand and dither? She liked that one.

It was a good point. She had dithered enough over the past three weeks, the time when she imagined the sliding scale into sadness had begun (a few tears, over nothing; playing dark Damien Rice songs over and over again to pull herself down the final few feet into the dark pit, and then alcohol to kick her fully down until she was submerged in it). Then, the thinking. Probably illogical. Certainly compelling, persuasive. She was tired, weary in a way which couldn't be explained away by lack of sleep. She was not hungry or thirsty, unless a craving for the next drink constituted thirst. She didn't want to move, to act, to do anything but sit and stare at nothing and let the music and the alcohol pull her further down, like a seal slipping into night waters and becoming adrift, slippery and sleek.

And so she decided to choose the road less taken. It was a quick decision, accompanied by a sense of relief. It would all soon be over. Alex checked in her pocket for her car keys, and set out to complete the sadness, to ride with it, to give in to it and let it claim her. She took one last look back at the house, safely locked and shrouded in darkness, and then released her hold on the gate and walked forwards into the unknown.

Gardening in the Dark

Chapter Two

The road less taken was arduous work when you were drunk. It involved concentrating very hard on putting one booted foot before the other, and attempting to follow a complicated line. Did the road have to be in a winding line? Alex mused as she focused on taking the necessary steps. Could it not be straight but just unused? The pavement seemed fully used as Alex meandered along it. Chewing gum stuck like little dots all over it, gleaming softly in the street lights' glare. Traffic approached behind her, shining out and illuminating her slight figure, then plunging her into darkness as the cars passed, leaving only two red lights to look at which shattered into shards if Alex screwed up her eyes.

The pavement was too bloody long. Alex was overtaken by ambulances, blaring and blue as they streamed past her, go-faster stripes of squat white which smeared against her vision. Perhaps she should just walk and walk until one day she walked herself right out of the sadness and came out the other side. Or running would be better, to run so fast that she left it behind. She continued to walk. She had decided not to cry any more, as the tears had been a waste of time anyway, time which she did not want, and they served no purpose. Walking was better, walking without crying. She felt a knot of nervousness in her stomach for what she was about to do. Nervousness felt good. Feeling, just as a thing, felt good. It seemed as if she hadn't felt for a very long time, even though the sadness had only lunged at her from above about three weeks ago. Three weeks is a long time to feel sad, if you do nothing but sit inside the sadness and let it weigh you down until you can't move any more.

So, on the plus side stood walking. Feeling nervous. On the negative side stood effort, the cold, the sadness. She felt as if she was walking with more weight than usual, as if she had to carry the misery along with her like a leaden cloud on her head, or a shroud about her shoulders. But, all that was immaterial as the decision had been made. She was not going to cry any more. A man in a too-large leather coat loomed up in front of her, and then was gone. Her body responded sluggishly, as Alex felt fear only after the man had returned into the darkness. It made her smile, if only in a detached kind of way. Funny that the body will respond predictably to life, even when the mind has decided to shun it. That Alex could feel fear was a plus. Fear was excitement, just with a different aim. It felt the same. She searched inside herself, trying to remember a time when she had been excited about something. The recollection evaded her. However, her nervousness was growing with each step she took, pushing the misery to one side in order to take over her body fully. She enjoyed it. It was an abstract, useless feeling, but at least it was there.

Eventually, her feet slowed, and she approached a building. It was squat, built with brown brick, and illuminated too much, so that when she stared at it in fear the brightness made her eyes hurt. She walked up to the entrance, stepped back, then walked around the corner and sat down on her haunches against the wall.

"This wall is where I'm supposed to be just now," Alex mumbled to herself. She reached into her pocket to pull out some cigarettes and a lighter. She carefully smoked a cigarette down to the last section, hoping that she would not be seen. She needed to think, but when she tried to sort out the jumble of fears and thoughts in her mind, nothing seemed to make any sense. But she had come this far. She was ready. She stood up again, brushed herself down, and walked once more to the glass doors which separated her from the lights inside.

Alex hesitated as she looked through the doors into the room. Inside was almost empty, with the exception of four people sitting in twos along the wall. She hadn't thought this far ahead and suddenly felt unsure. The other road, the travelled path, felt suddenly safer, sleepier, and more secure. She paused at the entrance, and the automatic doors opened for her like an invitation as she stepped forwards cautiously. It was terribly quiet inside. There was a walled reception desk, with an elderly woman in stern glasses peering at pieces of paper then tapping into a computer screen. Alex approached the desk with an overwhelming sense of trepidation.

"Be brave," she said to herself, and her body responded by pumping out all the blood from her arms and legs and making her heart hammer. "Bastard body," she whispered, as she used her will instead to propel forward until she could place her two index fingers on the smooth white of the reception desk.

"Hello," she said, and the woman looked up, bored and irritable, for it was past midnight and Alex certainly didn't look as if she was an emergency.

"Can I help you?" the woman asked, her voice reflecting the expression on her face. Alex paused. She didn't know the answer, so was not sure how to respond.

"I'm going crazy," she said, the words apologetic. "And I want someone to help me with that," she concluded. The sentence was all wrong, but how was she supposed to articulate the truth? The woman, surprisingly, accepted it.

"What's your name, your address?" she asked, as if people wandered in to the Accident and Emergency department every evening and announced themselves in a similar vein. Alex supplied the details, and the woman asked her to take a seat. Alex hesitated.

"Is it OK to come here, for that?" she enquired politely. The woman nodded, and smiled suddenly.

"Of course," she said, inclining her head and considering Alex fully for the first time. "Of course it is." With that, she motioned towards the rows of plastic chairs to the left of the reception, and continued tapping on the keyboard, studying the screen. Alex walked backwards in a half-stumble, and then went to sit on a chair. She selected one right in the middle of the room, as if that were somehow safer, and surreptitiously looked at the two couples who shared the vast white space.

The first couple were so obviously a mother and daughter, that Alex almost smiled. The younger woman was a miniature clone of her parent, as if the mother had reproduced asexually like a strawberry plant, borrowing no genes from any male supplier. They both shared beaked noses, light brown hair in wide curls, and pale faces. Alex couldn't work out which was ill, why they may be here. Perhaps they both were, being so similar. Perhaps if one caught something, the other developed it too, because their DNA was the same? They were chatting together very quietly, laughing together, and Alex turned away, feeling the sadness again with fresh apprehension.

The second couple were more difficult to feel at ease with. A young couple, in their late teens, sitting next to each other, the young man busy and annoyed. His wrist, pouring out blood. It made Alex's knees wobble when she considered it. Dark brown and bright red liquid had oozed all over his cuff, crisp now in places, seeping in others. Bodies are fragile, she thought to herself. It's easy to let them go.

Alex turned to the wall on her left, where there was a large flat-screen television suspended above the chairs in the waiting room. There was no sound, but a ticker-tape bar ran across the bottom, reminding Alex of the things she needed to know, accompanied by suitable images and narrative. Alex stared at it as it doled out advice to her, piece by piece:

'Don't forget your 'flu jab!'

'The correct way to wash your hands'

'Safety for Guy Fawkes night'

'MRSA – what you need to know'

Just as Alex feared that the information reel was about to come a full circle and reiterate the same advice, she heard her name called at the other side of the room. A man with a clipboard stood in front of some wide swing doors which sealed off the waiting area from the rest of the hospital. Alex's stomach lurched somewhere up near her throat, and she stood up unsteadily.

She followed the man as he walked through the double doors and held them open for her. He was smiley and young, a big round face that grinned at her, eyes twinkling.

Gardening in the Dark

"And what can I do for you, this evening?" he asked kindly. Alex walked in to the little room and sat down, lacing her fingers in her lap. It was too bright.

"I have no idea," she said. Her voice came out in a croak, and so she coughed and tried again. "I want some help, please," she asked. The nurse nodded and pulled a piece of paper towards him, and reached for his clipboard and pen.

"What do you need help with?" he asked her carefully, looking at Alex's face, meeting her eyes. She looked down quickly.

"I want to be dead and I'm frightened of myself," she said. The words were uncertain, as she had not spoken them aloud before, and she was unsure about how they would sound. Unperturbed, the nurse put down his clipboard and looked at her again.

"When did you last eat?"

"I don't know."

"How much have you had to drink?"

"I don't know."

"Do you want to harm yourself?"

"Yes," she replied, although this answer didn't seem to be the right one.

The man scribbled down some notes and asked her if she'd mind waiting. Alex said she wouldn't (after all, she only had one thing to do, and that could be delayed indefinitely). She genuinely didn't mind sitting in the reception area, watching people come and go, and letting her drooping head lose its weight by dropping to her chest.

Back in the waiting room, Alex found the same chair and sat down. She was mildly perturbed to find that the teenage couple seemed to migrate towards her. The young man stood up and bought something to eat from the snack dispenser against the wall, then came and sat right beside Alex, away from his partner. The girl stood up after a few minutes had elapsed. She quietly bought some coffee in a brown plastic cup, and joined him. Alex frowned and shrank into herself. She did not want to be in close proximity to other people. Not that it mattered, but she couldn't find it in herself to swap pleasantries, to smile back if someone chose to smile at her. It didn't happen. In the end, the couple fidgeted and changed seats, walking to the entrance, standing outside and then returning. The young man walked up to the reception desk and started shouting at the woman with glasses, who turned on her heel and locked herself in the little room behind the desk. Alex moved her head towards the large screen in the corner. It was flashing up adverts again.

'Don't forget your 'flu jab!'

'The correct way to wash your hands'

'Safety for Guy Fawkes night'

'MRSA – what you need to know'

Alex spent about two hours waiting, watching, and drooping. Perhaps she could stay here, she mused to herself, whenever the sadness proved to be too much to deal with. She would be safe, and she could survive quite well. There was a place to sleep, somewhere to sit, and a big screen. She walked up to the reception desk shyly and caught the woman's attention.

"Do you mind if I stand outside and have a cigarette?" she asked. The woman looked up, confused.

"Of course not." She seemed to be laughing at her, for her politeness. Alex turned and walked away. She went outside, and returned to her previous place against the wall. There were 'No Smoking' signs dotted everywhere, so Alex retreated around the corner and squatted on her haunches again. Her previous cigarette was still on the ground, crushed and creased into a little stub. She smoked methodically, then added her new cigarette end to the old one, and returned inside. The doors hushed open, light flooded out, and she returned to her seat.

Gardening in the Dark

"Alexandra?"

She started as her name was called, the angry name that was usually saved for trouble. This time, there was an older male doctor standing in the doorway. She followed him through the doors again, to another room. She started shaking, a low vibration that began in her stomach and radiated outwards. He asked her all the same questions that the nurse had, and Alex felt somewhat frustrated with him. She answered them all again, more quietly.

"Would you like me to ask our duty psychiatrist to come and speak with you, Alexandra?" the man asked. Alex shrugged.

"Is that what is supposed to happen?" she asked, confused. The man nodded.

"Yes."

"Yes, then. Please. Thank you."

"OK. I'll leave you here, and we'll get someone to come down and talk to you." And, with that, he was gone. Alex looked at her feet. She was wearing a brown corduroy skirt with buttons down the front, a blue jumper with a large baggy cowl neck, cinched at the waist, and her brown boots. She wondered briefly if she looked like a mad person, or just someone who was rather tired. She wasn't sure what she felt, so dropped the entire thought process and continued to stare at her boots. Outside the room, people walked up and down, speaking in hushed voices. A woman somewhere was crying, and Alex welcomed the sound because it meant that there was someone else, outside the room, feeling the same way as she was, someone who knew how to articulate the sadness. She felt envious. Alex moved her gaze around the floor, which was immaculately clean with no scuff-marks on it.

She looked up as a young woman with cropped blonde hair and casual clothes slipped in to the little room, her blue eyes concealed by an over-large pair of glasses. She had a lovely, smiling face.

"Alex?" the woman asked. She pulled out a chair with wheels and perched on it when Alex nodded. The woman was fashionable in an understated way, with no jewellery, just the large brown-rimmed glasses that worked to make her eyes bigger. She had a wide smile, with neat even teeth that made Alex feel more relaxed. She seemed easy to trust.

"I have some information here about you, that you told the staff this evening," the woman began. "And it sounds as if you are feeling very unhappy. Is that right?"

Alex nodded, her eyes cast down to her boots again.

The woman covered the same questions, and Alex found that answering them became easier on the third go, like practising a particularly difficult piece on the clarinet which improves each time you play it. Like the clarinet, her voice garnered strength and she began to find herself speaking more articulately, warming to her theme like an unused instrument reed which suddenly finds itself being picked up and tongued; licked into submission.

"When did you last have something to eat?"

"I don't know. I can't remember."

"How much have you had to drink?"

"I'm not sure. But I'm not drunk now," Alex said, suddenly wishing with a gnawing feeling that she were. The woman nodded thoughtfully. "I can see that. You don't seem drunk to me," she commented. Alex squirmed a little, shifting in her seat.

"Do you want to harm yourself?"

"No," she replied, this time with certainty. "I just want to be dead."

This, then, made sense. It was a stark sentence, and Alex felt a huge degree of relief as she spoke it aloud, without embarrassment. It opened something up inside her, as if someone had reached in and flicked a switch, and suddenly she could not stop herself talking. The words flowed on and on and Alex settled herself back in the plastic chair and watched them roll out, suddenly feeling a degree of contentment. The woman before her was paid to hear this. It was her job, and she would do something magical and then it would all be over.

"I want to be dead so much that I think about it all the time. I want to be cleanly, discretely dead in a way which doesn't cause any distress to anyone at all. I want to be a polite dead person, suddenly vanished, suddenly unfeeling. I want to be dead as if I am deeply asleep, as if I am swimming in nothing."

"Have you thought about how you will achieve this?" the woman asked, conversationally. Alex looked at her, feeling her cheeks suddenly flush with something akin to embarrassment or shame. This was rather personal.

"Yes," she answered, because of course she had nothing left to lose, and this woman was going to help her. Or not help her, which in itself would be a great help as then at least Alex could be sure that her chosen path led to nowhere, and she could safely and easily pick the other route knowing that she had exhausted all possible other paths.

"How will you do it?" the woman enquired. Alex took a deep breath, tasting the stale air, and then answered.

"I think the car is the best way. I think that the cleanest way is to shut all the windows, except the one by the driver's side, and use the exhaust with a long tube. And then stuff a fleece or a rug or something in the gap in the window. Put some nice music on, something quiet, and fall asleep and breathe the fumes in and out until I am asleep and then dead. Dead," she said. It felt good to say the word aloud, this ultimate taboo that was worse than saying the word 'fuck' at the top of your voice in the middle of an opera.

"Dead," she said again, and something about it, flat and lifeless, made her suddenly smile. The woman smiled too, as if she kind of *got* Alex. As if she had played the game at some point or another, and then decided to win it, rather than lose.

"Right," she said. "Thank you for telling me." Alex inclined her head dismissively. 'It's nothing' her gesture said, but of course that was the opposite of the truth. It was everything, this opening up, this sudden honesty.

The woman fired a number of questions at Alex, and she answered all of them. She understood questions; it was like being at a job interview, and Alex always got the job. Tell me about when it first started, tell me a bit about your current situation, tell me something about your background, and tell me if this feeling of sadness has happened before? Tell me what you did the last time? Have you ever tried to harm yourself before? Alex answered quickly and honestly. The woman watched Alex for a moment, and smiled.

"I'm not sure what the right thing to do is," she said, and Alex suddenly felt her youth, her inexperience. She understood that this woman was talking to her as if she was a human being, because she was hearing her. Alex suddenly felt an immense sense of relief, and began to cry, whilst still watching the woman and hearing what she was saying.

"I want to take you to a safe place, so that you can be with people, so that you won't be able to do anything to harm yourself. Because if I don't do that, I'll worry about you. Is that OK with you?" the woman asked. She moved her head to one side, waiting for Alex to answer. Alex really believed that this was a choice. She nodded.

"Yes," she said. "Thank you." With that, the woman smiled and nodded.

"OK. I'm going to leave you here for a few minutes, and I'm going to get you a bed sorted out for what is left of the night. Then, I'm going to send you to another part of the hospital with a security guard who can show you the way. He'll take you inside. Someone will meet you there. Then, I'm going to come and see you and make sure you are settled in. Is that OK with you?" she asked again.

Alex nodded her response, and then spoke. "Yes. Thank you."

Gardening in the Dark

The woman smiled again, and ducked out of the room. She had left her handbag on the floor, and Alex looked at it while she sat in the chair. It was an unambiguous handbag, with a large silver clasp. It looked exactly right for the woman. If someone had met her, and been asked to draw a bag which would fit her, embody her, this handbag would be it. It was young, fresh, and uncomplicated. It was an empathic warm brown colour which instinctively inspired trust; it was not ostentatious. It was simply a bag. Alex warmed to it. She continued to sit for a few minutes, and looked at the wall. There was a poster depicting parts of the body, showing organs and bones, and stating what a human being needed to do to take care of each part. Alex looked away. She was not interested in this. She looked back at the bag. She started as a young man hesitated at the entrance to the room, pulling open the concertina door.

"Alexandra?" he asked, and Alex nodded, claiming ownership of the rather long name. "Would you like to follow me?"

Alex stood unsteadily and walked after the man, who paused to let her exit through the main entrance. She passed her nurse on the way through, and he grinned at her and nodded, as if he was pleased to see her leave with someone. She smiled back, a thin pulling of lips over dry teeth, and hoped it was enough to thank him for being normal and kind. She wondered if he understood.

The two passed out of the main entrance of the hospital, and the man paused so Alex could light a cigarette, and then they began to walk. The silence between them was palpable, uncomfortable, and Alex felt like filling it but was too tired to think of anything to say.

"It's cold," the man said, opening up a conversation. Alex nodded agreement, and pulled on her cigarette. It felt familiar and comforting to smoke.

"Yes," she said, blowing the smoke out in front of her and seeing it rise. She wanted desperately to ask where they were going, but couldn't form the words in case the answer scared her. Finally, after about a five-minute walk which felt much longer, the man paused at a wrought-iron gate, and held his hand out to her, palm upwards, letting her know that she should stop walking. He pushed a button by the side of the gate, and it swung open with a soft click. Alex looked up, suddenly completely daunted, and saw a building like an old house, a mansion, in front of her. She didn't like the gate, didn't know enough of what was ahead of her to feel entirely comfortable with walking through it and leaving herself behind. She paused, scared, and looked at the man. He smiled.

"It's all right," he reassured her, young and gruff. For some reason she accepted the phrase and continued to follow him.

Together, they walked purposefully through a dark wooden panelled door, with a worn round brass knob, and entered an old building with a floor laid with brown tiles in a mosaic pattern. Alex scrunched up her nose. The building smelled like a library. They walked up some stairs together, and Alex became aware of her legs, which were leaden and shaking. She looked down at a blue carpet with stains swirled into a pattern, and then the carpet changed to red, as Alex was focusing on her boots and making sure they propelled her forwards.

A woman with mid-length brown hair let them in through a glass door with bars across it, and Alex noticed that the staircase banister had a thick plastic screen below it, in case people fell over. The door was messily littered with posters and notices. And then she was inside, and a woman was there screaming at Alex that she needed to go out for a cigarette, and a man was shuffling backwards and forwards with too-long hair and a house-coat, like something that Oscar Wilde would wear draped about his shoulders, over striped pyjamas.

"Oh, God," she breathed, quietly, and though she hadn't meant to say it out loud it made the woman in charge turn and look at her, smile, and take her hand, leading her past the shouting woman, around the corner to a little room.

"You'll be sleeping in here tonight, Alexandra," she said, and Alex flinched. "I'm afraid we don't have any beds free, but we can put you up in here until the morning so you can get some sleep."

Gardening in the Dark

Alex looked at the room. It was small and white and almost clean, with a camp bed in it and a small mattress. Someone had put two cotton sheets and a blanket on top, and even folded the corner of it back for her to climb into. She nodded her response. She felt terrified. Taking the other road would have made her feel more as if she were taking control. This road felt as if she were drowning, lost adrift on a big sea of water and not sure which direction to take.

She was told to sit down, and Alex selected one of the chairs because the bed would mean lying down and that felt too vulnerable. The woman slipped out of the room. Alex made herself small and tight in the corner and sat in silence, looking around her. The room was empty save for a tissue box, and three chairs, and the funny camp bed with the blankets. Alex stared at everything. The window was stained glass and partially ajar, with a five-centimetre gap, but had wooden blocks nailed into it to make sure it couldn't be opened up fully. Alex started to be more aware of where she was, but it didn't matter. She couldn't feel, so nothing mattered. She rocked slightly, for something to do, reminding herself to stop and pull herself more upright when someone came in.

The blonde psychiatrist was there again, in the doorway, and Alex looked at her, in fear.

"Hello, again!" the woman exclaimed, as if surprised to see Alex. "I need to check how you are physically, then I am going to leave you with Susan, who will look after you from now on," she said. Once again, Alex welcomed her forthright way of speaking. It all seemed very clear. The woman took a stethoscope and listened to Alex's front and back, asking her to breathe. She then took her pulse, and Alex looked down at the woman's hand holding her own, and studied it, aware that her heart was pounding. There was a tussle with a blood-pressure cuff, and then Alex was left alone for a moment.

Susan returned, and told Alex to climb under the covers and get some sleep. With that, Alex unzipped her boots and sat on the bed, moving into the top corner so she would feel a little safer, and covered herself with a blanket. The little bed creaked and groaned, and Alex bit her lip trying to stay as quiet as possible.

Susan offered her a drink, which Alex declined, then turned the light down to a tiny glow and left her.

"I'll be back to see you every five minutes," she said. "But I'll be as quiet as possible."

Alex nodded and turned her face to the wall. She wondered if she had made a mistake. If she had taken the other road, the dead road, she would be feeling nothing now. Instead, she was feeling small, confused, scared, alone and terribly muddled up. She did not feel tired. She studied the chairs, picking out a crude diamond pattern which moved about as she stared at it. Her eyes traced the irregular cracks in the walls; cracks which showed the building's age. She listened to the shouts of the woman who wanted a cigarette, and then she examined the tissue box carefully.

'Clean hands

Reduce the spread of infection'

The yellow box stated on its side. Alex considered this. Was it one statement, or two? There was no punctuation to give her more information. Was it telling her that clean hands make it less likely that infection is spread, or giving her both the command to clean her hands, and the one to reduce the spread of infection? She played the words over and over again in her mind and couldn't reach a conclusion. Susan popped her head around the door, which creaked loudly. Alex glanced up, Susan looked at her, and then she was gone.

'Clean hands reduce the spread of infection' she read again. And then she closed her eyes, and sat thoughtlessly until the light from the window grew gradually brighter and it was obviously daylight. It was five, then six, then seven o'clock, and every five minutes Susan stuck her head around the door to make sure that Alex was still alive. And she was, in a numb automatic kind of a way, and that was surely the road less taken?

Gardening in the Dark

Chapter Three

Ally was cleaning, her small hands circling the neck of a brass vase. She had rubbed the Brasso into the unforgiving surface, working the liquid dexterously into the very pattern of the metal, and now she was polishing it off. She liked Brasso, the strange ammonia-tinged metal tang of it, the way it glugged inside the bottle when she tipped it this way and that. She liked the smear of it on a clean cloth, the application, and the wait for it to dry to a crisp film. Polishing brass, however, was not as good as silver. Silver gleamed more, reflecting Ally's face in each piece. It looked *done* afterwards, so that it was obvious how much effort had been put in. 'Elbow grease', as her mother called it. You could measure out elbow grease in minutes, in the amount of polishing that had been expended. As Ally rubbed the last vase to a shine, she imagined how they would package elbow grease. In a small round pot, like Nivea moisturiser? Or, in a spray like Mr. Sheen furniture polish? It would smell like dripping. You would rub it into things, and they would be left with a lardy tinge. Not a shine.

Ally sat back on her haunches and looked at all the brass which marched across the mantelpiece like a parade. First, the two vases which had faded red and blue patterning on them. Then, a small bowl with a mesh lid, which caught the Brasso and held on to it, no matter how hard Ally tried to rub it to a shine. After the bowl, a large round plate depicting some scene from a Dickensian Inn. The men on it, bearded and static, raised their tankards to drink to some unknown toast. Ally refused to polish the plate fully, knowing that she would make it worse by dripping Brasso into the ridges. After the plate, another, smaller vase, similar to the other two but without the pattern. Finally, on the far end of the mantelpiece, a picture frame with no picture inside. The silver, overall, was much better. The sideboard was used to display all the pieces. There was a funny sort of cake stand thing that opened up like butterfly wings. There were vases, a candlestick (which Mother called a 'Candelabra', a word that made James and Ally snigger behind discreet hands), and other numerous odds and ends.

There were shelves under the mantelpiece, one of which housed a series of black irons. Ally didn't like the irons because their surfaces were matt and, unless she plunged them into hot soapy water, they refused to shine. If they had been hers, she would have painted them with clear nail varnish. She looked at them now, all pointing in the same direction. There was not much point in polishing them. The third shelf housed books, which collected too much dust and were not worth reading. The print was too small, even for Ally who was normally happy enough to read anything she could get her hands on. The books were also too heavy, which meant she couldn't sneak them in to her bedroom and hide them to read under the covers when she was supposed to be sleeping.

It had all been polished, now. Ally looked at it with something akin to satisfaction, but close to relief. She stood up quickly, gathering the rags she had used, and placed the lid carefully back on the Brasso. She walked towards the kitchen, looking down at the tired brown carpet in the living room as she went. She took care to tread on the most worn areas, where the traffic of feet had pushed the pile into disconsolate smooth surfaces, instead of the plush deep chocolate to be found under the sofa, or in the corner by the dining table. She entered the kitchen, put the rags in the washing machine, the Brasso back in the cupboard, and then returned to the living room. It smelled unusually clean, with lemony polish vying to overpower the fumy stench of the Brasso and the sharp smell of vinegary window-cleaner. Ally had polished the mantelpiece, dusted the coffee tables, and wiped down the dining table. She had taken all the silver off the sideboard and then replaced it in the right order when it had been cleaned. She had dusted and polished her way around the brown room, even down to the wooden stairs which snaked up the side of the wall. She had taken everything out, cleaned it, and put it back again. She stood in the centre of the living room and surveyed her work. All that was left was the vacuuming, and then she would be done. She could go in to her bedroom and play, read, or hide in the wardrobe and pretend she was somewhere else. Maybe, go outside and bicycle up and down the street, maybe even meet up with Caroline and they could go to the den.

Ally turned as her mother wandered into the living room and established herself, prostrate, along the sofa. She seemed in a quiet mood, not speaking, just interested in watching the television

Gardening in the Dark

and smoking cigarettes which she flicked into a glass ashtray balanced on her stomach. Tiger tried to jump up on to her legs, but she frowned and pushed him away irritably. Ally eyed her as she smoked, thinking how elegant it looked. Her mother would inhale the smoke luxuriously, and then breathe it out with a gasp. The smoke started out a light grey, like pigeon down, but when it had been inside and then came out again, it had more of a brown tinge. Ally wanted to be like her mother, lying elegantly across the sofa like someone in a film. She cleared her throat and looked at Maggie.

"Shall I do the vacuuming now, or leave it for later?" she asked. There was no one answer she would prefer. To leave it meant instant freedom, but to do it meant that it was over and done with. Ally didn't feel overly comfortable about Maggie being there; when she had to vacuum around mother. It would mean she would be watched, and that was a sensation Ally preferred not to have. Maggie stared at the television, not looking at her daughter.

"Do it now," she said, and Ally nodded and went through to the hall cupboard to get the cleaner. The hall was oblong with a bright red carpet, a vivid red that grew darker if you dragged your stockinged foot across the pile the wrong way. It cleaned well, showing the tracks of the wheels and brush where it had been sucked into clean submission. It was one of Ally's favourite parts of the house. She liked it most because of the hall cupboard. Mother called it the 'cloak cupboard', which conjured up images of pagan rituals and daggers. In fact, it was much more appealing than that. The hall cupboard looked innocent when you first pulled open the door. It was full to bursting with coats of all sizes and shapes: furs, parkas, waterproofs and jackets. It looked impenetrable, but Ally knew from much experience that a nine-year-old girl with skinny shoulders could slip between the giant fur on the left and the grey army coat, and disappear behind them.

There was magic behind the coats. Like the gateway to Narnia, it held endless space. There was another hanging rack behind the first, with an area behind that again, which was completely boxed off by the first row of jackets. Best of all, if Ally clambered her way up through the pockets and shoulders of the coats, she could make her way to the top shelf, and curl up there. The top shelf had blankets on it; pale pink and blue waffle, with silk trims. They smelled of dust, a warm fuzzy scent that made Ally feel instantly sleepy and safe. Though there was no window in the cupboard, Ally was right up close to the bare light bulb which swung in the centre of the ceiling. Sometimes, James, her older brother, would walk past the outside of the cupboard and flick the light switch off, leaving her stranded in a darkness so thick Ally imagined it had been knitted around her like the blankets. She didn't mind being left in the dark. If James turned the light off, she would curl up in silence and lie on the top shelf, waiting for him to turn it back on. Sometimes he would turn it back on, out of frustration at getting no response, or curiosity to see if she was, in fact, elsewhere. If he didn't, she would slither her way down the furs, sensual and cool against her skin, and climb through to the front, and out again. The cupboard was her favourite place bar one in the house.

Ally pulled the door open, and lifted out the vacuum cleaner from behind the layer of coats. It was a tall monstrosity, in beige plastic. It was hard to push; you had to tilt it to the right angle to get it to move from one room to the next. Vacuuming was one of Ally's least favourite jobs. She leaned back with the cleaner and dragged it into the lounge. Maggie was still on the sofa, laughing at something on the television. Ally was not looking forward to disturbing her. She pulled the cleaner to the top end of the living room, and started to unwind the cable. Maggie did not look up. Ally plugged it in at the switch by the irons. Maggie carried on laughing. Ally walked back to the cleaner, used the foot pedal to tilt the shaft, and turned it on. Maggie stopped laughing as if she could feel the electric current which had shot through the vacuum cleaner, bringing it to life. Ally noticed that her mother had started to frown, and turned her back on Maggie to vacuum under the sideboard. The noise was horrendous. The machine emitted a low purring sonorous groan which alternated pitch depending on whether Ally was pushing it forwards, or dragging it back. It smelled of cat and dust. She hated it.

The top section finished, Ally started on the middle part. This was going to be tough, as Maggie was watching her intently, all of her attention focused on Ally dragging and pushing the cleaner back and forth. The carpet changed colour under the brushes of the machine, and Ally tried to make stripes like they did on football pitches with the mower. She imagined the Hoover sucking at the top of the carpet, chopping it shorter. She pulled and pushed more quickly, the cumbersome appliance making her start to pant and sweat. Maggie watched, her frown deepening. Ally tensed as she came within reach of Maggie's arm, which was waving in the air, holding a partially smoked cigarette. Nothing happened. Ally reached the end of the room, opened the living room door to get to the red carpet in the hall, did some of that, and then turned the Hoover off and brought it back to the centre of the lounge. She unplugged it carefully, and the television sound became more prominent, as if the vacuum cleaner had pushed the noise to the side of the room, then allowed it back in again to the middle.

Ally took the wire and wound it up and over the top of the cleaner, backwards and forwards on the two hooks along the length of it. She took the plug and pulled it through the loop. It was immaculate, as was the living room which now looked somehow newer than it had before. Ally dragged the cleaner back to the hall, pulling it through the door.

"Alexandra!" Maggie called to her. Ally sighed and left the machine, popping her head back around the living room door. Someone on the television was discussing a recipe for cheese fondue. Maggie waited until Ally was fully in the room, and then smiled. Reaching out her hand, the one which held the ashtray on her stomach, Maggie took the ashtray and upended it in the middle of the carpet. Grey ash flew up in the air, and tan cigarette butts fell rapidly downwards on to the carpet. The whole mess sat in a circle in the centre of the floor. Ally's mouth dropped in surprise.

"You missed a bit," Maggie said, and turned to watch the television again. She was smiling a little. Ally felt her insides screw up into a hard tight ball of frustration and humiliation. She returned to the hall, took the cleaner, and dragged it back to the centre of the room. She plugged it in again and took the nozzle from the side of it, to suck up the cigarette butts. They flew into the bag somewhere. Ally hoped that one was still smouldering, that she could burn the house down with Maggie inside it. If that happened, she could run away and never be caught. Maggie watched as Ally completed the ritual of unwinding and winding the wire again. She was enjoying herself, her veined nose pink with pleasure. Ally seethed quietly, determined not to say a word to add to her mother's enjoyment.

Ally returned to the hall with the cleaner, and tucked it back behind the layer of coats. She looked up at the top shelf with longing. She would like to shut herself in and climb up there, and maybe take the book she had been reading. "Maybe later," she told the cupboard, and turned away from the hiding place and back to the living room.

James was coming down the stairs, and Ally watched him as he bounced down them two at a time. He didn't seem scared of the stairs; not as she was. They were just pieces of wood polished and varnished to a gloss, and they had no backs to them. Ally was afraid of the stairs, because they were slippery and sometimes James would lie in wait for her beneath them, a sly hand reaching out and grabbing at her legs to make her fall. The stairs twisted when they hit the bottom of the wall, turning around to release their passenger into the centre of the living room. James had a cloth in one hand, the furniture polish in the other.

"Finished," he said to Maggie, who grunted something at the television in response. Ally scowled from a distance. It wasn't fair. James only had to do the easy jobs, like the bathroom and bedrooms. Ally had the kitchen, a minefield of hidden dirt and concealed oil and mildew, and the living room with the brass and silver. James always got the good cleaning jobs. She bet he hadn't bothered to change the duvet in their parents' room, either. That was a tough job for Ally, who had to take a corner of the duvet and climb into the case with it until she found her way up to the ends. It took a very long time, and sometimes Ally would forget what she was doing and fall asleep inside.

"Ally, get me a drink," Maggie said, suddenly turning to look at her daughter, who was busy scowling at James. James swaggered over to the armchair and sat down in it, looking at the television.

"And one for me," James added, without looking at her. Ally snorted and moved forward to the kitchen again, taking down a glass from the shelf. The kitchen was a pleasant room, most of the time. The walls were papered with a small orange floral print, tiny flowers repeating again and again. Ally knew it by heart, could close her eyes and conjure it up. The units were made of a dark wood, and a scrubbed and worn pine table with two benches monopolised the centre of the room. The kitchen housed the hot water tank in an airing cupboard, an old microwave with oil spills and grease caked around the sides, and the oven which Ally detested because it was so hard to clean. The sink lay under the kitchen window affording a view of the back garden, the rabbit cages, and the field behind. The whole was framed by impressively brooding hills which looked like faces if you half-closed your eyes and stared at them for long enough.

Ally turned back to the glass. She reached into the freezer and retrieved the ice cube tray, which stuck to her fingers for a second as she prized the cubes out. She put them in the glass, returned the tray, and reached up for the bottle of vodka, which was three-quarters full. She poured a generous measure into the tumbler, and then filled the cap with some of the fiery liquid before drinking it down. It made her throat burn and her eyes smart, but for some reason she liked it. It made her feel grown-up like Maggie, and gave her something which James couldn't know about. She quickly topped the glass up with tonic water, and took a rapid swig from the bottle to soothe the burning of the vodka. With that, the drink was done. She carried it carefully back into the living room, navigating around the cat who wanted to rub his soft purring body around Ally's legs. She pulled the smallest coffee table from the nest beside the sofa, and placed the glass down.

"Thanks," her mother said, and Ally nodded a response before sitting down in the chair opposite to her brother. She looked at the television. It was 'Blockbusters', one of her favourite programmes. She liked the prizes, and the way a single person could win against two if they were good enough. The music started and she settled back in the chair to watch. Maggie was sitting up, her feet tucked beneath her, the cat sitting warily nearby right on the edge of the sofa. James was folding and refolding the edge of his T-shirt, bored. He didn't like quizzes on television, listening to Maggie and Ally as they vied against each other to get the answers right. He wished it were still early afternoon, so he could watch the wrestling. He was bored. He stood up and left the room, going to his bedroom where he could watch what he liked.

Ally watched Bob Holness. He looked like a nice man, someone whom you would want as your dad, or your grandfather. He always looked freshly laundered and pressed, and terribly proper. His voice, the sentence structure of the questions, enthralled Ally. She liked them because they made her feel clever, and gave her an opportunity to demonstrate her cleverness, which always seemed to please Maggie.

"What P –" began Mr. Holness, and Ally leaned forward eagerly. Maggie paused in the inhalation of a new cigarette, the vodka glass perched precariously in the crook of her free hand.

"– means a word, phrase or sentence which reads the same backwards or forwards?" finished Bob. Maggie looked at Ally expectantly.

"Palindrome?" Ally answered at the same time as the contestant, a slight young man in a bad shirt and tie, offered the same response.

"Get me another drink, Ally?" Maggie requested. Ally nodded and stood up. She reached for the glass and Maggie supplied it, empty except for the ice cubes shrinking in the bottom as if they were shy. She made another vodka, using the same ritual. With a swig of the tonic, she completed the drink and carried it back in to her mother.

"What B –" asked Bob Holness, and Ally took the opportunity to walk through the living room and into her bedroom. Maggie would be busy for a while, drinking and smoking and watching the programme. Ally probably had at least half an hour before Maggie wanted something. She padded over to the bed in her socks and sat down on it. Half an hour. She could spend it absorbed in a book, listening to a tape, or doing something else. She knew she had to be sure not to spend too much time thinking about it, because half an hour could spin away and disappear in a heartbeat, leaving you having done nothing but ponder how it should be spent.

Ally considered her room. It was very, very messy. She jumped slightly as she heard the door being pushed open, but relaxed again when she saw Tiger's striped head peeking around the skirting board.

"Come on, then," she said, and Tiger came into the room, sedate and lean. He jumped up onto the unmade bed and pawed at Ally's leg ponderously. She pushed him away.

"What are we going to do with the leftover time?" she asked Tiger. He ignored her, true to form. Ally looked back at the room. It was an unpleasant place, on the whole. The brown carpet was patterned with huge splotches of colour, which, in all their garishness, failed to disguise the ingrained filth residing within it. The furniture was an odd assortment of mismatched items: a pale brown suede sofa which had seen better days (Ally seemed to remember it used to live in the living room), and a white wardrobe made out of some kind of MDF or melamine, with a floral pattern etched on to the top of it (the wardrobe was not nice to look at, but Ally could sit either inside it, or on top, and be relatively well hidden). The bed was a simple mattress on a platform, with no headboard, and next to the bed was a shelf, painted white, which housed Albert, Ally's solitary goldfish. Albert was Albert VI, the preceding five Alberts having been consumed by Tiger over the course of the past eight months or so. In the corner of the room, the wall where the window started was coated in mildew, a damp, sticky mould which clambered laboriously up the wallpaper and stained it a clammy grey. The wallpaper itself was torn in places, a victim of the damp and the perennially low heating. It consisted of funny bumps of air coated in emulsion, which Ally loved to sit and squash with the tip of her index finger. The rest of the room was surprisingly bare. There were no posters on the wall, no clutter, in fact nothing but clothes and a single shelf crammed with books.

The room had not always been like this. A month or so before, it had been a busy and bright place, covered in mess. All of Ally's toys had been spilled, higgledy-piggledy across the floor. There had been socks mixed up with dolls, colouring books interspersed with shirts and blouses. The whole lot had been strewn all over the room. Months of toys pulled from cupboards and shelves and left where they had last been played with. Maggie had threatened twice before to take the entire lot away for good unless Ally tidied up after herself, but she simply didn't know how. No one had shown her how to return something back where it had come from, or shown her that things could have a designated place in which they resided, to make it easier to find them again once they had been played with. And so, when the third threat had been issued and Ally had still failed to comprehend what was expected of her, Maggie and James had marched into her bedroom, armed with crates and boxes, and removed each one of her treasures. Permanently. Except for Albert VI who, for some reason, had been granted leave to remain.

Maggie had warned that there would be no going back, that when the toys were gone, they would be gone forever. And Ally had tried, really tried, before the third and final warning had arrived, to be good. She had tried to put things back where they belonged, but truth be told they didn't have proper homes. The doll's house with the chipped roof had always lived in the centre of the room, because it had never been moved. The things under the bed lived there because they had nowhere else to go. With a distinct lack of storage, Ally had no choice but to await the final warning and sit back as her most important belongings were packed away and locked upstairs in the section of the attic that she was not allowed to access. Her teddies had gone, amid many tears and recriminations. They had been squashed into a box, including Sue the stuffed dog (whom Ally believed may have magical properties, as Sue could sometimes be seen to raise an eyebrow in sympathy when Ally cried on her in the dark), who was piled in with some of the other, less well-loved plush animals. James had relished every minute of it, throwing the bears and dolls into the crate with extreme swaggering nonchalance, safe in the knowledge that *his* room would never be defiled in such a way.

After the bears and stuffed animals, and the beloved Sue, Ally had to stand back as her mother and James went through her games. Backgammon boards, Ker-Plunk, Hungry Hippos and Snap had all gone into a large cardboard box, followed by Guess Who?, and Monopoly (good riddance, thought Alex, as she always lost anyway). The Dinosaur Game, where you had to make monsters out of cards with wriggly tails and funny faces, was another matter. The games went. Following the games, the Barbie and Sindy dolls were targeted. Ally didn't mind losing the brunette, whose hair she had cut short anyway to make her into a Ken, but the blonde beauties

Gardening in the Dark

and their wardrobes were a different matter altogether. That felt like pure hurt. Her room was stripped, depersonalised. Maggie hummed and hawed over the books, buying Ally enough time to reach under her bed and grab a handful of marbles before the rest of the room was decimated. Maggie left the books, thinking that, after all, there was a limit to how much mess could be made with them. Clothes, unfortunately, had to stay for practical reasons. Albert VI was allowed to stay, only for the fact that Maggie didn't know what else to do with him. James and her mother packed up Ally's entire room, and took it up to the attic, to the part where Ally was not allowed to go. She was told that the toys were gone, lost, irretrievable for ever, and that had proven to be the case. Following the decimation, Ally had had a birthday, and each of the toys had been given, played with briefly, then hauled up to the loft to join the rest of her possessions.

And so, she had little to do in her room, except to fling her clothes across the floor in fits of pique, talk to Albert, mourn Sue, or carefully and cautiously reach into the left shoe of her favourite red summer sandals, and take out the eight marbles which were hidden carefully in there. This Ally did now, knowing that Maggie would be busy for as long as 'Blockbusters' and the vodka and tonic lasted.

The marbles were beautiful, in an understated small round sort of way. They were a kingdom unto themselves. Ally had chosen well when she reached under the bed. There were six royal marbles, and two plain – a fact which never ceased to amaze her. She could have ended up with all eight being plain and boring, in which case there would have been no fun in playing with them. No one wants to play with civilians, whilst knowing that somewhere in a box on the top floor there was royalty which could be played with. However, her small hand had grasped the very best six marbles from the group.

The first marble had been a gift from the couple across the road, Keith and June. It was a battered old thing which had actually, judging by its appearance, been used as a proper marble. It was chipped and brown, nothing much to look at, but it was *big*. Size was everything in the marble hierarchy. This was the chief, and it was called Justice. After Justice came Diamond and Sapphire, both little spheres of porcelain with a respective orange and blue swirl. These were the King and Queen of their little empire. Crystal was the wild best friend of Diamond, the lady-in-waiting, dark and lustrous and beautiful. Then there was Jade (green, obviously, in a pond-water kind of see-through way), and two normal marbles, a red one and a blue one, which were the King and Queen's children, adopted despite their plainness, and saved from a life of debauchery and financial penury. They didn't have names. Then, there was Ruby, who was just another royal family member of indeterminate relation. Justice and Sapphire were best friends, as the only real males. The females sometimes sojourned to the right sandal for a holiday, or sometimes the whole kingdom made long arduous and exciting journeys all the way to the living room, and hid behind the sofa to have illicit parties.

The marbles were Ally's lifeline. She loved them all, allocated personalities to each, and spent hour after hour playing with them. They could perform courtly dances to Tina Turner and Michael Jackson songs. They had Olympics, learning to roll as fast as possible. They ate and slept together, had quarrels, fell in love and had judiciary disputes which needed each one to take part as jurors, plaintiffs, or witnesses. Sapphire and Diamond shared a great love, as proven by their miniature offspring, who were sometimes mischievous but usually good. The eight were Ally's entire world. She opened the wardrobe door and looked down at the sandals thoughtfully. Did she have time to get them out and play before Maggie called her back? It was unlikely. She shut the door again and left them to whatever it was that they were doing, quietly promising to come and see them later.

And so, there was not much to do with her precious time after all. Ally jumped back on the bed, displacing a grumpy Tiger who had decided to curl up on her pillow, and folded her arms behind her head. Another game she could play, when she was in her room with nothing to do, was to pretend something. She usually pretended that she lived somewhere else, or that she was desperately sick and being cared for by some kind people. She closed her eyes and imagined that she had broken her leg, and that people were coming to bring her food and look after her. They were kind with quiet voices, and they liked toys and especially liked playing games, cooking sweet warm things for her, and administering love and hugs.

Gardening in the Dark

"Ally!" she heard Maggie's voice, raucous and screeching, from the living room. Time to pour another drink. Ally pulled her legs off the bed and shook her head, dispelling the feelings of warmth and replacing them with a mild, frustrated despair. She walked through to the living room again, Tiger following behind.

Chapter Four

Morning arrived with infuriating slowness, the short grey light rising like torture through the fuzzed pane of the window, throwing feeble tentacles of light into the room where Alex lay. She pulled herself upright and stood unsteadily, her legs numbed by too many dragged minutes of inertia. She felt nothing. She was neither alarmed nor surprised to find herself still alive. She walked out of the room slowly, making sure her footfalls made no noise, and imagined herself to be invisible. Residents of the ward walked to and fro, zigzagging with imagined purpose from one room to the next. Alex shrank into herself. She found the bathroom, a large white square around the corner from her room. It was stripped of personality, and she took refuge behind the locked door for a few minutes to gather her thoughts.

She was horribly sober, with a crashing headache that made her feel as if her brain had enlarged and was pushing against the sides of her skull. The bright light in the bathroom added to it. Alex was shaking, and she looked at her hands curiously as if they belonged to someone else. They appeared monstrous and unfamiliar, twitching and jerking. She tried to take stock of her situation.

She was in a mental hospital. She was sober, with no access to alcohol. Rather than making everything feel good again, her decision the previous evening had made things seem far worse. She was still desperately unhappy, but now the unhappiness was stripped of sedation of any kind, and she had no means to alleviate it. She was frightened (a good thing – she still felt), and confused (a bad thing – she was not in control of her present situation). She took some strange solace from the fact that the bone-creakingly heavy depression was still cloaked about her shoulders like an old friend.

She resolved to give them a week. If you were going to die, a week was a relatively short stretch of time. It was life, the future that loomed ahead in all its despair and futility, that was an unbearable distance to navigate. A week was short and rounded, soft edged. She could manage a week.

Gardening in the Dark

She jumped as someone pounded on the bathroom door, then she clambered over to the sink and splashed her parched face with water. She opened the door in some terror, and stood back as a large woman pushed past her and sat on the toilet. Alex looked away and left the room, pulling the door closed on the strange woman.

She found her way to the smoking room, and retrieved the packet of cigarettes and lighter that she had relied upon the evening before. She looked about her. The room reminded her of something unsavoury from when she was at school. A small utilitarian and rather filthy table had been placed under the window, and a fan blared out a whirring sound which thankfully drowned out her thoughts. Two plastic chairs, brown with cigarette burns in them, were placed on either side of the table. Alex sat down gingerly and lit a cigarette, her eyes travelling over the bare yellowed walls and to the window. Outside, in the crack afforded by an open pane, Alex could see a tree. It was dappled with early morning sunlight but looked bleak and naked, its leaves partially fallen and the remainder decaying and brown. It felt like the room.

Alex hugged her knees to her chest and rocked. She could feel the sadness weighing her down, slumping her shoulders and taking away her energy. She was in a pit. The pit. It was a constant, hovering in the shadows ready to catch Alex's eye and throw her off guard when she least expected it. It was like death, wrapped in a rotting shroud in her peripheral vision. It was the millstone around her neck, the Jiminy Cricket voice which whispered in her ear that everything she touched would turn to shit. It was Philip Larkin judging her to an eternity of raw, real death. It felt like hell, as if the mouth of hell yawned and gaped every time she turned around. It felt like damnation, like decay. She thought of it, when she could bring herself to, as simply 'The Pit'. All powerful, all-consuming, it stayed with her, casting curses on to her light. Diminishing and dimming her. Reducing her both mentally and bodily to the very least she could ever dread to become.

She lit a cigarette slowly, noticing that her hands were still trembling, and resumed her sluggish thoughts. Her life, when she looked back at it, had always seemed to be this way. Either the pit, or the high. Extremes. Polar opposites. Light and darkness. All and nothing. Black and white. Hard and soft. Alex was all of these things, but never simultaneously. She was either a deity or powerless. Art or science. Round or flat, high or low, low, low. Alex stood and pivoted on her heel clumsily, and looked back on the last ten years of her life. Had she been one of the diagrams produced by an irregular heartbeat, she could not have been less stable. The rise and fall of her life seemed laughable. She traded up all her serotonin in short blasts, and then waited for the flat blackness to open up and claim it back. She was being punished for living too hard. She was dying quickly, burning out and fading away. This time, she felt, the pit was too deep and dark to be overthrown. This time it would never end.

Alex was awoken from her reverie by someone pushing the door open. She started guiltily, as if the woman who entered could read her thoughts, know her innermost fears. She sat back down quickly, pulling her limbs tightly in, her arms wrapped closely about herself.

"Hello," Alex said quietly, as the woman nodded and took the vacant seat opposite, opening a rusting tin of tobacco and taking out some cigarette papers. The two sat in silence, Alex aware of the uncomfortable feeling in her stomach which came from a silence she wasn't sure how, or if, to break.

"Would you like a real cigarette?" she offered suddenly, pushing her pack across the filthy table. She wanted to dispel the silence, to pretend at least for a moment that she was somewhere normal, where sadness didn't permeate the walls and feel like a thick coating of tar across the entire room. The woman considered her closely, lank brown hair half concealing her face, which was already partially obscured by over-large horn-rimmed glasses. She shook her head dismissively.

"No," she replied. Her owlish eyes were languid and large, with sorrow written into every line around them. Although she was young, her face looked as if she was tired beyond belief.

"How long have you been here?" Alex asked curiously. The woman reminded her of the Lady of Shallot, trapped in a turret and unable to leave. She had pallid skin which suggested a lifetime of confinement.

"I don't know," the woman replied, and turned her ashen face towards the window. Alex drew on the rest of her cigarette as fast as she could, blowing the smoke out in front of her to obscure the woman's face. She suddenly stubbed it out viciously. She felt that madness was contagious, that if she stayed too long in any one place she would become contaminated, subsumed by it. It was a scent which poisoned the breath she took, cloying and weighty, and she felt a sudden surge of panic at the thought of it, the inescapable insanity which was entering her breath, travelling through her body in each of the cells of her blood. It sickened her. She returned quickly to the room she had stayed in overnight, almost running past the curiously bored gaze of the residents gathered in the hallway.

She looked about listlessly at the colours in the room, drab and grey. There was no beauty, here. She started as the door was pushed open and Susan, the nurse who had checked on her throughout the night, walked in. She had shoulder-length brown hair and big eyes, and a lot of lines creasing the brown skin of her face. She managed to retain a freshness about her, as if she were constantly outside, refusing to allow the smell of the ward to permeate her lungs, skin and clothing.

"Alexandra!" she exclaimed, smiling, as if Alex were a long-lost friend and Susan had not spent the entire night watching her for signs of self-harm or attempted suicide. "How are you this morning?"

Alex tried a smile, but her lips were parched and snagged on her teeth.

"Are you ready to get up and look around now? Have you had enough sleep?"

Alex nodded. Susan, content with this, busied herself in the room straightening the covers of the makeshift bed and then bundled Alex out of the door. She guided her by the elbow and introduced her to a series of staff who were loitering in the hallway. Alex had assumed some were residents. She kept her head down, staring at her boots, as Susan made the introductions. There was a tiny smudge on the left boot, which looked like something small and brown had died on it.

Susan showed her the kitchen, conspicuous for its soft edges and lack of knives, and the canteen area that smelled of stale school meals. She showed her the bathrooms, upstairs and down, and the smoking room. Alex nodded appreciatively and watched the smudge on her boot as her legs were propelled from room to room. They moved with a life of their own, and Alex felt slightly surprised that they functioned so well.

"…And this will be your room. You'll be sharing with Doreen, she's a sweetie," Susan finished, pushing Alex into a small room with two narrow beds in it separated by a limp blue curtain. The nurse heaped a blanket, toothbrush and paste, a towel and soap on to the bed in the corner, smoothing the white waffle blanket beneath it with a practised palm. Alex nodded and mumbled as she was shown a small cabinet on wheels where her possessions could go, and a plastic jug and tumbler of water. She made her way onto the bed and curled up in a corner of it, knees and arms closed possessively around her shaking frame.

"Susan," Alex started to say, but the word was dry and brittle so she cleared her throat and started again.

"Susan." The nurse paused and turned to look at her new charge, her head slightly to one side.

"I can't stay here," Alex finished, and she felt lighter as the words left her mouth. Susan stood upright and bit her lip.

"You can. Just for a while. Just until you're better," she replied, and touched the top of Alex's head gently, before leaving.

Alex sat in the corner of her bed as her companion in the room moved about, attending to her toilet, lining her meagre belongings up and then realigning them. Doreen was fat and dark, her eyes bagged and lined, her face set in stone as if it was unaccustomed to smiling. Alex smiled at her a lot, a hollow grimace, and Doreen looked at her appreciatively but couldn't muster the energy to reciprocate.

*

Doreen snored. Alex lay awake the second night, listening to the regular fat breathing of her companion, and thought about the nights she had spent with other people, in such close proximity.

She had had a few relationships which lasted for a while, bringing her together with other bodies that rose and fell in the darkness, their breathing giving her something physical to match as she whiled away the lonely hours of the night. She liked sharing with people, being so close, but Alex found Doreen difficult to become accustomed to. Doreen was quiet and closed, like the solemn ending of a spiritual book. Alex could find no way of penetrating her closedness, and lacked the enthusiasm to try. She was completely self-absorbed in her own pain, wilted and selfish. On the second morning, outside the window of their hot little room, Doreen and Alex watched as the sun rose, having slept and stared through the interminable hours in between.

On the third night, Alex thought of love. Being so close to someone else suddenly made her question everything with a new depressive candour. She had occasionally loved before. She had loved in an easy, accustomed way that came of familiarity; she had slept and loved through short tempestuous relationships which seemed, now, in the stark drab grey and blue room, somehow unbelievable. Had she really sweated and heaved her way through nights with various men, trying to connect with someone? It was difficult to imagine, with the sound of Doreen's regular breathing, and the dim light that came from the entrance hall, the low murmur of the night staff. Alex sat through the third evening of her incarceration in the hospital with a feeling of unease, half waking, half dreaming, which left her feeling as if her soul had upped and deserted her, leaving her somehow halved and crippled. Her dreams, when she slept fitfully, were bizarre and inconsequential, but left her with a bitter heaviness when she awoke. She was aware of a feeling of low disaster, as if her dreams had tainted her mind without her conscious awareness. "I'm dying, I'm dead," she said to herself, and the words sounded self-conscious and ridiculous in the new grey light of her third morning in the hospital.

The routine of waking, bathing, eating and sleeping impressed on Alex a sense of practicality. The function of the ward was to keep people alive, at whatever cost. As long as she awoke every day, performed her ablutions and functioned, she would comply with their requirements. Even better if she would take the medication that they proffered three times a day, preferably without questioning what it was. She was not sentient and reasonable enough to be told what she was taking. All she knew was that it made her have strange dreams, of corpses and death, that were not so far removed from the thoughts which occupied her mind in the daylight hours. She took the pills one by one, in a haze of numbness and impending death. In many ways, she was already dead. Her body performed perfunctory acts out of habit, while her mind secreted itself away and withered. Was she being saved? She was still alive.

In the stillness and half-light of her room, she woke up sharply and sat bolt upright, her mind full of craziness. Stark images crowded her thoughts. She was running, falling. Her teeth were being pulled out one by one and she was screaming, a wide-open bloody maw of pain and destruction. Alex tried to cling on to something sensible, and fixed her eyes on the dresser beside her. It was small, wooden, and functional. She stared at the glass of water which stood on the top, focusing on the curved meniscus and the tiny bubbles which had formed during the night. Her body, back and legs were drenched with sweat. The bedclothes were damp and turning cold even as she tried to still her ragged breathing.

She was shaking. The alcohol had left her body and every fibre in her physical being screamed to be appeased. It was a sideline, this addiction. It was not something she had thought of before, nor anything she had encountered. She was surprised to find herself without the palliative effects of drink. She had never had to go without before. She was shocked that her body was responding to loss, just as her mind was coming to terms with the loss of a will to live. It was betraying her, causing a surge of anxiety to rise up in her stomach. She was utterly dumbfounded by it. It was a betrayal. The fact of her body behaving in a certain way, outside of her control, infuriated her. She settled back into the bed and slept again, twisting the sodden sheets around her confused body.

Routine came quickly. With the absence of any other stimulus, Alex's body and then mind quickly became accustomed to the machinations of the ward. They awoke at about half past seven, with the sounds and activities of people rousing from slumber and talking, laughing or crying around her. She awoke naturally, without feeling, pulled from sleep, as the sleep she had was so tenuous and fragile that it took little to rouse her from it. After that, in this place of wakefulness and fear, things were straightforward. She showered. The act was comforting in some way, even as she was humiliated by the constant presence of a nurse watching her, scrutinising her ablutions in case she found some way to harm herself.

It wasn't as if she didn't constantly think of ways. They knew what she was thinking; could read it in her sallow face. She thought of palming a blade, drawing it across her arteries in a warm bath until the blood ran crimson and plentiful into the steaming water. The thought of death was a quiet pleasure, a comfort. She searched the windows for ways to complete her life, and wondered how many other distraught and empty bodies had chosen to stop living in these rooms. It was a gentle thought, no longer holding the fear it had a few weeks ago. Death had been a constant companion, and she welcomed it as a familiar friend. She tried to think of more ways, but not too hard, lacking the energy and the resourcefulness which she would have had if she had been less miserable. It took some level of initiative to creatively end one's life, in a situation where she was watched and checked up on every five minutes. She lacked the energy to elude the gazes of those around her. She continued to live. She breathed.

She hadn't eaten for days. She ached with heaviness and couldn't contemplate sustaining her body, this physical bruise which she was forced to drag around after her, while she took it from the smoking room to her bed, backwards and forwards throughout the day. She didn't want to feed this thing; give it nourishment. It was a simple decision which came from her sense of powerlessness.

"If they fail me, here, I still have a choice," she whispered to herself in the middle of the night, while Doreen cried and stumbled through sleep in the cubicle next to her. It was a quiet determination not to be trapped by life, even as the staff on the ward seemed utterly determined that life should be preserved.

By not eating, she was in some sort of control. As the third day passed she thought about it curiously. She felt no hunger. She needed nothing, because she wasn't really alive. She was fascinated by the way her body had shut down about her, slow and clumsy as if it had retreated into some form of hibernation to allow her dull mind to survive. She wondered if she were not already dead, which would explain why her body didn't need to perform the usual functions. It didn't seem to need to eat or to relieve itself. It asked only for sleep, hour after hour, and Alex was more than happy to oblige.

They kept giving her pills. Alex took the small plastic container of water with apprehension. She didn't want to give herself sustenance. She took tiny sips; just enough to wash down the medication, without questioning what she was taking, and then slept heavily for hours. It was enough, for now, to fall back in to the safety of the building, to allow herself to be shepherded from one room to another without thinking. Perhaps some form of healing had started from the moment Alex resigned from having responsibility for herself. She smiled out of the window, unseeing. She had made a choice. Either they would heal her, or she would die. It was enough. They didn't try to talk to her, or ask her how she was, and she was grateful. She didn't want to answer any more questions. The evening of her admission felt as if it had occurred a lifetime ago.

She watched women coming and going with dead eyes.

She was surprised that the staff didn't try to talk to her, other than empty words. They would come to her in a regular procession, rouse her from sleep during the day, just to go through the same vacuous questioning which didn't seem to achieve anything.

"Alexandra are you OK?" they'd ask, pulling her from uneasy oblivion.

"Yes, thank you," she would answer. It was a lie, of course.

Gardening in the Dark

"Have you eaten anything?"

"No, thank you." She was terrified that she would be overruled, as not eating was the only thing left over which she had some control. How long does it take for someone to die, with no food? It didn't really matter; she had time.

Time stretched before her, a dim and fogged truth. She would sleep and survive her way through it. They discussed practical things with her which she didn't hear, about how the medication would soon take effect and she would feel herself change. She trusted them, knew that they were only there to ensure her body continued, that they didn't really care what was occurring in her mind. As long as they could see her breathing, that was good enough. They watched her body rather than searching her face. She hid Alex behind her hair, behind her cardigan which was large enough to conceal her thoughts from them. They weren't enemies, they were just inconvenient.

Her life seemed to be structured by sleeping and dreams. She was allowed to pad from her room to the smoking area in silence, a ghostly Alex. She sat with the night staff, trying to avoid dreams which were too vivid, leaving her body drenched in sweat and the scent of anxiety, half-remembered. They asked her what she had dreamed about and she couldn't articulate her experience, too vivid was it to evoke in mere words.

She was amazed how quiet it was in the night, one single lamp burning and casting a small glow into the shadows, making a tiny part of the darkness recede. The rest was cloaked in warmth and blackness, secure. She remembered the first night they had brought her in, and she shook her head in wonder. From what had then seemed to be inhospitable and terrifying, the ward had already taken on some feeling of safety. She belonged there, functioning quietly from one room to the next. Drugged and drowsy and warm, it was becoming easier to exist. By the fifth full day, she was almost alive with it.

She tried to connect, at any level, with the other people there. Alex was a woman who needed some form of reassurance of her humanity, even in this, the most inhospitable and severe of circumstances. She surveyed those around her with a greedy need, wondering how she could assert her own sense of self and awaken that of those around her. She was constantly alternating between feelings of fear and loss, and loneliness. The people she found herself with were all broken, dissipated, somehow lacking, but she felt herself being suddenly awoken with a bizarre, voyeuristic curiosity. What freak show was this? Even in the midst of her own selfishness and suffering, she cleaved to the sadness she felt around her, wondering if she could be the person responsible for alleviating it in some way. Her inherent politeness led her to smile at people even when she felt as if she couldn't breathe for her own sorrow. She smiled, and elicited weary smiles in return. Most of the inhabitants of the ward seemed as if they hadn't smiled for a very long time.

She was beginning to belong. She was still alive.

Gardening in the Dark

Chapter Five

Somewhere between the sheets of a deep sleep, Ally was shaken awake. She pulled to the surface of the early morning reluctantly, and saw Ben at the side of her bed. She held out her arms to him sleepily, pleased to see him.

"Morning," she mumbled, but Ben held his finger to his lips and cautioned her to be silent.

"Do you want to come to London with me, Ally-Cat?" he asked, his face twinkling even as he glanced over his shoulder to be assured that Maggie and James were safely asleep in their respective rooms. Ally sat up quickly, her eyes shining.

"Really?" she asked, suddenly wide awake, excited and nervous at the same time.

"Yes. But you have to be very *very* quiet, and you have to be ready in less than five minutes," Ben answered, smiling at her enthusiasm.

With that, Ally jumped out of bed and started running around the bedroom, picking up items of clothing and hopping into her jeans, hardly believing her luck. A whole day with her father all to herself, away from the house, on a Saturday, when she should be meandering around the living room doing the chores. It was too good to be true. As she got dressed, Ally was conscious that to be too loud would mean that Maggie could come down and discover her, and the knowledge that it could end before it even happened lent an element of caution and quietude to her movements. Within five minutes, she was dressed and ready, her hair brushed quickly and scraped back, her trainers on and coat fastened. She crept through the hall and lounge into the kitchen with trepidation, terrified that Maggie may awaken at the last minute and scupper their plans.

Ben looked at her approvingly, and motioned to her to follow him out of the back door. When Ally pulled the door to behind them, she broke into a run, down the side steps and out to the front drive where the van was parked in readiness, its engine running with a deep rumble. Ally, still warm from her bed, gasped at the cold air which greeted her. It was a foggy damp morning, and Ally held her hand out in front of her as she went to the passenger side of the van, amazed at how dense the air was. She was rarely up so early, and it felt illicit and strange. She liked it.

Ally climbed in to the passenger side, her knees shaking with excitement, and hauled herself into the seat. The van had three seats in the front: a double one for passengers, then a gap for the gear lever, and Ben's own seat. It smelled of road and business, and Ally wasn't keen on it, but anything was preferable to staying at home. The material of the seat felt cold when she sat down, and she drew herself up into a tight ball as Ben jumped in to the driver's seat.

"Belt up," he said sternly, and Ally uncoiled herself reluctantly and fumbled for the cold seat belt, which she had to tug on a couple of times before it would release. She pulled the belt across her, and it dug into her neck a little, as she was still rather too small for it to fit properly. At least Ben didn't make her sit in the back any more. She felt suddenly grown-up and refined. They were going on a business trip together. To London. Ally had never been to London, but she knew it was where Buckingham Palace, the Queen and the Prime Minister were. Big Ben! She was suddenly terribly, terribly excited.

"What are we going to do?" Ally asked Ben, not caring about the answer particularly. Ben had eased the van quietly out of the driveway and they were off down the steep road of their cul-de-sac, suddenly completely free of Maggie, of James, of the house. They had made it, undiscovered. Ally breathed a sigh of relief and her exhalation came out like fog. She blew on her hands just to see the clouded air again.

"I have to do some deliveries in various parts of London, and then I can take you around afterwards and show you some stuff," Ben said, his voice sounding relaxed and pleased to have the company. "I've been wanting to take you for a while," he added, and Ally smiled and hugged her knees to her chest. London was a magical place. Ally had seen it on the telly.

Ally didn't mind sitting in the van. It was better than the car, because she was higher up and she could see out of the whole of the front window without moving her head or craning as she had to when she was in the back of the car. It smelled strange and industrial; diesel scent and metal tools and grease. The smell clung to her after she had been sitting in it for a while, and she closed her eyes and breathed it in, because it smelled like her father when he came home. Ben flicked on the radio, and sang along to all the music, even the things Ally wouldn't have thought he knew the lyrics to. Someone had written 'Clean Me' on the side panel of Ally's door, which made her laugh even though Ben seemed annoyed about it and sighed, and rolled his eyes.

"Original," he said. Ally thought it was, too.

"It's as if the van is asking you for help." She giggled, and Ben didn't answer, but smiled at her suddenly.

Ally wondered to herself as she listened to the hum of the van, which grew louder as they gathered speed, then quieter when they approached roundabouts. What would be the cost of this trip? She thought about the infinite pleasure of being with her dad, but understood that it would have to be paid for. It was a trade-off. It seemed that everything was measured out in currencies which Ally couldn't understand. She grew quiet, thinking about the trouble that would ensue when they returned home back to Maggie and James, but shook herself out of her reverie as Ben pushed a CD in to the player and began to sing along to the music. He was playing Electric Light Orchestra, and the sound of strings and Jeff Lynne's voice flooded the car, swelling out to the windows, with a bass pulsing in Ally's stomach. She began to smile, despite herself.

Ben's voice was deep and warm, like melted sugar. Ally liked listening to him sing, more than Jeff Lynne. She concentrated on trying to learn the words, wondering if she would be able to sing like her dad when she was older, or if her voice would always stay piped and reedy like an out-of-tune clarinet.

Ben pulled into a service station and parked up, leaving Ally for a few minutes. She sat up and watched the other travellers as they pulled their cars into spaces then disappeared into the petrol station. When Ben returned, he was holding a huge milkshake in his hands. He handed it to Ally with a grin, and she took it in reverence. It was massive, in a cardboard cup with a straw, bigger than her two hands put together. It was absolutely forbidden and Ally felt a thrill of pleasure as she looked at it. The straw was pierced through the lid of the plastic cup, and she pulled it out a short way to look at it. It was coated in thick shake, and it looked like frosted snow. The cup was too cold to hold properly for a long time, so she pulled her sleeves down and nursed it carefully. It absorbed her completely. Her cheeks didn't have enough suck in them to drink it properly, and she told Ben but he said it would soon start to melt and then she could drink it. It was divine; the most beautiful thing Ally had ever tasted. At the beginning, she wanted it to go on and on and never end, but eventually it seemed as if there was too much of it, and she started to feel a bit sick. She put the cup down surreptitiously on the floor of the van, and held it upright with her feet. Ben didn't seem to notice; he was talking on his mobile phone and looking at the road intently.

He suddenly pulled up in a lay-by, and there were lorries in front and behind.

"Are we allowed to stay here, because there're lorries, and we're smaller than them?" Ally asked, worried that they would be told off by the traffic police.

"Shh," Ben said, unclipping his seat belt and leaning over to her. Ally suddenly grew tense, knowing what was coming. She wriggled away, but Ben was undoing her seat belt too, and pulling her towards him. She started to panic, imagining that all the men in the lorries nearby could see what he was doing to her, and she closed her eyes and gritted her teeth, taut and tense like an elastic band at breaking point. She started to count, and by the time she had reached two hundred it was over, and Ben did her seat belt up again, and pulled out of the lay-by. He turned the music up on the radio, and Ally held her breath and looked out of the side window, imagining there was a big chopper on the side of the van that was sweeping across the sides of the motorway and cutting everything down.

London wasn't as exciting as Ally had imagined. They stopped outside a few shops in different places, Ally sitting patiently inside waiting while her father went and spoke to people, sometimes opening up the back of the van and poking about inside. His voice sounded different when he spoke to people in London; more confident, louder, more charming and he laughed much more. Ally fell asleep a few times, because she had been woken up so early, and kept starting awake, feeling nauseous with the diesel smell and the twists and turns in the road and the backwards and forwards motion as the van stopped and started at traffic lights. She was, however, always glad throughout the day that she wasn't at home.

Ally thought of Maggie and James, wondering how they would react upon realising that she was not there. There was a note from Ben to say that they had absconded for London like the heroines in Ally's school stories, the girls who sneaked out in the middle of the night to go on adventures. It had felt like the middle of the night, and, similarly to those girls who lived at boarding schools, Ally was afraid of being caught, afraid of being found out. She hoped her punishment was not going to be too severe.

"Can you make sure I don't get hit, for this?" she asked suddenly. Ben looked at her, his lips pinched into a thin line. He frowned.

"I'm not sure, Ally-Cat," he said. "I'll try."

Ally knew that Ben didn't have any power, though. It would be OK when she was there standing next to him, but when her dad disappeared to go off to work again, or go to the pub, or do whatever he did that meant he wasn't at home, she would once again be at the mercy of her mother. She would have to hope that Maggie was not in too bad a mood.

Maggie was jealous. James was jealous. They all wanted to spend time with Ben but Ally was his favourite.

Ally took the opportunity to educate Ben about her mother.

"Do you know what she does? She stops me from going to school sometimes, so my grades drop down. She keeps me at home so I can go to the shop and do the cooking," she said, her voice conspiratorial as if Ben were a friend, and an equal in her gossip.

"I know, Ally," Ben replied, staring straight out on to the motorway, which seemed to go on and on with no curves.

"And sometimes she hits me for no reason, and screams at me and James. And sometimes when she can't hit me herself she asks James to do it and he's even harder," Ally continued, suddenly desperate for Ben to know about Maggie, just in case he didn't.

"I know, Ally." Ben's voice was quiet and sad, but not angry like Ally had hoped.

"Can't you do anything about it? Can we go away somewhere together and make sure she can't find us, and you could leave her and James because they are each other's favourite anyway, aren't they, Dad?" she finished, finally understanding that Ben, who sometimes seemed like the most powerful person in the world, was not going to help her.

"I wish I could."

"Why can't you?" she asked, and even as she asked she felt some fear, because if James and Maggie weren't there then Ben might come into her room all the time, not just a few times a week, and that would be almost unbearable. There would be nothing to hold him back. So, Ally didn't plead very hard. She spoke more about Maggie, instead.

"Sometimes she hits me hard, and she calls me a bitch and a whore, and sometimes she says if I scream or cry I'll get taken into care. What's 'care'? She says it's not like what it sounds but I think it sounds quite nice."

Ben had gone hard and quiet, his eyes focusing straight out of the front windscreen. He didn't answer any more, and Ally felt a sudden nervousness and became abruptly quiet. She retreated into her thoughts.

Sometimes when Maggie was being miserable and crying, she'd ask Ally to choose which parent she wanted to be with. Ally always picked her mother, knowing this was the right answer, but she wouldn't even hesitate. At least Ben didn't hit very often, and – when he did – it seemed to be because she had done something wrong, and she sort of understood. And he didn't make her bleed as Maggie did, or leave scars behind or bruises.

Her mind kept flicking guiltily back to the house in Derbyshire. Maggie would be up, maybe, provided she had decided it was a good day to get up. James would be awake. He would have had a shower by now and probably would be dressed in his paisley shirt, the blue one that Ally sometimes tried on when he was at school and she got back early, or if she was kept behind.

Maggie would be on the sofa now, and maybe someone would have come over for coffee and they would be watching television, or Maggie would be reading, or maybe it was a good day and Maggie was baking, but somehow because Ally was in the car driving to London she imagined it would be a bad day back at home. She was probably shouting at James. Would James have to do the cleaning, still, if Ally was out with Ben? Probably not. It would most likely be saved for her, for when she got back.

Ben and Ally stopped talking. They pulled up on a kerb and Ben showed her Big Ben, the Thames, and Buckingham Palace – but they couldn't get out and look properly because of all the traffic, and the Queen wasn't there, after all. Ben explained to her about how the flag was up or down depending on Her Majesty's presence.

London smelled funny and there were too many people. Compared to Derbyshire, it was a strange, loud and busy place. Ally saw a dog running and sniffing along the pavement. He looked mangy and dirty, as if he needed a bath, and he also didn't seem as if he had had very much to eat. Ally looked at him, turning in her seat and craning her neck to see what happened to him. Did he belong to anyone?

"Did you see that dog? He wasn't on a lead," she said to Ben, hoping he could give a good explanation, like maybe the owner was around the corner and the dog didn't like being on leads, so he was allowed to walk by himself. But that didn't explain why he was so skinny if he had a proper owner.

"He's probably homeless," Ben said. Ally frowned and tried to see the dog again, but the van had moved along the line of traffic and it had disappeared.

"Oh."

"Why are dogs sometimes homeless? Can't they match up people with dogs so they've always got somewhere to live? Is that what they did with us and Tiger?" she asked.

Tiger had been Ally's sixth birthday present from Ben. She still remembered it even though it was a long time ago, because it was the most exciting moment of her life, the best thing that had ever happened to her. She had thought she wasn't going to get a present because Ben was at work, but he came home at tea-time and Tiger was round his neck like a funny, scratchy, hissy scarf. She hadn't been allowed to play with Tiger at first, in case he was scared, but then – by the day after – everyone except Ally seemed to have lost interest. James was too cool to care about a cat and so she could play with him. He chased bits of string and scratched her hand to ribbons but she was proud of her war wounds, and everyone at school was jealous of her.

"Not like Tiger. I got Tiger off a farm. He was the littlest one there and the others were all black," Ben said. He sounded as if he wasn't really concentrating but Ally had more to find out.

"Do dogs all have homes, and then some run away and go to live in London?" Ally asked.

"People do that, more often. Dogs can sometimes be born on the street, or sometimes people leave them outside because they don't want them to live there any more. Cats are different; they are more likely to run away because they feel like it."

Gardening in the Dark

"Does everyone start out having a home?" Ally asked.

Ben smiled. "Yes. Sometimes they decide they don't like their home, though, and then they move somewhere like London and live on the street until they find one they like more."

"Can we do that just until we find one we like more?" she asked. She felt suddenly excited. They could live on the street for a day or two and then pick a new home which didn't have Maggie in it.

"It doesn't work like that Ally," Ben said. He was almost laughing.

The rest of the day seemed to fly by, and then suddenly they were headed back for home, and Ally felt the rise of nervousness as she thought about Maggie being angry because they had gone to London without her knowing about it. Her mother would be furious, and she would probably shout when they got back, if she was still awake. Ally frowned until she thought about how jealous James would be that she had gone all the way to London with Ben and had a milkshake, and she was going to tell him that she saw the Queen and that they had had tea together. She smiled out of the side window, and then saw some people fighting in the street outside a pub and she stopped smiling.

"I wouldn't want to live here," Ally said aloud, thoughtfully, then coloured slightly in case Ben would take that as an insult to the day they had had. "Though I've loved today," she added quickly. Benjamin smiled at her, and she relaxed. He wasn't offended.

"I wish I could take you out with me every day, Ally-Cat," Ben said, his eyes crinkling at her. Ally felt suddenly flushed with warmth. He loved her the best.

"I wish you could, too," she said, and the warmth and knowledge that she was his number one kept her drowsy and safe until the van pulled up outside the house. It was dark and Maggie would be inside, but Ally kept her eyes closed so Ben would have to lift her up and carry her, huddled in her coat, all the way in. She must have fallen asleep at some point, because she couldn't remember getting to her room or being put to bed, but she woke up in the middle of the night sick with terror, because they had disobeyed Maggie and that meant that Ally was going to suffer. She was going to pay. She slept again, uneasily, images of London and flashing lights, the milkshake and Ben, and Maggie being angry ran through her mind until she stopped dreaming.

Chapter Six

Time had passed fluidly, and Alex could no longer remember how much had elapsed since she had first arrived on the ward. One morning, as she dragged her leaden body out of bed and collected up the toiletries which they had given her on her first night, she lifted her head. Something seemed different, as if the air crackled with a strange charge. It felt as if an electric spark were coursing through the ward. Alex sensed nervously that if she ran her hands through her dishevelled dark hair, it would cleave to her fingers, lifting up and away in a burst of static. She could feel an unusual bustle in the cubicles around her, an expectant and pregnant hum.

"What is happening today?" she asked Doreen warily, and the older woman smiled a little and nodded, fussing with her hands to smooth her lank hair and pull at her bobbled jumper with barely contained excitement.

"I think it must be Monday. Monday is Ward Round," she replied, nodding again enthusiastically. Alex stood, nonplussed in the middle of their small room, and tried to make sense of the words. What was Ward Round? Wards were square. People came and went all the time, so there seemed to be no reason to have a separate round of visits. She chewed on her lip, feeling a swell of concern, and then left the room in search of a free shower.

The staff seemed more animated as she walked past them, greeting her enthusiastically and carrying on a number of conversations simultaneously, punctuated with raucous laughter. Alex showered quickly, and then padded back to the reception area where a number of the nurses congregated each morning. She sidled up to the group nervously, and tugged at Susan's arm unobtrusively. Susan turned and smiled, her face enquiring. Alex rarely spoke to the staff.

"What is Ward Round?" she whispered cautiously. Susan patted her hand.

"It's where you get assessed. Your consultant will be here to see you later, to find out how you're getting on," she responded, matching Alex's tone and volume to ensure Alex didn't feel embarrassed. Alex nodded and backed away. This didn't explain the undercurrents of excitement on the ward. Unless they all wanted to escape, and like an interview with a jailer who could offer parole, it was a chance to be sane and prove they were capable of being released? Alex returned to her cubicle and sat on the bed. What would her consultant say to her? Was she mad? Could she leave, and if she were allowed to go right now, would she want to? She felt a surge of terror at the thought of being sent out into the world to deal with her demons alone. She wasn't ready. What if they believed that Alex was self-indulgent, that she was seeking attention? What if they didn't believe in her own peculiar brand of madness, and it transpired that it was simply a self-absorbed introversion, or a result of too much drink? She watched Doreen covertly as the woman pottered about folding her clothes and dragging a brush through her brown hair. Doreen was humming quietly, seemingly content and satisfied with her lot. Alex wondered how long the older woman had been incarcerated, with only the ward and the staff to form her world, her version of normality.

What if they didn't let Alex out? What if they, rather than thinking there was nothing wrong with her, decided she was as crazy as Doreen? What if these walls were her future? This thought was even worse than the idea of being cast out with her shadows. Alex scratched her neck, worried. She felt a sudden sympathy for the lost souls who walked the rooms, pacing out their individual universes. Had any of them ever been out walking in the long grass by the river? Looked up and felt a free sun on their face? Known the chatter and laughter that hung like smoke in a busy pub on a weekend evening? What about driving? Swimming? Running fast and exhilarated along a deserted path? Supermarket shopping, selecting ripe plump fruits and colourful vegetables, going home and cooking them? Alex searched the ward in her mind, the kitchen and smoking room, day room and hall; there was no joy here. Ward Round, apparently, provided the weekly diversion.

"God," she said to herself, before standing up impatiently, brushing creases out of her trousers and walking to the smoking room. She felt a sudden desire to be out in the open, to stretch her legs and run. Or to sleep. A cigarette would have to do. She pushed open the door, lost in thought, and jumped as she realised the room was already occupied.

"Hello," she said, looking at the woman who sat before her, long tousled hair and a flowing black velvet skirt, bare feet and a way of tugging on a cigarette that smacked of insanity. Alex was afraid. This was Lois, notorious on the ward but as yet unintroduced. This was the woman Alex had encountered on her first night, as she was admitted. Lois was the one shouting and creating a scene, demanding to smoke in the early hours of the morning. Smoking was a comfort, Alex recognised that, but she couldn't imagine being so desperate to do it that she would lose herself in the need. Lois glanced over her and smiled a twisted lopsided grin. Her eyes were manic, darting about and capturing each corner of the room in a matter of seconds. She reminded Alex of a caged bird. Her legs pulsed with energy; she jiggled and tapped against the table her bare feet rested upon. Alex sat opposite Lois warily in the only other remaining chair, so that they were uncomfortably face-to-face.

"Who are you?" Lois asked suddenly, her birdlike eyes suddenly resting on Alex, taking her in quickly. Alex cleared her throat, feeling an irrational terror.

"Alex."

"That's a man's name."

"Yes."

"You've got nice eyes."

"Thank you. You've got nice hair."

"I'm not mad."

"No."

"Pete says I'm not mad. Margaret shouted at me so I shouted back but that doesn't mean I'm mad. Margaret wants my bloke but she can't have him but maybe she can, do you think she can?"

"No."

"Are you mad?"

"I'm not sure."

At this Lois, started to laugh. She had a beautiful, open smile and a laugh that bubbled in pulses of joy out of her broad mouth. Alex grinned back, suddenly relieved.

"Are you a singer?"

"No."

"Writer?"

"Sometimes."

"Margaret said you were a famous author. That you wrote those Jane Austen books."

"I didn't."

"That's my name. Austen."

"Yes."

"Don't you ever sing, then?"

"Sometimes. When no one can hear me."

"What's the point in that, if no one can hear you?"

"I don't know."

"Margaret swears at me, so I swear back."

"OK."

Gardening in the Dark

Alex shifted in her seat, her cigarette coming to an end. She looked at Lois, who looked back and started to grin again. Alex smiled too, until both of them were giggling over nothing.

"You're pretty."

"Thank you. I think you are, too."

"Do you? Really?"

"Yes."

Alex left Lois smiling, and went back to her cubicle. She felt as if she had achieved something small but important. She had met someone and made them smile, and it had all been fine. She thought of Lois, the energy that pulsed through her, making her move constantly. She beamed again, picturing the woman's crazy eyes and wide smile. Lois was focused on smoking; it seemed to be what she did. When she wasn't sitting in the smoking room hunched and rocking over the charred remains of a rolled cigarette, she was poking over the ashes in the bin, trying to find some tobacco which could be re-used. As Alex thought about the woman, Susan came into the cubicle and drew the blue curtain back. She smiled as she saw Alex.

"There you are. Your doctor is here, and ready to see you."

Alex stiffened, suddenly feeling sick. She felt caught off guard, having been temporarily distracted. She wondered if she should have prepared herself in some way, or thought more about how to behave when her turn to be questioned arrived.

"I'm afraid," she said, in a matter-of-fact voice to Susan. The nurse shook her head brusquely.

"No need. Come with me."

Alex stood with wobbly legs and walked behind Susan. She was led down the corridor and near to the front door. She wondered if she was going to be taken outside, but Susan suddenly halted and pushed Alex into a room to the right. She stepped forward and found herself confronted by a series of eyes, all looking her way. She blushed and grew hot, suddenly petrified.

"Come in Alexandra." An imposing voice spoke, and Alex walked to the centre of the room, hesitating until she was asked to take a seat at the centre of the circle of eyes. She sat down quickly, and looked at the floor. She couldn't bring herself to look up. She saw a pair of smart sensible court shoes directly in front of her.

"I'm Dr. West, your consultant," the court shoes said, and Alex nodded. The shoes continued to introduce people. There was an occupational therapist (brown sandals, small feet), the staff nurse Mark (trainers, white socks), Susan (navy blue shoes, scuffed) and four other people with standard issue anonymous hospital footwear.

Alex lifted her eyes. The doctor was impeccably dressed, with a sharp navy suit and a crisp white blouse. She was intimidating and didn't smile. Alex tried a nervous grin that was completely ignored.

"How are you feeling?"

"I'm OK."

"Are you having any adverse effects from the medication?"

"No."

"Are you eating?"

"No."

"Drinking fluids?"

"A little."

"Alcohol?"

"No."

Gardening in the Dark

"Do you still want to commit suicide?"

"I don't know."

"Do you want to harm yourself in any way?"

"I don't think so."

"Anyone else?"

"No."

"Is there anything you need? Or want?"

"I'd like to go outside sometimes."

"If you were to go out, would you drink?"

"No."

The doctor shifted in her seat slightly and stared at Alex. Alex looked back.

"I'm going to change your medication, Alexandra. I'm going to prescribe something to increase your appetite. I'll see you next week to check how you're getting on. Unless there's anything you'd like to ask us today?"

"No."

"OK. Thank you."

With that, Alex and Susan stood up and left the room. Susan paused when Alex was outside, and patted her arm.

"Was that so bad, then?" she asked, smiling. Alex shook her head and went back to her cubicle, feeling suddenly exhausted. She climbed under her blanket and slept almost immediately.

*

Alex had dreamed heavily, and was shaken awake by one of the nurses on the ward. She didn't recognise him, and shrank away as she tried to remember where she was. Behind the blue curtain, Doreen was moving to and fro with some purpose. The sun was streaming through the thick glass window, lighting up the surfaces of her small cubicle with her few belongings on them. She sat upright slowly, regaining her sense of self as she untangled her legs from the twisted white blanket and damp sheets.

"Alexandra, you don't have any clothes to change into, do you?" the nurse asked in a concerned voice. Alex rubbed her eyes and looked about her. Her handbag was tucked down the side of the bed, and she had borrowed a toothbrush and paste, a cheap navy blue comb and some soap, when she first arrived. Other than these few objects, lined up neatly on her bedside cabinet, she had nothing. They had given her a thick flannel nightgown, and she had washed it every day in the machine, taking care over it and sitting in front of the machine watching it circling round. It killed time. She placed it in the tumble dryer and then ironed it with agonising precision each afternoon after it had dried, only to wear it and soak it with night terrors each evening. This had become her reason for being, this flannel dress which had obviously been worn to rough bobbles by numerous previous borrowers.

"No," she responded. She had nothing, here, to call her own. She had become possessive over her comb, her toothbrush, the nightdress. Although they were not really hers, she had taken ownership of them and that was enough.

"I think you could call someone and ask them to bring you some things in, couldn't you?" the man asked kindly. Alex looked at him, and shook her head.

"I don't know. Am I staying here?" she asked, not really concerned to hear the reply.

"Yes, for a while," he said, then left her and went to talk to Doreen, a patter of inconsequential questions which rushed forward without pausing for an answer from the dull fat woman sitting on the other side of the room. Alex swung her legs out of bed slowly and looked at her toothbrush. It would be nice to get some real things, things which belonged fully to her. She would like a deodorant, a proper toothbrush, perhaps a change of clothes and something that was her own to sleep in, even though she had grown fond of the flannel nightdress. She thought about what the nurse had said. Whom could she call, and speak the unsayable; that she was in a mental hospital and needed some things? She didn't know. She didn't want to consider it. They had taken her mobile phone from her anyway, and she didn't know any numbers at all off by heart. She knew everyone around her would have assumed she had gone away on business, undertaking some freelance work somewhere in the country, and they wouldn't be concerned. She didn't want anyone to know where she was.

They asked her once more as the other residents went into dinner and she was sitting in the smoking room.

"Is there anyone you can call?"

Alex considered it again.

Whom should she call? Whom did she trust enough with this broken shard of information, the stripping bare of her? Who could be relied upon to listen without censure, to respond to the sentiments beneath the alien words? She gazed into the distance uncertainly. Who would come to seek her out like an oyster in a pearl, and not be thwarted by the wrought-iron gates, the shuffling steps of her fellow inmates? She needed soap. She needed her own soap that smelled like home. She needed a change of clothes that would serve in some way to remind her of who she was.

"Please may I have my mobile phone?" she asked, and the nurse smiled, relieved, and nodded.

"I'll fetch it for you, from the office," he said, and walked briskly away.

Alex decided to contact Stuart. A text, first. Something short and sharp which would break the ice, allowing her to plunge into the depths of the icy water which she felt surrounding her. She concentrated fully on the little screen of her phone.

What to write?

It wasn't such a big deal, anyway. She was just in hospital. The fact that she was craving death, and despair clouded her every thought, was somewhat immaterial. Hers was a practical request, for clothes.

She turned the phone on and looked at it. It beeped at her instantly, flashing up that she had a number of messages and missed calls. She looked at the list of missed calls and smiled to herself. Stuart had been looking for her. 'Where are you?' her phone asked, and she shrugged. It enquired again and again. 'Where are you? I'm worried!' it said, and she smiled at her phone. She was here, it was all right.

"I'm in hospital," she wrote. "Please don't worry. Would you come?" She hesitated before pressing the send button, and then the text was gone, pushing its way through the barred windows and out in to the afternoon.

Alex sat on her bed and looked out of the window. She thought about the people in her life that made a difference. She had lost contact with her family many years ago, and this had left a gap in the centre of her that made her feel hollow sometimes. Other than that, she had filled her time with good friends. There were those who were there for her when she was upbeat, happy to run alongside her as she soared. These were the people who seemed to fade away when Alex encountered a pit of depression. While she loved their company, they were not there for her when she needed them. And then there were those whom she sometimes confided in, who tried to understand when she felt low, and tried to talk her round. They didn't succeed. Alex got to a point where she felt guilty for talking about her sorrow, and put on a brave face because she could hear herself, whinging and moaning, and realised she needed to hide the way she felt.

And then, there was Stuart. Stuart was perfect. With his dark hair and piercing blue eyes, Stuart was Alex's best friend. They had met in a pub, on an innocuous and tedious evening when Alex had gone out with some of her more shallow female friends. She

Gardening in the Dark

had stepped into the pub with a leaden heart, looking forward only to the point when she had drunk enough to feel woozy and light.

Stuart had been sitting in the corner in a long coat and trilby, his silhouette looking like a throwback from the brat pack, a cigarette hanging from his mouth. He was dapper and immaculate. A lean and lithe figure, he was the sort of person who made women and men alike turn in the street and look after him. His sideburns were too long, tapered into triangles like some villain from a Bond film. He had turned with a ready smile, high cheekbones and a perfectly trimmed tiny moustache and beard.

Stuart was terribly, terribly gay. He wasn't camp, but gay in a perfect way. He understood how to speak his feelings, and how to interpret those that Alex shared with him. He knew when to laugh at her, when to cry, and when to ignore her moods and terrors and focus on making her laugh. He had had numerous relationships, and was rumoured to have slept with all manner of film stars and musicians. He could walk into a room and command the lust and adoration of any person in there. And yet, he was there for Alex. He had liked her instantly, casually placing an arm around her when she was near him, drawing her to him. He was infectious and funny, and she always felt proud to be walking down the street with him. When he drew the covert glances of strangers, Alex would blush furiously, as if she was somehow being noticed by them, too.

Could she trust him with this? Much of their relationship had been shallow, to date, based around drinking and going out. They had never had the opportunity to test it. Alex imagined the text message floating through the window, surprising Stuart amid a group of people. She pictured him pausing in mid-conversation, reaching in to his pinstripe trousers and glancing at it.

Alex held her breath.

The phone beeped almost instantly. Alex exhaled slowly and picked it up again.

'Tell me where and when, and I'll be there' she read.

Alex pulled the phone to her chest and hugged it. She felt scared and relieved both at once. She went to the bathroom and threw up.

He was coming.

'Thank you' she wrote. She told him where she was. He was coming. She sat on the bed nervously, thinking about Stuart – letting himself into her empty house and packing some belongings, all the time wondering what she was doing in the hospital. She looked around her little room and imagined Stuart on the ward, laughing and incongruous with his vitality and life.

Within half an hour, Susan came to find her, telling her she had a visitor. Alex glanced down at herself suddenly, realising for the first time what she must look like. She looked like a patient in a mental hospital. She raked a nervous hand through her dishevelled hair and then went quickly to the visitors' room. Stuart was standing uncertainly, clutching a bright pink holdall crammed with oddments. She ran to him and they hugged, Stuart lifting her off her feet before putting her down and standing back.

"Christ, Ally, you look like shit!" he exclaimed, and Alex burst out laughing. She led him by the hand to an empty room and they sat down together. Stuart was completely relaxed, eagerly asking her questions about how she had arrived at the hospital, how long she would be there for. Alex deflected his queries, instead gesturing to the holdall. They looked through the items together, Alex laughing at the impossibly frivolous things he had thrown in for her. Admittedly, he had thought of jeans and socks, underwear and T-shirts, but he had also packed an evening gown, a teddy bear, odd items of make-up and some luxurious toiletries.

"I'm not on holiday, you know," Alex chided him, holding up a satin basque that she had bought a few months earlier for a new lover. Stuart grinned and blushed.

"It can't do any harm, even in a place like this!"

They talked for a while, Alex revelling in the sound of his familiar voice, holding his hand and listening as he discussed work, his home life, relationships and new conquests. He in turn listened as she recounted stories about the residents on the ward, their foibles and eccentricities. All too soon, Stuart was asked to leave and Alex found herself saying goodbye.

"Are you eating? You look like they're starving you."

"I will eat."

"I'll bring you something."

"Does that mean you're coming back?"

"Every damn day. I promise."

With that, Stuart gave her an enormous hug, and pushed something into the fold of Alex's jacket. She went to her room with the holdall, Susan having searched it, and sat down. Surreptitiously, she pulled out Stuart's parcel. She smiled as she unwrapped a sizeable bottle of vodka. He knew her well. When she was sure that she was fully concealed behind her blue curtain, she unscrewed the cap and drank deeply; the first alcohol she had tasted since she was admitted. She felt the warmth of it as it slipped down her throat, and the stretchy luxurious sensation of it reaching the tips of her fingers, the soles of her feet. Concealing the bottle carefully in the bottom of the holdall, under her bed, Alex lay down again and drifted to sleep, holding on to the echoes of her conversation with Stuart, and thinking about his next visit.

Chapter Seven

James was bored. It was the weekend, and Ben was home. Maggie was in the kitchen doing some cooking that was making decent smells float through the living room, coming under his bedroom door and making him panic slightly. He didn't want his bedroom to smell of Sunday lunch. He wanted it to smell of him, or nothing.

James shifted on his bed, turning on his back to look at the ceiling. He liked it when Ben was home, because it meant things were a little calmer, but he felt jealous. Jealous of Ally, who hung from Ben's arm like a monkey, clawing at him for attention. Jealous that Maggie, his allocated parent, would never have a laugh with him, challenge him to a game of Monopoly or backgammon, and make him laugh. Ben seemed to have all the smiles in the house, bestowed about him genially, while James brooded and Maggie stalked about with a permanent frown that made her face look wizened and witch-like. Ally was just pathetic and needy, with no self-respect or awareness, soaking up smiles and affection like a parched sponge. It made James sick.

Maggie had been cooking for what seemed like an eternity. His parents had been fighting quietly over Ally. His mother would call her and get her to do something like peel potatoes or pick up carrot shavings from the floor where Maggie had scattered them. Ben would then shout at her and ask her to help him to wash the car. Maggie would call her back ten minutes later, angry and bitter, and demand that she wash up or lay the table. Ally was running from one to the other as if she were on a spring. James almost felt sorry for her. But not quite. It wasn't about Ally, he knew, but rather about control and some argument between Maggie and Ben that James couldn't quite fully understand. His parents seemed to hate each other, but they still shared a bedroom and lived under the same roof. James had mates whose parents got divorced. He liked the thought of that, the opportunity to have two homes and choose where to be at any given time. If things got bad, he could go and stay with Ben, and then when he was bored he could come back and stay in his room again. Double Christmas presents. Parents vying with each other to win popularity. It seemed like a good solution to the perennial problem of Ben and Maggie.

He wondered whether to mention it to them. He could just walk up to his father and say, man to man, that the situation was bizarre at best, and wouldn't Ben rather be off having fun instead of being here? Maggie used to say that they stayed together for him and Ally. That seemed stupid, to James, who would be much happier if he and Ally didn't share a house, and even better if he could choose which parent to go with. Maybe he would be able to live with Ben, lads together. They could drink beer and watch the wrestling and there'd be no more girly shit like crying and arguing. No more Ally vying for attention and usually winning out.

Ben could get a decent bachelor pad somewhere in the town. They could have a computer and a big telly, and a fridge packed with decent food. They could put their feet up on the furniture and then James could invite his mates over. He could stay out late and roll in pissed or off his face, and Ben wouldn't be waiting up for him with a belt in his hands. Maybe he wouldn't even have to go to school. Maybe Ben would let him buy a bass guitar, so he could learn to play and get his meal ticket out of the place one day. He'd make his fortune and then buy his own place, and have groupie girls with long legs and big tits screaming after him when he got out of his limo.

It was all theoretical, though. If Ben moved out, he'd take Ally. James would be left mopping up puke and avoiding his mother. James sat upright and rubbed his eyes, shaking his head to dispel the daydream which for a few minutes had made him feel like someone else. He looked around his room critically, checking for dirt. He found none.

Ally knocked on his door and called him, her voice reedy and a bit pleading.

"Dinner's ready. Maggie wants you to come now, she's dishing it up."

James swung his feet off the bed and frowned, ignoring Ally as he walked out of the room, pushing past her roughly. He walked into the lounge, dragging his feet and scowling. Ben was sitting at the head of the dining table, Tiger weaving around his legs. Maggie was walking to and from the kitchen, steaming plates of roast dinner in her hand. It smelled good. James sat down next to Ben, his stomach growling as he sniffed the air. He kicked out with his feet as Tiger approached, pushing the cat away from him roughly. Ally sat next to James, pulling her chair a little closer to him, so she was out of the reach of Maggie. Ben was grinning at them both, picking up his knife and fork in anticipation as Maggie placed the last plate down on the table.

"Looking good, Mum!" Ben exclaimed, and Maggie grunted and unfolded her napkin. Ally sidled off the chair to the stereo, flicking some buttons and turning it on.

"How is it?" Maggie enquired, her eyes looking a little unfocused as she watched them all eat. Ally made appreciative noises without looking up. Ben balanced a green bean on his fork and nodded. James scowled to himself and jabbed at a piece of meat with his fork, before pulling a piece off and surreptitiously dropping it beneath his knees onto the floor for Tiger.

Maggie stood up suddenly, and walked unsteadily to the kitchen to get wine. Ally pushed her glass forward hopefully as her mother returned, but Maggie ignored her, filling first her own glass and then Ben's. Ben watched his wife carefully as she poured, and James imagined he saw disapproval in his eyes.

"Can I go out and play, after lunch?" Ally asked, and Maggie took a long draught of wine before answering.

"No. You've got homework to do. After the washing up. And the ironing is piling up."

Ally looked down again and played with some green beans on her plate. Ben sighed and shifted in his seat, avoiding Ally's eyes. Instead, he looked at James, his mouth down-turned, but James looked away, shrugging. It was nothing to do with him, and if Ben had any sense then he'd keep out of it too. As if realising that this wasn't the right time to start an argument, Ben drank some wine and continued to eat, his leg jiggling about under the table, making the liquid in his glass dance up and down like a tiny tide. James watched the wine for a while, pushing food in to his mouth and chewing quickly. He hated weekends, hated when they all had to sit together and eat. You could slice the heaviness and tension in the room with a blade.

Once they had eaten, Ally cleared the table and started washing up, and James slunk back to his room to stare at the wall. He could hear Maggie making her way upstairs unsteadily, probably to lie on her bed and drink. Ben seemed to have wandered off outside somewhere. James hesitated and then pulled a tin out from under his bed, rummaging in it for a joint. He found a half-used one and finished it, pushing the smoke from his lungs out of the window. Ben was out of sight, and James could see the open door of the garage if he craned his neck to the right. There was little or no chance of his being caught smoking. He heard the sound of the radio in the living room and started humming along, the music pushing to the forefront of his mind which was becoming nicely muddled. He hated Sundays.

Stubbing the last of the joint out on the brickwork beneath his open window, James exhaled one last time and flapped at the air in his room, trying to dispel the last strains of smoke that hovered at head height. It smelled sweet and slightly ashy. He went over to the bed and lay on it again, holding his hand out in front of him so he could study it. Maybe he could be an artist. He could sketch masterpieces, getting a load of money so he could escape. That would bring the women in. That would make Donna look at him.

Donna was a beauty in the year above him at school. She was brunette, her long hair permed into soft curls that cascaded over her inordinately large breasts. She smelled of apples and cinnamon and cigarette smoke. James sometimes followed her surreptitiously, watching the way she walked, her hips undulating with a tantalising wiggle that made his mouth water. He started to blush as he thought of her. Donna barely knew he existed. He needed a plan to catch her attention. On Fridays, she wore tight jeans that stretched over her bum, causing little creases and folds beneath the cheeks. She had a soft tinkling laugh that reminded James of fairground rides and ice-cream van jingles. James sighed, pulling her voluptuous image to mind. He unzipped his jeans and slipped a hand beneath, thinking about Donna's eyes, blue and piercing, and the cream-white skin of her pale throat. And her breasts. Too big for a hand to hold them. Ripe and full.

James sat up suddenly. Donna would never date him, because he couldn't invite her over as his mates did. He briefly considered the image of Donna in his house. She would have to pick her way through the discarded spirit bottles in the living room before accompanying him into his bedroom. She'd have to hold her breath to avoid gulping in a lungful of stale cigarette smoke. She would have to be blind not to notice the dust and mess, the way Maggie's jumpers were usually stained and creased, the stale smell she gave off when she was drunk. No apple scent in the world could combat all that. James imagined Donna's face as she surveyed his little kingdom and then turned baleful eyes back at him. Disgust and surprise. James had to be cleaner, more neat and tidy, than anyone else to stop the filth of the house permeating his skin, giving off strange odours of sadness and desperation. He stood up. He was hungry again.

Maggie called it having hollow legs, amazed and proud of how much food her son could put away. She seemed to get a kick out of feeding him, as if James's eating were a spectator sport. He imagined what it would be like to have hollow legs. He could flip the top off them and store things inside. He giggled suddenly.

Standing up, James decided to check on his mother. He could hear Ally and Ben in the kitchen now, and that meant Maggie was upstairs stewing and brooding by herself. The Sunday routine meant that she would be completely out of her head, rocking and crying to herself, slowly imbibing more and more chemicals in an effort to knock herself out. James didn't question it, it was so normal to him. He left the room reluctantly, leaving the door ajar to allow the last of the smoke out.

Maggie was unconscious in her room, sprawled at a peculiar broken angle across the bed. Her face was pale, and as James pushed the door open cautiously he caught the unmistakeable stench of vomit. He shuddered and walked over to her, his sleeve pulled out over one hand to cover his gagging mouth. He stared at his mother for a moment, pausing to hear the sound of her breathing.

Gardening in the Dark

It was regular and deep. She had thrown up over one side of the bed, but was obviously sentient enough to roll over so she wouldn't choke on the vomit. It had happened before. Ally and James had dealt with it quickly and quietly, neither communicating to the other but both fully aware. James grabbed some tissues and a plastic bag from beneath the bed and cleaned up roughly, his stomach clenched and arms goosebumping against the smell and look of it.

There were a couple of bottles of cough mixture lying empty by the bed. Maggie had a habit of drinking it neat from the bottle. He lifted it to his nose and inhaled. It smelled of menthol and blackcurrant, reminding him of being small and tear-streaked, coughing through the night. He picked over the medicine bottles scattered across her bedside table. Valium, Temazepam, Diazepam. He shook some into his upturned palm and looked at them before slipping them into his pocket. He retrieved a packet of cigarettes, half-squashed beneath her inert weight, and pocketed them too. Opening a window to let some air in, James covered his mother with a sheet and settled her head more comfortably on a pillow, instinct making him roll her head to one side to stop her from choking if she was sick again. He hurried downstairs to get some bleach, and to scrub the cloying scent of her from his clothes and skin.

He walked to the kitchen quickly, intent on being clean again, thinking about his mother with a mixture of love and revulsion. He paused in the doorway, shaken from his wandering thoughts by some unfamiliar sounds. His eyes widened.

It was a tableau, a grotesque tapestry image sewn into the air. Ben and Ally were bent over the kitchen table in a shocking embrace. Ben towered over his sister, grunting. James froze and stared. Ally looked up quickly, a gasp of shock issuing from her clenched mouth, her tear-stained eyes round and horrified. She stared at her brother, and James stared back, his lip curled in disgust. For a full few seconds the two considered each other, before his sister bowed her head and submitted once more to the situation. James backed away from the kitchen door and back to the living room. He stood for a moment, his mouth open, scratching at his eyes as if they burned, and then he fled to his bedroom.

He opened the window and lit a cigarette, his hands shaking. The smoke burned his throat, making him want to retch. He needed air. He needed to breathe. He climbed out of the window and jumped clumsily, then started to run. He covered distance quickly, his breath jagged and painful, his legs pumping against the concrete so hard that they sent jarring pain up through his knees. He ran to the train track. It was deserted.

Gasping for breath, James started to panic as his body slowed, which in turn made his thoughts run faster. He felt at once numb and sick with the speed of his brain, the flashing images that crowded him. He felt as if his skull were becoming stretched and taut with the weight of his mind. He sat for a moment, his hands over his ears, then his eyes, fists balled and pushing against the pictures behind his lids. He took a joint from his pocket and lit it quickly, his hands shaking, and took pull after pull of the acrid smoke until he felt his heartbeat begin to slow.

James barely looked up as a train went past, screeching its presence with an eerie wail. He stared at the tracks. When they were children, he and Ally used to clamber down and put two pence pieces on the rails, waiting with excited anticipation as the train sailed over them. When they retrieved the coins, they would be rolled paper-thin and misshapen, the Queen's head becoming squashed and deformed. The slight thrill of danger; the possibility that they could be squashed flat, too. Jumping out of the way just in time.

James put his head down by the side of the railway track and began to sob. He normally didn't cry, couldn't remember the last time he had felt so bad. His tears washed away the scent of Maggie, leaving his insides feeling a little lighter. More tolerable. The sobs were loud and desperate, a wail of despair that wrenched his stomach and made his shoulders heave and shudder. A lifetime of misery seemed to surge up from some hidden place inside him. He cried for himself.

He cried for his mates' parents, all perfect, and his friends who didn't know what it meant to come home and feel the sting of their mother's hand as she lashed out. He cried for the love that Ben bestowed upon his sister, who was ugly and stupid. He smoked another of Maggie's cigarettes and cried for jealousy, for revulsion, cried loud and hard to try to run from the image in his head. Ben and Ally. Ally and Ben. He sat forward and threw up by the side of the track, the nicotine and smoke making him nauseous, coupled with the image of his father and sister. He cried until he wanted to breathe again; he cried himself inside out.

That's why Ben didn't love him. That's why he would never be good enough, because Ben wanted a girl. Maggie wanted a boy, and that didn't bear thinking about either. He imagined himself murdering Ally. It felt good, a small kernel of bitter and acid satisfaction. He would sneak into her room in the middle of the night and smother her with a pillow, until her face went blue and she stopped breathing. Then he'd go to borstal, and that could be a blessed relief.

It was too much. James wanted to be normal. He wanted to sit in class and feel that he was the same as all the others, not that he was part of something mad. He needed to be able to come home to a house that was clean and safe, where he could bring Donna and they could sit and have cups of tea and chat to his parents, all smiles and baking and clean carpets. He almost laughed, the image in his head so different to his reality. It wasn't fair.

James stilled and thought about Ben. He hadn't always realised what was going on. Only when he awoke to the sound of Ben's footsteps creeping across the hall, Ally crying and white in the mornings. And Maggie, dirty and disgusting and smoking her cigarettes and pissed and vomiting and her witch voice and the same filthy clothes, drugged and bruised on the sofa. Mumbling to herself about other men, always wanting some other life.

James imagined being dead. He climbed down on to the tracks. The light was on green. A train was coming; he felt the low rumble beneath his feet and reached into his pocket for a two pence piece. He stood straddled on the tracks, and turned the coin over and over in his hand, across his knuckles. It had taken him hours to learn how to do that. He did it brilliantly.

And what was the future? He asked himself as he stood with the tracks reverberating beneath the soles of his trainers, his tears still splashing down unchecked. He focused on the coin, spinning faster and faster over his hand, rolling between his fingers.

The future. There wasn't one, he concluded, as the vibrations grew louder and louder.

"Don't be a chicken," he said to himself, as the train came into view. He stopped, mesmerised as it rounded the corner, and suddenly it blared at him and he was shocked by the noise and he jumped, becoming athletic and responding with each fibre in his body attuned.

He stood by the track. He was so very alive. He had a body that would take him on and on, regardless of how his mind swirled. There would be a future, one day soon, away from them all. He was going to stay silent. It was too nauseating and vile to put into words, to articulate.

Her face. Ally's face. He hated her.

James stayed by the track until his legs, shaking, started to calm. He held tight to the coin, no longer rolling it fluidly across the top of his knuckles.

He didn't want to be dead.

Then James turned and walked home, a part of him suddenly and resolutely sealed and complete. He vowed to never feel again.

Gardening in the Dark

Chapter Eight

They had talked to her again and again about the need to leave her cubicle, socialise. They had diagnosed her with manic depression, or Bipolar Affective Disorder, having asked her to fill in forms outlining how loud she sang in the shower, or if people around her got frustrated when she started new projects. If she was promiscuous, or spent too much money. She had burned with shame, recognising some periods in her life as they were catalogued by the questionnaire. Apparently she was very 'manic', very 'depressive'. At last she had a label, a neat tidy category.

She hadn't asked more about it, at the time. She had been shocked by the term, which sounded harsh and made it seem as if she belonged on this quirky ward, with people who shuffled and dribbled. She had asked if anyone else there had the same thing, and they had walked away, tight-lipped with confidentiality. She had scrutinised the other residents and found nothing among any of them that even vaguely reminded her of herself. She wasn't being carted off every week for Electroconvulsive Therapy, and she didn't scream or fight or chip away at the walls with bleeding fingernails. Alex had looked about surreptitiously at the people she found herself surrounded by, and shuddered. How was she to socialise with people who frightened her, who reminded her at every turn of where she was, and – much worse, much more terrifying – who she herself had become? Was it natural to encourage socialising in a place where everyone was suffering and vulnerable; where anything one said or did was risky, in that it could potentially damage someone?

She agreed to it, because she was tired and it was easier to comply than resist the constant gentle pushing and persuasion that they seemed to be so adept at. One morning, after she had showered and neatened up her possessions (hoping to herself as she aligned her meagre belongings that she was not becoming more than a little like Doreen), she made her way to the living room. She hadn't been in it before. It was sectioned off by a dark wooden door, with elaborate panelling. She looked through its glass window with apprehension. There were a lot of people in there, it seemed, and she felt suddenly afraid of pushing the door open and walking in, being stared at or studied for signs of her own madness, by the mad eyes of those within.

"Come on, Alex!" – and Mark, the staff nurse with the floppy brown hair, had pushed open the door from behind her and propelled her in, shielding her and leading her to a seat in one of the armchairs, concealing her partially from view until she was sitting. It happened quickly, and Alex smiled her gratitude at the sensitive young man who had picked up on her apprehension and relieved her of it. It happened quickly, to Alex whose mind was working very slowly, and she felt as if Mark had clicked his fingers and magically transported her into the room without giving her a moment to compose her face in readiness to approach those faces which she would encounter.

"Good morning," Alex mumbled, and studied the television with intense concentration. Nobody responded, and she relaxed a little. If she stared at the screen, she would perhaps pass unnoticed. There was a talk show on, a daytime chat programme with a smug presenter who walked about the stage with an air of tedium, as her guests argued and swore at each other. Alex frowned at it. It couldn't be a good idea for the inmates of the ward to see this, surely? As if they weren't low enough without observing that people on the outside world were just as bad. What hope was there, for them, if the supposedly sane acted with more bizarre behaviour than the people who were held at the hospital? Alex turned away from it, trying to stop the voices of the shouting family on the programme from working their way into her mind. She looked about her cautiously.

Doreen was sitting in an armchair opposite Alex, her head tilted back and her mouth wide open, a small puddle of drool forming on her chest, which rose and fell gently as she dreamed. Alex felt something akin to mild affection as she looked at her. Doreen was young in her mind, stuck somewhere in a dark childhood, still locked in a shed waiting for her father to come back and release her and her siblings. Alex smiled and turned away. Doreen was a sweet and damaged thing.

Gardening in the Dark

With a sense of shock, Alex realised she was being studied. She looked to her side, at a young man who was sharing the sofa with her, and was almost affronted to find he had turned to face her, and was watching her carefully, a wide smile lighting up his face. Alex recovered from the initial surprise of his directness, feeling that he lacked the discretion necessary in such a volatile and complicated environment. She stared back, determined not to be cowed by his direct gaze, which seemed to cut through her, analysing her innermost thoughts.

"Hello," the man said, and his voice was rounded and warm. "I'm Martin."

Alex attempted a smile, a slight curving grimace, as she turned and faced him fully for the first time.

"Alex," she said, extending a hand. As the man took it, she looked at him. He had a nice face, with glasses and almost-black hair which was a little too long. His eyes were wide and bright, and looked as if they had a smile playing behind them which changed their colour from second to second. He was unshaven, with a roguish few days of stubble that framed his angular chin in dark shadow. His nose, long and pointed, gave him a curious expression as if he were accustomed to hunting things out, ferreting for answers and meaning beneath the veneer of things.

"Pleased to meet you, Alex. And may I enquire how you are feeling today?" Martin asked, his face betraying a hint of mischief and sarcasm beneath the apparently innocent words. Alex found herself smiling, for perhaps the first time, with a genuine feeling of pleasure to be addressed in a normal, carefree way, as if Martin was unconcerned about her reaction to his words. She felt suddenly much more normal.

"Absolutely superb, today," she said. "On top of the world, in fact. And you?"

Martin grinned, flashing even white teeth, and settled himself to face her fully.

"Perfect, thank you. Never better," he replied, his eyes twinkling, and Alex giggled. Surrounded by these people who rocked and drooled at the television, their conversation seemed, frankly, insane. Martin smiled again and flicked his eyes over to the television.

"Is this show a favourite of yours? I have to admit I've never watched it before. It's been quite a revelation this morning," he said. Alex shrugged and turned her eyes to the television.

"They are all freaks, on this programme. I watch it sometimes when I'm not working," she said. Martin nodded seriously.

"All freaks?" he said, and looked about him, taking in the room with his eyebrows arched. Alex suddenly realised the irony of what she had said, and started to laugh. Martin joined her, covering his face with his hands, and the two of them laughed harder. Alex tried to be discreet, not wanting to disturb the people around her, who were all engrossed in the programme, but the laughter would not be contained and she snorted with the effort of trying to keep it down. This made Martin laugh harder, and soon the two of them were given over to the hilarity. The harder they tried to control it, the more the mischievous laughter erupted. Alex clutched at her stomach and wiped tears from her eyes.

Suddenly the two of them were startled by a sound from across the room, and Alex realised that Doreen had awoken, and had begun to laugh too, a rich warbling of mirth that Alex had not heard before. She was looking at the two of them, caught up in their merriment, her face creased into a huge smile. Alex looked at Martin, and the two of them were off again, becoming more and more noisy, drowning out the television. The people around them looked up, curious, until the entire room was suddenly full of laughter. They were laughing at each other, their situation, and each person was feeding on the laughter of the person next to them. Alex rocked backwards and forwards, her eyes streaming, and felt suddenly alive. The room was full of the warm rich sound of laughter, and it felt like an old friend that she had missed, as if someone dear to her had just skipped into the room and flung their arms about her.

Gardening in the Dark

"Well," Martin said, his giggles subsiding as he looked around the room, "I've missed that." Alex nodded, wiping her eyes again, and grinned at him.

"Me too," she answered. Martin turned to her.

"I haven't seen you smile since you arrived," he commented, and Alex felt herself suddenly stiffen, remembering with a jolt exactly where they were, and who she herself was.

"No," she responded, drawing her legs up to her chest and crossing her arms about them protectively. Martin noticed her reaction, and bit his lip.

"Sorry. It's not done to talk about anything real, here, is it?" he commented. Alex smiled a little, and shook her head.

"No. You can talk about the weather. Or the food. Or any pets you may have, and we can play Scrabble perhaps, but you can't ask any questions, and neither can I," she agreed ruefully.

"Well that's a stupid rule," Martin said. "We're going to be terribly bored if that's the case." And he turned back to the television with mock disgust. Alex smiled.

"Well it's up to you," she offered, allowing him in for a moment. Martin turned back to her and smiled again.

"I'm Martin, as you know. I'm here because I have Bipolar, and I've been sectioned."

"What does that mean?" she asked. She was immediately curious, as finally she had met someone who could be the same as her, who may be able to shed some light on her situation. She leaned forward eagerly.

"It means I don't dribble and shuffle, and I don't spend my entire life in a pit of depression – just part of it. The other part I spend being very, very happy," he responded. He was entirely unselfconscious. Alex smiled.

"Oh. Me, too," she said, and together they looked about the room. Alex suddenly realised that all the people in the room were different from her. They stayed at the bottom of the pit, wandering lost from day to day, and didn't get the bubble of joy which Alex knew would soon be coming to claim her. She could be saved, temporarily, while they would remain the same, shuddering from Electroconvulsive Therapy and drugs which made them shake, while at least Alex knew she would soon swing with the regularity of a pendulum into a better place.

"Me too," she said again, and grinned at Martin, this person who may be the same as her, in this odd place.

"What does 'sectioned' actually mean?" Alex asked. Martin shrugged and smiled again.

"It means that I am detained under the 1983 Mental Health Act, for up to six months, for assessment because I am deemed to be harmful to either myself or to others," he quoted seriously, but his eyes twinkled again and Alex didn't feel disconcerted by his response.

"Oh. That's a shame," she said, and suddenly the two were laughing again.

"Could be worse. Could be dead," Martin countered, and that set Alex off laughing harder, as Doreen began to giggle across the room, her usually blank eyes sparkling across at the two of them. There seemed to be limitless opportunities for humour, in this most humourless of places, and Alex felt more relaxed and at ease than she had since her admission.

"And you?" Martin asked carefully, turning to the television again as if to give her enough space to formulate and state a reply. Alex bit her lip.

"I'm not entirely sure. Voluntary, I think. Bipolar, too," she said, matter-of-factly. It seemed strange to state her madness aloud, to offer it up in statements which reduced her entire life to a small thing which could be labelled and volunteered in that way. She cringed inwardly at the transition from negation to ownership, wondering if it were quite right to be claiming the label as her own. After all, how did one articulate it so simply, this bleak and life-destroying illness which had haunted her for so many years? Martin nodded and turned back to her.

"That's a shame," he said, and again the two were laughing. It was a good response, Alex thought.

"You don't eat," he commented, and Alex flushed in surprise that he had noticed. She had never seen him before, and felt disconcerted that he knew so much about her.

"No," she agreed, and looked down at her hands. How to explain that she was hedging her bets, that she needed to feel safe that the people at the hospital would offer her some reprieve from her madness, before she would relinquish control and remove her only chance of making a choice? Martin studied her for a second.

"Hedging your bets?" he asked, nonchalantly, and Alex looked at him, mouth open.

"Exactly," she stammered, and he nodded, completely accepting.

"What is Bipolar, for you?" Alex asked, and Martin smiled, his face looking almost nostalgic as he considered the question.

"It's everything, up and down, high and low. It's paying for all your happiness in one fell swoop with the bleakest darkest most irrational depression you can have, and then saving up all your happiness into one earth-shattering period of devastating brilliance. It's opposites. It's creativity and genius and prolific activity, or complete sluggish inertia. It's fast forward, and then slow motion, in one big cycle that leaves you feeling confused and out of breath."

"Oh," Alex said, suddenly realising that he had summed up her life in one simple paragraph.

"Do you feel sometimes like you want to do everything, try everything, be everything?" she asked curiously.

"Everything. I've set up and destroyed hundreds of businesses. I've made fortunes and then squandered them. I play golf, do rally driving, sing, paint, draw, model, do photography, calligraphy, philosophy, bricklaying. Plastering, Reiki, sports massage and nutrition. Counselling, paragliding, scuba diving and debating."

"Squash, badminton, swimming, horse-riding, tennis-playing, drawing, playing guitar, sax, cello, flute. Drawing, painting, sculpture, pottery, glass-blowing, writing, composing, running, engineering, decorating, landscape-gardening, glass-painting, flower-arranging, translation, tapestry, dress-making, cooking and topiary," Alex added to his list. They grinned at each other.

"And your favourite?"

"Gardening."

"Gardening works for me, too."

The two looked up as Susan entered the room and watched them for a moment. She smiled and surveyed the room, taking in Doreen who was still giggling and murmuring to herself in the corner, and then paused to watch television for a moment. The family on the talk show were shouting, getting up out of their seats on the stage and pointing fingers at each other, shaking fists and storming off-camera. Alex and Martin fell silent and watched it for a moment. Doreen looked across at them eagerly, hoping for another outburst.

"Are you allowed to go out, off the ward?" Martin asked suddenly. Alex shook her head.

"No. Not yet. They're scared I'll try and hack myself up or something."

"That will change in a few days, I expect. Unless you do actually try and hack yourself up."

Alex lifted her knees and hugged them to her chest. She didn't want to do anything like that. She wanted to learn more about who she was, and more about the intriguing young man next to her. She watched him out of the corner of her eye as he gazed at the television, lost in thought. He had a nice nose, she decided, and lovely large piercing eyes with dark lashes. Too long for a man, really, lending his face a soft femininity in opposition to his square jaw and pronounced features. She started and blushed as he suddenly turned to her.

"What do you see?" he asked. Alex shrugged.

"Someone I would like to spend more time with."

"Me, too," he replied, candidly.

"Why are you here?"

"The flatness went on for too long. I became afraid it wasn't going to shift."

"Me, too." Alex stood up sharply, suddenly confused. She went to the kitchen and leaned her hands on the cold metal of the draining board, looking out of the wide barred window. Her mind was reeling as she stood by the sink, absolutely thrown by Martin's complete understanding of her situation, the darkness in her that she had felt unable to articulate. He was the same as her. It was unthinkable, unfathomable, that this genteel and funny man could have lived through the same bizarre life as she had, with so many similarities that it almost normalised Alex's own experiences.

"Shit!" she muttered to herself, as she wandered into her cubicle and looked about her with new eyes. She had laughed for the first time, opened up, felt herself almost alive as they had talked. Perhaps, after all, she was not completely alone? Perhaps the way she acted, the odd decisions, impulsiveness, creative insanity and heaving lows were, after all, something routine? A way of being that could be categorised, marked and accepted? And if this was the case, perhaps they could be treated, held in check, and maybe, unthinkable as it may be, she could regain her life? Alex shook her head and went to find Mark, the nurse. She wanted to breathe, get away from being looked at for a few minutes, to reorganise her mind and place the new information in it.

The staff nurse was lounging in the hallway, picking at a loose thread on his shirt.

"Mark, are you busy?" Alex asked. He looked up, pleased to have a distraction.

"Not at the moment. What do you need?"

"I'd like to go outside. Can we go outside for a walk?"

"On the street?"

"No, not yet. In the grounds. Doreen said there's a fishpond, and trees, and a stream."

"Right you are. I'll grab a coat and we can go now."

Alex felt a small flush of pleasure, the first she had noticed since she had been admitted. She was looking forward to smelling the damp grass, lifting her head up to the sky. She hovered by the main entrance to the ward, impatient to get outside. She could almost smell the clean scent of fresh air coming through the bottom of the solid wooden door, infiltrating the heavy mustiness of the ward.

"Come on, come on," Alex muttered, and then checked herself, wondering if she could be kept on the ward for longer if she was caught talking to herself. She grinned at the thought; she was starting to get paranoid. Mark returned, pulling a jacket over his shirt, and pressed some buttons to get the door to open. Alex pushed out first, almost running down the steps to get outside. She stopped abruptly as she got to the bottom step.

Her senses were tingling. She had goosebumps at the nape of her neck, spreading across her arms. A thousand things seemed to happen simultaneously. She smelled the rich scent of fresh earth and flowers, the musky brown smell of crushed leaves and damp twigs. Her eyes smarted against the naked light that hit her face. Her skin shuddered against the unfamiliar sensation of the breeze that lifted her hair from her damp neck and cooled her. Mark stood by, watching, smiling at her reaction.

Gardening in the Dark

"It's hot on the ward. You don't realise how warm it is until you step outside."

"Step outside," Alex echoed, and shook herself.

"Where do you want to walk?"

"You choose."

They set off down an immaculate path towards the back of the hospital. Alex sniffed the air, and her pace began to speed up.

"I haven't walked for a long time, not really," she commented, and Mark picked up pace with her, his long arms swinging by his sides.

"Good day for it," he remarked, and Alex felt gladdened by the inane conversation that wasn't focused on pills and sleep and nightmares.

Mark led her along the path until they got to a small copse, the trees looking strangely tall to Alex, as if she were seeing them for the first time. She noticed the bark, the way it was stripped and gnarled in places, the way the roots lurched out of the ground in a tumult of brown entwined strips. She heard birdsong, and craned her head up, shielding her eyes to catch sight of the perpetrators.

"It's lovely."

They stood in front of the pond, and Alex looked into the water pensively, watching a myriad of carp in different shapes, sizes and colours darting backwards and forwards, threatened and intrigued by the long shadows which Alex and Mark cast over the still water. She could smell the water itself, a green earth scent that made her want to push her arms into it; become submerged. It smelled real.

"I met someone, today," she said, and looked at Mark. He smiled.

"Martin?"

"Yes. He's Bipolar, same as me."

"Yes."

"How long is he in here for? Why did he get admitted? Is he the same as me?" she asked, wanting to know everything about her new acquaintance. She wanted to ask how he managed, what he did, how he had been admitted, how old he was. Martin represented some form of future to Alex, recognition that you could understand madness and drive forward with it. Mark frowned, his lips pursed.

"I'm not prepared to discuss Martin with you, just as I wouldn't discuss your situation with anyone else," he said, suddenly terse. Alex felt her face flush in embarrassment.

"Of course. Of course not. I'm sorry." She had forgotten, for a moment, that Martin was not there to make her increase her self-understanding, but rather to improve his own. It was nothing to do with her.

"You forget about real life, and etiquette, and normality, in there. It feels like I've been in there forever," she said, watching the fish. Mark nodded his understanding, still reticent.

"Do people get cured? Of Bipolar?"

"No. But they learn to manage it, to stop themselves from swinging from one extreme to the other. Life can be as good, or even better, than for other people. You can learn to harness the creativity, without compromising your stability. You can tap into the special qualities it brings you, without falling into a depressive state. There is some great medication available, and counselling and workshops and resources to help you get to grips with it. To be honest, I think if you're going to have a mood disorder, you've picked a great one!" he quipped. Alex smiled at his candid comment.

"Is it hereditary?" she asked, suddenly reminded of something. Mark hesitated.

"We think so."

Gardening in the Dark

"Oh." Alex shuddered suddenly, and felt her temporary positive mood shift down and down. She had inherited this, then. Along with alcoholism, low self-confidence, and erratic behaviour. Along with sharp green eyes and a full mouth, the small bump on the edge of her nose. Her brown hair. All this was passed down, and now she had a new thing added to the list of qualities. Madness.

"Oh," she said again, and sat down for a moment on the side of the pond. The carp swam up to meet her, and she stuck a wary hand into the water. Mark watched as the fish came closer and nibbled on her fingers.

"I wonder if they're hungry," he mused. Alex didn't reply.

"I wonder if you're hungry." Alex looked up.

"What did you have in mind?" she asked. She was starting to trust them.

"Start small and work your way up and up and up to a feast! What's your favourite food?"

Alex shrugged. She couldn't think of anything, it had been so long since she had eaten; it was as if her body had forgotten how to do it. She poked at her stomach, unresponsive and flat, and thought of Martin's comment – 'You don't eat' – sounding as if she were only part human; dysfunctional.

"Are you going to help me?" she asked. It was an open question, taking in everything. The fishpond, the pit, the searing-hot flat depression. Mark nodded.

"Of course. It's what we do. That's why you're here, isn't it?"

Alex nodded. Mark hesitated, and then sat down next to her.

"Alex, don't get too involved with the other people in here. You need to focus on yourself, right now. I have a feeling that underneath that depression you're a sociable kind of person, and naturally curious, but it doesn't do to get close to anyone here. Don't accept where you are. Hold on to this, once you are outside, and you'll do better. Do you understand?"

Alex nodded. In the distance, she noticed Lois meandering through the trees, making barking noises at the trunks, ferreting in the grass. She understood.

"Don't get too close. Don't get involved. Above all, don't get your feet under the table and get used to the routine, Alex. You don't belong here," Mark reiterated. Alex nodded again.

"This is the beginning," she said. She looked about her at the fish, bright streaks of gold and white in the clear water, the mowed grass and neat hedges and borders. The impressive red brick of the hospital kept deliberately out of sight behind her back.

"This is the beginning," Mark agreed. "Come on, let's find you something to eat."

Alex's body stirred and stretched inside. It was responding, the robotic automatic response of an animal to the sense of approaching nourishment. She lifted her arms above her head and stood, eyes closed, feeling the light and the breeze playing along her features.

"Come on, then," she decided. Now there was a Martin, and a Stuart. And something to eat. Mark paused and held out his arm, and she took it carefully as they walked back to the building, Alex pausing outside for one last glance at the real world before she bowed her head and followed Mark inside.

Gardening in the Dark

Chapter Nine

"And then he said you're not supposed to kick the ball with the front, you should use the side," Matthew concluded, looking at James for approval. James shrugged and turned his attention back to the playground.

"Everyone knows that. It's called toe-poking when you stab at it with your foot. You need to control the ball," James said pompously, although he didn't care for football at all. Matthew nodded eagerly, not deterred.

"Exactly. That's what he said." Matthew was talking about his brother Martin, years older and already escaped from Primary up to Big School. James was jealous. Martin was cool, listened to rap music, and shaved tramlines into his hair. James wanted a Martin instead of an Ally. Allys weren't cool in any way. They were an object of ridicule. Even now, as James leaned on the stone wall of the upper playground and looked down at all the titches in the junior yard, he could make her out. Tiny, stupidly dressed and incompetent, surrounded by older girls and being picked on again. He sighed.

"Did you watch the wrestling on Saturday?" he asked Matthew, hoping to change the subject and talk about something upon which he was more of an authority. Matthew joined him in leaning against the wall. The two were looking cool, staring down at the younger kids. It never failed to give James a sense of pleasure, knowing that they were getting older and bigger. He liked lording it over the lower playground, walking with long strides past all the children who still peed themselves and cried a lot. James wouldn't cry, these days. He had practised carefully in his room, finding ways of stopping. He chewed the inside of his cheek if he felt tears were about to start, and the shock of it usually made them go back in to wherever they came from.

"Nope. I was out with Martin," Matthew said, in a reverent voice. James sighed and turned away for a moment. He located Ally surreptitiously, just as she was being punched in the stomach by one of the older girls, Lindsey. James bit his lip lightly and watched, curious. Ally had fallen to the floor, clutching her stomach. It made James feel mildly uncomfortable to see her there.

"Hey, isn't that your little sister over there?" Matthew asked, suddenly. James shrugged and carried on watching. There were now a circle of larger girls surrounding Ally. Lindsey was definitely the ringleader, though. She was leaning over his sister like a skinny willow tree, her blonde hair obscuring her face. James quite liked Lindsey but he was sometimes scared of her because she was from the estate, and estate kids were always that little bit tougher than the others.

"Yep," James answered, his face colouring. Matthew drew in his breath and leaned over the wall to get a better view.

"She's getting a bit of a pummelling, James," he commented. James closed his eyes for a second, feeling sudden warmth hit his cheeks. Ally was just…embarrassing. He wanted a Martin, who knew how to kick a ball properly and would maybe help James at sport, instead of a little bawling creature that kept being bullied because she wore stupid clothes. And her clothes were *stupid*. James had started to notice how Ally always seemed to wear the same few dresses, and they were all getting threadbare and too short in the arm. He was desperately ashamed of her. He wondered if his own coolness would be brought down, once people started to notice Ally a bit more. She was normally unobtrusive, hiding in corners and reading books, and James preferred that much more. At this moment, she was making a spectacle of herself. The crowd around her was growing slightly, as interested onlookers, half-scared and half-jeering, joined the group to watch Ally being bullied.

"If it was my sister, I'd go and sort them out," Matthew said matter-of-factly. "I'd pick out that big blonde one first, 'cos she's obviously the worst one." James rubbed his eyes and carried on looking, indecision starting to make him hesitate. It wasn't really his thing, to go to Ally's rescue. He didn't mind seeing her getting a bit of a beating. It was only what he himself would do sometimes, practising his wrestling moves on her when Maggie and Ben weren't looking.

"Martin always used to stick up for me," Matthew said, and with that James turned to his friend in frustration. He felt cornered.

"Shall I?" he asked, uncertainly. Matthew shrugged and nodded. "Martin would," he repeated, and James was shamed into turning from the wall and making his way down the wide steps to the lower playground.

"Damn it," he said to himself, then slowed his steps. Lindsey was quite big. And scary. And she probably knew how to fight much better than him. Although she was just a girl, she was a *tall* girl. James pushed his shoulders back and his chin out.

"I'm a wrestler. I'm Giant Haystacks and I'm unbeatable. I can pick someone up with a single finger and fling them into the corner of the ring, bruised and bloody. I'm seven feet tall and three feet wide and I am the scariest and toughest of them all," he whispered to himself, feeling his body elongate and fill out, muscles springing from each limb like Popeye on spinach. Unbeatable. Giant Haystacks. By the time he reached the lower playground, James had transformed into an ogre, with bushy eyebrows and long hair, and a body that looked like the side of a badly pointed brick wall. A giant.

He strode over to the group of girls purposefully. He was unstoppable. They were laughing at Ally, a miserable little heap of torn dress and some blood. Crouched over, trying to crawl away. James walked up to Lindsey and tapped her on the shoulder, hard. Lindsey spun around, the smile on her face suddenly freezing and a look of confusion creeping in to her eyes.

"That," James said, pointing at Ally, who had raised a tear-stained face in shock, "is my little sister." His voice was very firm, a giant's voice. He felt a thrill of pride and nerves when he heard it. "And no one –" a sharp poke to Lindsey's stomach "– but no one –" a swift hard push, that made her fall back against the wall "– hurts my little sister," he concluded. The group of girls fell back, trickling away unobtrusively like dirty water. Lindsey looked suddenly very small, and her face seemed to have changed colour because all her freckles stood out as if they had turned very dark. James smiled inside, but kept his face stern and furious. He reached out for Lindsey, taking her by the neck and trapping some of her blonde hair in his hand, then pushed her up and up against the wall like Giant Haystacks did with his least worthy opponents. He looked into her face, stricken with fear, and hissed at her quietly.

"Do you understand?" he asked, seething. Lindsey whimpered and nodded as best she could, into James's hand. He glanced down and saw with some satisfaction that her feet had left the floor. He also noticed that she appeared to have wet herself, which was a good thing (she was scared) but also a bad thing (James felt as if he might be sick). He put her down roughly, and she stumbled back away from him. James reached down and pulled Ally up, turning her around so she could see her tormentor more fully.

"Look, Ally," James said, his voice ringing out across the lower yard. "Lindsey has pissed herself." Ally stood half-behind James and looked, letting out a small snigger as her face relaxed. The crowd that had assembled to watch Ally now returned in groups of two and three, laughing and pointing at Lindsey until she fled, running across the yard and into the juniors' bathroom. James folded his arms and watched for a moment, and then began to walk back to the upper playground.

"James," Ally said, suddenly beside him again and tugging on his sleeve. James flicked her off impatiently.

"What?" he said. Ally smiled up at him suddenly, her face full of pride and what very much looked like the face Matthew pulled when he talked about Martin.

"Thank you," she said, and James felt a strange swelling up in his stomach, that was like being hungry and full at the same time. He shook his head at her, shrugged, and went back up the concrete steps two at a time, bouncing and suddenly weightless.

"That was cool!" Matthew greeted him as he turned the corner into the top yard. James noticed that a crowd of older boys and girls had been watching him, lining the wall and cheering him on. He hadn't realised. He smiled suddenly. He felt fantastic.

Gardening in the Dark

"That was a wrestling move, wasn't it?" someone walked up to James shyly and asked. James nodded, feeling suddenly terribly smug.

"I wish I had a little sister," Matthew said. James looked at him, surprised. He turned again to look at the lower playground, where the crowd had dissipated and Ally was in a small group of short girls, talking animatedly. He supposed it was all right, sometimes.

On the way home, James allowed Ally to walk beside him instead of making her trail behind. She bounced about by his elbow, talking about what had happened. Her face was shining.

"She can't look at me now, James. She's ashamed and you frightened her and it's going to be *brilliant* because now the bigger girls won't do anything to me because they know I've got you there and sometimes you could just look over and you might see them, and then POW! You'll come and get them and I can tell you if they do anything behind your back and you can come and get them then as well!" Ally garbled, skipping along. James looked at her suddenly. She was quite small. She had a bruise across one side of her face, and it looked puffy as if it might hurt quite a lot, but she didn't seem to notice. In some ways, James mused, she was quite brave. Not brave like him, because he could pick up spiders, but brave in a quiet sort of way because she just sort of put up with things. James thought again about what Matthew had said, about wishing he had a little sister, and he tried to weigh up why it could be a positive thing.

On the one hand, having a sister was not good because she was annoying, embarrassing, and just wasn't cool. And sometimes she smelled bad. On the other hand, James could get more respect by sticking up for her at school. And sometimes it was nice to have her creep into his room when it was dark, and sleep on the floor by his bed, because they could talk about things that they wouldn't ever mention in the daylight. Also, it was good to have someone to hit when he was in a bad mood.

"Maybe you're not all that bad," James muttered to Ally, who carried on glowing and skipping, her face a beam of smiles.

James slowed down to let Ally keep up with him, her shorter legs working at double time for each step that he took. He gave her a sideways glance.

"Your face is bruised," he said, keeping concern out of his voice.

Ally shrugged. "S'okay," she answered, brushing her fingers across the livid mark on her cheek. James winked at her, suddenly proud. She might not have held her own in the playground, but Lindsey was tall and willowy, and even James had felt slightly worried at the prospect of taking her on.

The two walked quickly, Ally chewing on the ends of her hair and James lost in thought. They both slowed down as they walked through the village and along the alleyway which led up to their cul-de-sac. James wondered for a moment if he could talk to Ally the same way as he did when she crept into his room at night. The sun was bright, with a warm wind. The weather seemed incongruous with confidences.

"What mood do you think she'll be in?" he asked. It was a non-committal kind of confidence, an opening into something darker. Ally's footsteps slowed even more, so that James had to pause to let her catch up with him again.

"I dunno. Bad, maybe," she said. Her brow was furrowed and James wondered if it was harder for Ally to deal with their mother, because she was smaller. "It depends on the music and the curtains," she concluded. James stiffened slightly, surprised that his sister, whom he thought was very stupid, could have worked out a similar system to himself for determining the state of Maggie's temper on a particular day. If the curtains were closed and there was no music, she would be lying prostrate on the sofa in darkness, the air thick with cigarette smoke and filth everywhere. If they rounded the corner and the windows were open, with some music blaring out, then she would be in a good mood. Sometimes overwhelmingly good, cooking and singing, dancing to the music and catching James as he walked past, pulling him into a waltz.

Gardening in the Dark

They walked on, past the dog at number seventeen that hurled itself at the wrought-iron gate, slavering at them. Ally drew in towards James and he didn't push her away. He felt suddenly protective of her. He was afraid of the dog – he'd once been frightened out of his skin when it leaped up at the bars and he'd been daydreaming – but something about Ally's faith in him made him suddenly tough. He looked up at the bungalow as they approached it, and suddenly smiled. The windows were wide open, and as they walked, footsteps quickening now they knew what Maggie was going to be like, James caught the strains of Dean Martin crooning a song. Ally started humming the words, getting them wrong, and James understood that she, too, felt a surge of relief that Maggie was going to be on good form.

As he neared the back door, James found himself wanting to push Ally away. Maggie didn't like her very much, and James wondered if siding with Ally would somehow make Maggie angry with him. Ally, too, seemed to instinctively draw back from James, as if she realised that their new-found companionship would have to draw to a close once the natural hierarchy of the house reinstated itself. Ben and Ally, Maggie and James – this was the natural order of things, and James didn't want anything to upset it. He would always rather have Maggie on his side than against him, even if he was jealous of Ally's relationship with their father. Ben was fun, bought presents and played games, but he was never about for long enough to be a worthwhile investment. Maggie, on the other hand, was scary and mean, but it was safer to have her on your side. James shrugged to himself as he walked through the back door, sniffing baking-scents in the air, the kitchen warm and homely.

"Hi," he said, walking up to Maggie who was up to her arms in pastry, kneading something in a Pyrex bowl.

"Hello darling." Maggie beamed at him. Her face was shining and there was a smudge of flour on her round cheek. "Good day?" she asked, and James felt suddenly that they were in the middle of an advert for washing-up liquid or gravy powder, and his mother was playing her role quite well.

"Not bad," he answered, and Ally hurried past him into the lounge, not bothering to greet Maggie. James saw her pocket an orange on the way past the living room table, and looked the other way. Then Ally ran straight to her room, as usual, trying to keep out of her mother's way.

"What you been up to?" he asked Maggie, who was pushing the dough mixture on to a marble slab and rolling it out. Maggie shrugged.

"Not much. I've been down to the shop and got some ingredients, I made a chocolate cake that needs icing and now I'm doing scones. And I've cleaned. Everywhere. Apart from Ally's room because it was a tip," she said, cutting the dough into circles and laying them in equal lines along a baking tray. James leaned in and took some of the dough, pushing the raisins into the mixture with his finger before popping it into his mouth.

"What's for tea?" he asked, wondering if Maggie had cooked for them. She smiled proudly, rubbing dough from her hands.

"I made a stew. With dumplings. Your father will be back later on and he'll probably be hungry," she said. James smiled. Ben coming home, a cooked tea, a clean house.

"Fantastic," he said, and started to help Maggie clear the side, scraping up dough and scrubbing the marble down. Maggie started singing along to the music that was coming through from the living room door. Ally suddenly appeared again, lured out of her room by the smell of cake and casserole that mingled with Maggie's cigarette smoke, making the kitchen fogged and homely.

"Good day?" Maggie asked Ally, and she grinned and nodded.

"Fine. You?" she asked, sidling up to the side and taking a currant that had fallen down the side of the marble on to the worktop. Maggie slapped her hand away, laughing, and took Ally's arms, getting her to stand on Maggie's stockinged feet, dancing in time to the music. James smiled too, watching his mother parade Ally around the kitchen to 'King of the Road'.

Gardening in the Dark

"What shall we do, kids? We have over two hours before Ben comes home. We should do something interesting," Maggie stated, her hair gleaming and flowing over one shoulder, face carefully made up and her beige apron keeping her favourite navy blue dress free of flour. Ally laughed as they spun around, and James clambered up on to the kitchen side and watched them, humming to the music. Maggie was in an excellent mood. The baking, the clean house and her exuberance all heralded the start of a good few days. James felt a thrill of excitement starting in his stomach. She would be unstoppable, keeping them up until all hours, planning and being busy and inventing exciting things to do. She would be feisty and fun for at least a week. It felt like Christmas, in that these moods were slow in coming and he looked forward to them for a long time.

Chapter Ten

Alex turned back halfway along the road to the Gatehouse, and looked at the hospital. It was an austere, red-bricked building developed at a time when lunatics were to be kept well back from the general public, out of sight. She gazed quietly at the windows which stared back like dead eyes into her regard. She pictured a broken person behind each barred eye. Doreen muttering to herself on the second floor, shuffling in threadbare slippers and crying into her soaked sleeve. Martin, confused at times, staring through the smudged glass trying to glimpse normality in the trees, or in the patterns of cloud in the sky. The building was weighted with sadness and mental decay. Alex lifted her hands to her face and she could smell the building on them, as if the hospital's essence had permeated her skin, oozing out like recrimination as she stood and stared.

"It's time to go in, Alexandra," her companion said to her, gently coaxing as if Alex were a sedated monster that had a tendency to lash out if provoked or spoken to in the wrong way. Alex returned her attention to the path ahead, turning around.

"Where is 'in'?" she asked, mildly curious as to how she could be going somewhere different, without leaving the grounds. She felt a sudden dread that she wasn't going to talk about alcohol to someone, after all, but rather any minute now she was going to be seized and straitjacketed, dragged screaming into a cellar somewhere and ministered with electricity until she was frazzled and lost.

"Over here. The Gatehouse," the young nurse replied, and his eyes suddenly smiled at her, as if he understood. "It's a lovely little building. I haven't been in, but I'd like to. I'm still a trainee, here, and I'd love to find out more about the facility and what they do. I'd like to ask you about it when I come to take you back…" The nurse hesitated and fell over his next words, and Alex grinned, wondering if he was about to say 'home'.

Gardening in the Dark

"Of course," she said, and the two proceeded to walk towards the imposing wrought-iron gates which signalled freedom, normalcy and mundane things like taxis and cafes. Alex lifted her eyes towards the gate as they approached, thinking hungrily of speeding straight through them and running down a normal street, heading for the pub or cinema, or a friend's house.

"Later," her companion promised, and steered her gently to the left, to a tiny building at the entrance to the hospital grounds.

"Right. Shall I...?" Alex asked, and he smiled and held his arm out towards the door, a discreet dark blue arch with a brass knocker in the shape of a lion's head.

"Are you...?" Alex began, and he shook his head.

"I trust you. I'll come and pick you up in exactly one hour, from here. Don't let me down and run away or anything. That would get me into trouble."

"OK," Alex said, and turned to the door, raising her hand to touch the knocker. She lifted it hard and brought it down, and the sound it made was solid and warm on the wood panel beneath.

Alex didn't turn around as she waited for the door to open, but knew that her chaperone would be standing at a discreet distance waiting to make sure she was admitted safely to the Gatehouse. Despite this, Alex still felt a mixed thrill of fear and excitement at the prospect of something different happening. A change of scene. She wondered if the smell of the hospital was still clinging to her clammy skin as the door swung open with a creak, for all the world as if she were in some old horror film about to meet her doom. She stepped in cautiously.

"I'm Alex," Alex stated, and her voice croaked so she cleared her throat and said it again. It came out better this time. She stepped further inside and found herself in a tiny hallway, with a rickety staircase to the left, and a few haphazard doors scattered along the length of it. Behind the door, a woman who seemed to be constructed purely out of an enormous smile gestured her in.

"Come in, come inside. The waiting room's over here. We've got a new coffee machine. Owen will be here in a sec, I think he's in with another client. Have a seat! It's this way. How are you, how are you?"

Alex blinked and smiled and nodded, and made a 'humph' noise. She walked through a door at the far end of the hall and sat carefully down on a small wooden chair in one corner of the room where she found herself. It was warm and scattered with noisy posters all over the walls, and reminded her of the lovely woman who had invited her in.

She took a deep breath. The woman followed her in, and fussed about neatening things, straightening a pile of magazines on the table and walking over to the coffee machine.

"Coffee?" she asked, her voice breathy and happy. Alex coughed.

"No, thank you. I've just had one," she said, and then laughed inwardly because it wasn't true, and she would like one but politeness and a sense of propriety had pushed the words out, automatic words that fitted not in this environment, or the one she had just walked from, but in a world of churches perhaps, or office buildings and interviews.

"I thought it was going to rain, Alex. It is Alex, isn't it? But then the clouds all blew away and it looks as if we're in for a nice spell, at last, which may sound like a great thing but actually the Gatehouse is shockingly receptive to weather, and if it's cold we literally freeze, and then in summer we toast in the rooms. The windows are that lovely old-fashioned sash type which may look nice, but you try and get a breeze through into the rooms on a hot day. It's nigh on impossible!"

Alex nodded and smiled and gripped the edges of her chair. She wondered fleetingly if this woman had walked down the path from the hospital, just as she had, for there was something almost maniacal in her manner of speaking. But perhaps that was because this was normal, and Alex hadn't encountered normal for quite a while.

Gardening in the Dark

"Here's Owen," the woman suddenly announced, and Alex looked up to see a man put his head around the door and search the room.

"Owen, this is Alex, Alexandra. She's come to see you!" the woman declared happily, as if Alex had popped in off the street for a coffee and a chat. Alex smiled at her, and then turned her attention to the man's head, which was made up mostly of a shock of grey hair above a brown face, though the face was too young for the hair's colouring. He must have been in his early thirties, and his hair was haphazard and unrestrained as if it were stretching up to the ceiling to look about.

"Owen," the man said, and his voice was smiley. "Good to see you, Alex." (Because suddenly they were old friends, and Alex understood this from the way the man smiled, and how he held his hand out warmly and practically dragged her from the wooden chair and out of the room).

"Three flights. Or maybe four, or two, depending on who is using what room. We swap about all the time," he said, and Alex followed him up the winding narrow stairs passing door after door, suddenly out of breath because she hadn't eaten for a very long time and her body was only accustomed to mild panic, and inertia.

"This one," Owen said, and then hesitated as his hand went for the door and began to push it, but then halted suddenly.

"No. The next one," he decided, and stepped back and ushered Alex into a small room with two comfortable chairs, modern against the Gatehouse's decrepit decor. There was a small table with tissues, and a water dispenser. The sash window was open, letting a welcome breeze rustle the top of Owen's hair which looked like a hedgehog with its spiked grey strands.

"Which chair?" Owen asked, and Alex hovered and then perched on the one nearest the door. Owen swung into the other, his long legs clad in faded jeans with a small rip above each knee. They looked at each other. Owen had a wide-open face, with lines around his eyes from smiling, and a jaunty eyebrow piercing. He looked…normal.

Alex smiled. Owen smiled back, and the two settled themselves into their respective seats. Alex became aware that her body had started to relax for the first time since she had entered the hospital grounds.

"So?" Owen said, and looked at her expectantly. Alex worried that she was about to endure the sort of counselling sessions she had been subjected to as a child, where her interviewer sat in silence for an hour, waiting for her to say something momentous. She had a fleeting memory of being in an office, at fifteen, and standing up in a rage after an hour of silence, walking from the room and slamming the door so hard a clock fell off the wall and shattered. She had never understood that sort of counselling, being naturally a little shy. How was she supposed to walk into a stranger's office, and begin to chat happily about herself, that most guarded and uncertain subject?

"I don't know anything about you, but I want to tell you some things," Owen said, his voice warm and undulating up and down like a musical scale. Alex nodded and breathed out. Good. Owen was going to talk.

"Everything you say in here is confidential. I won't make you say anything you don't want to, but in the same way, you can use this time exactly as you want. If you would like to sit in silence and take the time to think, that's fine too, but talking may be more interesting for us both. And you're safe here," he concluded. Alex smiled and nodded.

"Thank you," she said, and her voice sounded very normal. "But I don't know what to talk about," she added. Owen nodded, completely understanding.

"Tell me about why you are here. Have you come from choice, or have you been referred?"

"Referred. I think."

"Who by?"

"A...psychiatrist." The word stuck like sand in her throat.

"OK."

"At the end of the road. The hospital."

"OK."

"I'm staying there. I've been there for a while, I think. And I drink too much and they want me to stop and so they sent me here to talk about it."

"Do you want to talk about it?"

"I don't think so. But I like sitting here."

Owen nodded and searched her face. Alex looked back openly. She liked him. Owen was scruffy and smiling, his jeans baggy and frayed at the bottom, his hair pushed up in all directions. His skin was brown and slightly wrinkled. His eyes were open, as if Alex could look right inside and see everything lying beneath. They sat in silence for a few minutes.

"I'm not an alcoholic," Alex decided. Owen continued to look at her.

"Why do you say that? How much do you drink?" he asked. His voice was friendly, non-judgemental.

"I don't know. A couple of bottles a night. Wine, mostly. But more recently spirits. Or anything."

"Do you want a drink now?"

"Yes. Very much. They've put me on some pills to make it easier to stop, but I keep thinking about it. My hands shake. I don't feel very well. I wonder if that's because I need a drink."

"It takes a while for your system to get used to going without alcohol, once you're accustomed to it. Do you think your system is accustomed to drinking a lot?"

"I suppose so." Alex looked away, suddenly ashamed.

"But you aren't an alcoholic?" Owen suggested. Alex shook her head.

"No. I'm not vicious and violent or aggressive. I don't lash out making people afraid to speak to me. I take care of myself. Usually."

"It sounds to me as if you have experience of someone with a drinking problem, maybe?" Owen hazarded.

"Alcoholics are vile. They destroy everything in their wake. They shout and cause damage."

"…and lie in the gutter, their trousers coated in piss and vomit, unwashed and unfed, waiting to get their next fix, which they drink out of a brown paper bag. Special Brew, usually. Or cheap cider," Owen finished. Alex stared at him.

"Oh. Shit."

"Let's start again, then, shall we?" Owen asked, and Alex nodded. Her hands were shaking, so she sat on them, and chewed her lip. She felt floaty and ethereal, barely there. This was not happening to her.

"Let's go at your pace. Where do you want to start? Shall I ask you questions, or do you want to tell me what speed to go at? You can also tell me at any point if you need to take a break."

"OK. It's OK."

They looked at each other again, the silence palpable in the room as Alex drew a breath, taking sustenance from the air.

"I think I have a drink problem."

Gardening in the Dark

"Right."

The room filled with words as Alex began to speak. She told Owen of the day she admitted herself to the hospital, the way she had drunk and drunk until the house was empty of alcohol, then stumbled out to take a chance on a different path. How the preceding weeks she had hidden inside the house, crawling out after dark to stock up on booze before going back and consuming it. How food had become obsolete, the alcohol giving her nourishment. How she forgot about time, where she was, people; everything, in fact, but the all-consuming need to drink herself into oblivion. How she would drink herself unconscious, and wake up the next morning with a head like leather and start the process again. How she knew she was damaging herself, slowly rotting away from the inside, but this knowledge made her thirsty for more; to drink and drink until she was completely destroyed.

Owen listened carefully without interjecting. He watched her face, and nodded periodically. He was without censure.

Alex drew breath, her eyes suddenly filling with tears.

"I expect you've heard all this before," she said, suddenly, moving from her personal experience back out into the room, listening back to her own words as they floated between them. Owen simply nodded.

"Where do you get your view of what an alcoholic *should* be like?" he enquired. Alex shook her head, her hand automatically covering her mouth.

"I don't know," she replied, and Owen grinned and shook his head too.

"I don't know – the stock response for 'I know full well, but I'm damned if I'm going to tell a complete stranger all about it'," he translated. Alex shrugged, suddenly sulky and annoyed.

"What does that have to do with anything? There are views of alcoholism all over the world. In the media, in pubs every evening, in the house next door to you with the parent who beats his kids. On daytime talk shows on television, demonstrating the evils of excess. I'm not one of those people. I'm not. I'm a quiet drunk. I don't get rowdy and inflict myself on people. I haven't hurt anyone through drinking, ever. I just get slaughtered and then sit in a corner until I fall asleep. I even throw up discreetly, for fuck's sake," she snarled. Alex was angry, the shake in her hands visibly worsening. Owen stayed motionless, watching her calmly.

"Right. Let's steer clear of that, then. Let's focus on how you are going to get through the next few days, before you come and see me again."

Alex looked at the room, the small table in the centre of it, the box of tissues at an angle, the way the light had moved around from one side of the window to the other as she had been speaking. She saw the tiny speckles of dust in the air, and imagined them to be her words, swirling into oblivion. She felt suddenly deflated, hopeless. Owen's words had piqued her, and she felt as if she would be furious, if only she had the energy to indulge the emotion.

"I'm tired," she said.

"Well fuck me, Alex, I'm not surprised. You've suddenly found yourself penned up in a mental hospital for the first time in your life, after spiralling into a pit of depression that you can't get out of. You've been doing a pretty damn good job of doing yourself in quietly for a while, now. You don't understand where your head is at, and that seems perfectly reasonable to me. You have a man outside waiting to escort you back to the hospital, and you've just been ordered to come to a strange place, to meet a strange person, and offload all your secrets to him, at the same time as being berated for drinking. You're drying out against your will, pilled up to the nines, and you are just *tired*?" Owen said, his body now animated, his smile starting despite himself.

"Not just tired. Terrified, confused, angry, scared. Alone. So miserable and afraid," Alex admitted.

Owen shook his head again and stood up, walking towards the window. He looked out and passed a hand over his silver-grey hair, making the spikes bend under his palm before he dropped his arm and they sprang upright again. Alex sat silently, twisting a tissue in her hands again and again until it ripped.

"What's it like, Alex, in there?" he asked, tapping his head. He kept his back to her.

"Like a nightmare. I'm not allowed to sleep during the day, because they try and keep you in a normal routine. I can't sleep at night because I dream a lot. I'm scared to sleep. All the people in there have dead eyes, as if they have already shrivelled away inside. Most of them shuffle like the caricatures you see of insane people. People cry a lot, and they are all broken and damaged, you can't reach out and hug anyone, and you can't speak to them. And no one speaks to me as if I'm a real person. In fact, you're one the first person to do that.

"I can't eat because my throat is choked up with something that I don't understand. I don't want to drink any liquid apart from booze, because I don't really want to survive in there. I'm not allowed to go out and breathe fresh air, or look at the grass, because they're afraid I'll kill myself. And yet they don't know why I want to die, or want to listen to see if they can change the way I feel. They label you, mark you, watch you, but don't fucking *listen* to you.

"Some of the people have been in there for years. Imagine that, Owen? Not allowed outside. Not allowed to do anything apart from sit in front of a censored television amid other destroyed people, because they're not able to function in the real world. They don't leave the grounds. In fact, some are so afraid of the real world that they choose not to. Their whole universe has been reduced to a kitchen with no knives, a day room with no reality, and a bedroom cubicle permeated by the sound of other people's sorrow. And now I have become one of those people, those objects. I'm not afraid of the outside world, I'm just afraid of myself. And maybe that's worse, in a way, than those other people sitting like vegetables waiting for the next pill round, the next meal. Because they simply can't function in the real world. I'm capable of it, but for some reason I seem to have chosen not too. And what does that make me?

"And you know, I'm proud of the fact that I'm drinking myself to death. I'm proud of the fact that I went so long without eating, not doing anything to save myself. It's the first time I've damn well been in control for years, and it actually feels good, feels like a positive thing. And I know I'm not going to get out of there, because I'm a failure and I'm afraid of my life, of myself, and the only thing I can do is try and damage everything so badly that it can't be repaired, and then find a way of dying so that I can escape everything.

"I know I sound self-indulgent. I know there are people out there with real problems. People going through financial problems, or divorce, or assault and all those other things. The thing is this just makes me feel worse. I have a great life, a good job, a nice house. Good friends. And yet I am constantly either flying up into the air with my head full of craziness, or crawling about in a pit of shit hoping to die. And that makes me feel ashamed, because I have no reason for all of this. I know I'm capable of achieving things – in fact sometimes I think I'm more capable than anyone I've ever met. And yet, I'm stunted. Stumped. I don't know what to do.

"I don't know what to do," Alex concluded, and the passion left her voice and she sat in silence once again.

"Thank you for trusting me, Alex," Owen said gently. Alex pushed her knees up to her chest and wrapped her arms around them.

"Is that bullshit?" she asked, deflated. Owen turned back, and grinned at her.

"I'm afraid you won't get much bullshit, in this room. I'm not very good at all that," he confessed ruefully. Alex smiled. She felt as if he were a friend. She was suddenly shocked at having confided in him, but not afraid.

"What are we going to do, what plan can we put into place to manage the next few days until you come back here, Alex?" the counsellor asked. Alex shrugged.

"You're the expert." There was no sarcasm in her voice.

Gardening in the Dark

"I suspect you've had enough expertise recently. What do you need to do?"

Alex searched her mind. Outside in the garden someone coughed, and she glanced through the window to see another couple, counsellor and counselee, sitting together. They were relaxed and animated, speaking in low tones frequently punctuated by a laugh or an emphatic nod. Alex watched for a moment. She turned back to Owen.

"Drink," she said, her stomach suddenly contracting at the thought, and a real smile appearing for the first time.

"So, drink. How do you get hold of it?"

"I can ask someone. Stuart, my friend. He brings it for me."

"Right. If that's what needs to be done, to survive, then that's what needs to be done."

"Is that wrong?"

"Of course. And I'm not, as your counsellor, recommending it. But right now I suspect that you have bigger things to be concerned about than how much alcohol you are, or aren't, consuming. Just try to limit it. Don't put yourself in danger. And don't get caught," Owen finished, sitting back.

Alex nodded.

"That's a plan," she said. She was going to take meagre control of her situation, in the only way she knew how.

"And then, Alex, next time I see you, we'll see how the land lies, and see if we can't build a better one, together."

Alex nodded, and suddenly began to cry, the tears falling silently in two rivulets down her pale face. Owen stood up and pushed the tissues towards her. He laid a tentative hand on her shoulder, and Alex rocked backwards and forwards, allowing her feelings exposure in the safety of the room.

"I'm afraid to cry, in there, in case they keep me for longer," Alex admitted, between gulps of air. Owen shook his head and walked to the window.

"We won't communicate anything that goes on in this room, to them. We're a separate entity. You can tell by the furniture, in fact –" he said, gesturing towards the mismatched chairs, desk and table "– that we are a charity!"

Alex smiled suddenly and dried her face, covering her cuff and sleeve with tears.

"Thank you, Owen," she said, and stood up. The counsellor turned around and grinned at her.

"You're very welcome." And the two of them made their way downstairs, past the reception area and to the hallway.

"You OK?" he asked, and Alex nodded.

"Actually, I am," she said, meaning it. She felt lighter, as if she had left some of her crap up there in the little room, as if Owen could sweep it up with a broom and stash it in the cupboard.

"Good luck, Alex. I'll see you very soon. Keep it together," Owen said, and with that she was outside again, blinking and sniffing in the bright afternoon, looking for the escort to take her back to the large brick building, to the relative security of her cubicle, and her mobile phone. She needed a drink.

Gardening in the Dark

Chapter Eleven

They had been having an adventure, a magical mystery tour. Ally was sitting in the back of the car next to James, with Maggie and Ben in the front, singing along to a sixties compilation tape. Maggie's voice rose high and clear and out of tune, making James and Ally catch each other's eyes and smile. Ben's low hum cut underneath her, a deep baritone that sounded like some old-fashioned jazz singer. His voice slipped so low that James and Ally could almost feel its reverberations in the soles of their feet. It made them giggle; it was like someone tickling their ears with silk and gravel.

Between them, they were making some passable noises and even James wasn't cringing and looking away in disgust.

They'd been to the coast. Ally had a new bright orange bucket and spade, and James was given bagfuls of pennies to spend on the slot machines in the arcade. He had come up about quits, after a long stretch studying the form, pouncing on machines that other people had ploughed money in and then left full and ripe, ready to drop. They had eaten candy-floss, Ally getting sticky and pink with it around her mouth, Ben swinging her up on to his shoulders so she was taller than everyone, able to look ahead and spot things before the rest of the family could glimpse them. She had seen a pair of sleek seagulls perched on a table picking over chips, making the people on the adjacent tables shriek with fear. She had watched a big black dog barrel straight into the sea, splashing towards the centre of the universe, his tongue lolling and damp ears sticking up as the only signs he was swimming.

James had found a pound coin on the pavement, and Maggie and Ben had bought them all ice creams, the soft white fluffy type that came out in a spiral. Ally had dropped her flake on the floor and didn't cry. The sun was warm and bright, leaving Maggie and Ally spattered with freckles as if someone had flicked a brush of brown paint over their faces. Ben's arms were glowing cherry red, and when Ally grasped one it smelled of sunshine.

James was in a good mood, his lip lifting despite himself as Maggie and Ben's singing got even more raucous. Ben lit a cigarette and puffed smoke rings out that hovered over Ally's head. James put his finger through each as they drifted to the back of the car, making them writhe about and break formation. Maggie handed out mints, and Ally sucked happily, looking out of the window as the sun went down. She felt tired, but was determined not to sleep, not to miss out on any fun. Ben messed about with the steering wheel, making the car veer from side to side, James and Ally falling into one another and giggling.

"Teach me to drive, Ben," Maggie said suddenly, and Ally noticed that she seemed girlish and very beautiful. She seemed to have lost weight and her face was back to the cheekbones of the old photographs from her wedding day. Ally wondered how she had not noticed before. Ben smiled mischievously and looked to the back of the car.

"Right kids. You remember when we went to the theme park and you both went on the roller-coaster? This will be the same, only worse! Strap yourselves in and we'll give it a go," he said with a laugh in his voice. Pulling up to the side of the road, he jumped out of the driving seat and ran around the back of the car, and Maggie raced around the front and jumped back in again. They both did up their seat belts and James giggled nervously. Ally chewed on her mint loudly, excitement and fear making her jump around in the back seat.

"Roll up, roll up! Tickets one mint each," Ben said, gripping the dashboard in mock fear. James thrust the half-eaten packet of sweets into his father's outstretched hand, giggling.

"We want to stay on it around and around, please sir," he said, and Ben laughed and nodded his head.

"See how you feel after the first go!"

Maggie looked at the steering wheel and was suddenly quiet, looking at the knobs and dials which always seemed terribly complicated to Ally, and then the engine growled into life and the car moved forward in kangaroo hops, until Ally and James were

Gardening in the Dark

thrown together in a heap of limbs, giggling and trying to extricate themselves. Maggie had started to laugh, as had Ben, the two of them sniggering like children in the front. James looked at Ally in delight. This was how he imagined it to be, when he heard about other people's families. There was a sparkle between his parents that he had rarely seen, as if they were in love.

After a few minutes, Maggie gave up, laughing too hard to drive properly, and their parents scrambled back into their usual seats. Ben started the engine and drove off quickly. As they approached the bottom of their village, Maggie laid a hand on his arm.

"Can we go to the moat? Can we see if there are ducks?" she asked, sounding like a child, her face flushed with pleasure. Ben smiled and nodded, pulling the car around and up the dirt track that led to the moat and river. James grinned at Ally, as they realised that the outing had not yet come to an end. Ben stopped the car and they all got out, Maggie reaching for Ally and giving her a piggyback, Ben doing the same for James. James kicked out at his sister as he went past, and then Maggie and Ben were racing each other, looking like strange humped animals as Ally and James bounced about on their backs, squealing and trying to reach each other's outstretched hands.

They walk-ran down to the moat, and Maggie pointed out the ducks who raised their heads in a flurry of fear and quacks and dispersed at the sight of the monstrous giggling party that was descending on them. Dropping Ally down gently, Maggie chased after them, slipping on the rocks and screaming, and then she was suddenly waist deep in water, laughing.

"Come on in, the water's lovely!" she said, and James didn't hesitate but jumped in with her. Ally was more cautious, inching in to the moat until she was submerged up to her thighs. The water was shockingly cold, in a way that made Ally's blood seem to shrink back from her legs, until they were pale to the point of whiteness, and bumpy. She sat on a rock, dangling her legs in the water up to the thighs, and watched Maggie and James perform a clumsy waltz in the freezing water. Ben crept up behind Ally quietly, and she felt his arm around her quickly as she shivered, and he gave a sudden push and she was in the water up to her armpits beside James and Maggie.

Ally opened her mouth, shocked and gasping with the cold, as tears of surprise welled in her eyes, before bursting into a fit of giggles. Maggie clambered out of the moat, pulling James with her, and the two hauled Ally out. They ran after Ben quickly, forming a chain to drive him into the icy water, and he fell head first, splashing about as he tried to regain his balance. Maggie and the children jumped in after him again, and the four play-fought for a while, pretending to duck each other, sending huge waves along the surface of the moat.

"OK, that's enough now," said Ben, but was ignored as Maggie pretended to be a shark, going after James. Ally coughed suddenly, as she noticed with horror that their neighbours were wandering down the path to the moat, on a ramble with their little white dog.

"Mum!" she hissed, torn between embarrassment and giggles as the older couple approached. Ben caught her eye and winked, then stood upright in the water as their neighbours walked up to the side of the moat and stared at the family drenched and laughing in the centre of the water.

"A very good evening to you, Mrs. Thompson, Mr. Thompson," said Ben in his clear low voice, sounding terribly respectable, and the Thompsons lifted up dazed hands in speechless greeting, then continued their walk, stopping every six or seven steps to look back at them all.

"That's enough," Ben said again, and this time Ally and James felt that it was too, as they extended cold and shivering hands to Maggie and the four of them dragged themselves out. Ally ran about in her trainers, feeling them squelching.

"We do this in cross country at school," she shouted. "If you run long enough the water goes warm." With that, Maggie started to chase her back to the car, Ben and James following arm in arm at a distance.

Gardening in the Dark

When Ben caught up with them, Maggie linked her fingers around his. Together, they hauled bin liners out of the boot and covered the car seats with them. Ally and James looked at each other in the back of the car, wondering at the change that had happened to the family. Ally hugged her knees to her chest in delight. Even James hummed away to the music, looking out of the window with a benign grin on his usually sour features.

As soon as they arrived back home, they rushed to get out of their wet clothes and Maggie put the washing machine on to get rid of the pond smell. There was a flurried queue for the bathroom, and then the four sat in the living room shivering. Ben built a fire, stacking the wood and coal up with expert hands, and Maggie went to the kitchen to make hot chocolate.

"Let's toast things," Maggie said, and Ally beamed, knowing that this meant marshmallows. Ben put on a Rolling Stones record and the four of them sat in blankets, hair steaming before the fire. They ate marshmallows and biscuits, and laughed at the thought of the Thompsons walking past when they were in the moat. The room grew darker as evening approached, and Maggie stretched luxuriously.

"Pour me a drink, Ally love?" she asked. "And you two can have one, too."

"Not the kids," Ben said, and James saw his father's brow furrow and a shadow pass over his face. Ally ignored him, coming back in with four glasses of wine on a tray. Before she had a chance to sit down, Ben was up and at the door.

"Too late," Maggie said, lolling back on her elbows by the fire like a sleek cat.

"I have some things to do," Ben muttered, disappearing to the garage. Ally looked after him in consternation, but was soon distracted by Maggie who was flicking biscuit crumbs at them both and laughing.

She fell asleep, woozy with wine, wrapped in her blanket by the fire.

*

"Ally, I'm bored. Wake up!"

Ally opened her eyes, heavy-lidded from sleep, and sat up as she registered Maggie's words. Her mother was dressed in a long floating nightgown that whispered as she moved. Ally stretched out a sleepy hand to touch the cool silk.

"What's going on?" she asked, her mind still half-full of dreams. She was warm and stretchy, reluctant to fully awaken.

"I'm bored. Let's do something," Maggie repeated, and Ally grinned suddenly.

"What do you want to do?"

"Something fun. Something outside, maybe."

"It's late, it's dark."

"Look, though, the moon is full and it's shining silver into the back garden."

"Let's do some gardening, then?" Ally suggested, shaking her head even as she said it. It was a crazy idea. Maggie, however, seized upon it immediately.

"Fantastic. Let's nick some plants from the other gardens and plant them in ours!" she said, laughing. With that, Ally was persuaded. She got out of bed and pulled on her shoes, looking comical in her white pyjamas.

"Is it cold?" she asked, and Maggie shook her head.

"It's fine. It's lovely."

The two of them crept out of Ally's room, stepping carefully over floorboards that they knew to squeak, and arrived at the back door in silence. Giggling quietly, they slipped out into the moonlight.

Gardening in the Dark

The garden looked totally different. Bathed in crisp pale moonlight, Ally noticed the way the leaves and bushes took on new forms in the semi-darkness. She stood for a moment absorbing the heavy silence and the way the breeze lifted and swayed the flower heads and leaves. Maggie ran forward in her bare feet, looking like an angel or ghost, lifting her hands above her head and swaying in the soft breaths of air. She called quietly to her daughter, and Ally ran to join her, dancing with her to Maggie's own inner music. Ally wondered what would happen if they were discovered, two luminous shimmering beings in white, curving and moving in the cold moonlight. She smiled and Maggie's returned expression caught the light, her teeth bright and silver. Maggie pulled her towards her chest, and Ally shivered as she was encircled in the pale warm white arms, ghostlike and unreal.

Maggie starting singing to herself, a gentle low hum, and Ally ran from one end of the lawned garden to the other, inspecting their playground.

"We could plant things here, Mum. Or here," she whispered, but her mother was lost in her own music, turning around and around so that her gown lifted slightly and billowed in the breeze she was creating. Ally looked down and considered the patch of earth on the edge of the lawn. It was forlorn and empty, a brown smudge in the moonlight. She pictured it brimming with colour by morning; filled with daffodils and tulips, hostas and hebes.

"Here, Maggie," Ally insisted, and her mother was suddenly beside her, abrupt and silent.

"Yes. Yes, this is a perfect spot," she said, nodding in agreement. Ally smiled in delight at the approval. She ran to the shed and got some trowels, ducking her head against the unnerving wail of the rusty door as she swung it open.

The two of them crouched and prepared the area, pulling at roots and grasses to make a good space for planting. A light drizzle started, and Ally paused and looked at her mother anxiously, hoping that it wouldn't stop the activity, but Maggie was wholly absorbed in her task, pulling and tugging at large clumps of grass with almost frenzied movements.

"You know, Alexandra, when I was young I was given a patch of earth just like this, to grow things in. I grew everything you can imagine. Big ripe tomatoes and peas in pods, sunflowers so big they looked as if they had caught the light. I loved it. I miss having the time to do things like that, now. There's never enough time. We should do things at night, the two of us. Imagine how much we could achieve if we didn't have to sleep!"

Ally looked at her, bewildered. She was sure that she would need to sleep at some point. It wasn't a school night, but the day after would be, and she would probably fall asleep in the afternoon if she stayed up for so long.

"When I was young, Ally, I was really beautiful."

"But you're beautiful now. Daddy thinks so!" Ally exclaimed, and Maggie grinned and shook her head, looking at her daughter as Ally tugged at a stubborn piece of grass in the ground.

"I used to have men following me up the street, just in case I'd smile at them. A string of callers all wanting to take me out. I had a pair of white boots right up to the thigh, that showed my legs off, and a very short skirt. That was fashionable, then. We used to go out, a group of us girls, me and my best friend Pam, and all our other friends, and hang out at the club. We didn't even look twice at some of those men. We'd dance all night, drinking Martinis and smoking cigarettes, and the girls all stuck together. We never had to pay for anything – not the drinks, or the lifts home. We'd dance to our favourite tunes on the jukebox, and it was perfect, Ally.

"And then one day, this handsome man came in, and all us girls fell silent. He had the biggest flares on you've ever seen, and a way of smoking his cigarette that made us weak at the knees. He was rich, too. You could tell from his clothes, and he pulled up on a big flashy bike. I'd never felt anything like I did at that moment. I felt like my insides had turned to jelly. He walked over to us, and ignored everyone, and just held his hand out to me. Without a word, we danced, and I felt like the best, luckiest girl in the world. He smelled good, like fresh linen and rain.

"Do you know who that was, Ally?" Maggie asked, her eyes sparkling as she turned to her daughter, looking flushed and luminescent, her face glowing with the memory. Ally shook her head, desperate to hear the answer, desperate for it to have been Ben.

"It was your father!" Maggie exclaimed, and smiled. Ally grinned back, imagining Ben as this debonair and mysterious stranger who had walked straight up to her mum and asked her to dance without saying a word.

"Wow," she breathed, and then the two fell silent, both occupied in different thoughts as their patch of earth grew clearer and the soil softened into powdery clumps beneath their hands.

"OK, Al," Maggie said, and then she was up and running across the lawn, towards the wooden fence that separated their garden from the woman's next door.

"Cover me, I'm going in!" Maggie exclaimed, wielding her trowel and slipping quickly over the fence. Ally stood in terror, even as a laugh escaped her when she considered Maggie, looking like a gangster with her trowel, brandishing it like a loaded gun in her white nightdress.

"Oh shit! Oh shit!" Ally whispered, rooted to the spot as she heard scuffling sounds coming from the other garden. She jumped in fear as something sailed across the fence and landed with a plop by her feet. She looked down and saw a hardy geranium on the lawn, none the worse for having discovered flight. She smiled. One by one, the neighbour's plants came sailing over to Ally, and she busied herself gathering them up, feeling like a hunter gathering up the spoils of an outing.

"Maggie!" she hissed as the tenth plant (a particularly handsome holly, with beautiful variegated leaves) landed on the lawn. "That's enough now!"

With that, Maggie returned stealthily, her breath raspy with giggles, and landed beside her daughter again.

"She'll never notice. Her garden is crammed to the rafters with plants and flowers, and I filled in all the holes!" her mother said, and Ally hugged her tight before heading back to their patch of soil, her arms full of plants that scratched her bare arms as she hugged them close. They started to plant quickly and methodically, Ally making the holes and Maggie pushing the plants in, haphazard and random across their newly dug earth.

"We should move somewhere warm, Ally, and then we could live in a big villa with a terrace, and a big swimming pool. We could drink sangria every afternoon, and have barbecues and go for walks on the beach looking for shells," Maggie suddenly said. Ally pushed back on her haunches and considered her mother, wondering how her thoughts could skip so readily from one subject to the next.

"Just the two of us?" Ally asked hopefully. At that moment, it sounded like the most perfect plan in the world.

"And Tiger," Maggie said, pushing her fingers deep into the soil and sniffing at a handful. Ally grinned as she lifted up a bunch of chives, their roots white and juicy, and handed them to her mother.

"Or we could buy a big boat and moor it right in the middle of a huge lake, so that anyone who came to visit would have to swim across to see us. We'd have a little music system and we could put it on as loud as we wanted, because we'd have no neighbours."

"Or a big camper van that we could drive all over Europe, getting wine and cheese in France, trying spaghetti in Italy, sausage in Germany, oranges in Spain."

Ally grinned and separated two geraniums out. For a brief moment, she allowed herself to be caught up in the dream.

"Or," she added, "we could buy big bikes and just cycle about from place to place. We could knock on people's doors and ask for food, and then sleep in sheds with hay, and we could carry Tiger in the basket on the front of one of the bikes."

Maggie nodded agreement, making a hole for the geranium. When the last plant had been laid in the ground, and the soil patted back into place, she stood up clumsily and walked backwards, holding out her hand. Ally jumped up too, her arms itching with the scratches on them.

"Close your eyes," Maggie commanded, and Ally did as she was bidden. Maggie took her by the shoulders and walked her away from their new garden.

"You've never seen this bit of garden before. Imagine what it was like before we started, all drab and boring with no life. Bring that image into your mind and hold it…

"…hold it…" She was led back to their patch, eyes closed and arms stretched in front of her.

"And…open!" Maggie said, and Ally did so, eager to see the change.

It looked fantastic, in an insane kind of way. The geraniums hustled the holly, the hosta and lavender vied for attention with a large gaudy clump of roses. Even in the pale light, Ally could see the cacophony of colour they had made.

"It's perfect!" she breathed, and Maggie nodded, satisfied.

"We did a magic job!" she agreed, dusting off her hands smartly.

"We'll have to invite some people round for tea, so they can see it," Ally said, wondering if this was a new beginning, and now they had done the garden perhaps they could do the house, too, to make it lovely inside?

"Round for tree!" Maggie sniggered, and the two began to laugh again.

"Come here, Ally," Maggie said and held out her arms, white-sheathed and sheer, her long tapering fingers reaching for her daughter. Ally ran to her and the two hugged, then Maggie was picking her up, swinging her up towards the stars.

"See, you can fly," she said, laughing, and Ally looked into her face, suddenly beautiful in the moonlight, and imagined her years ago, the model with no temper, bright and optimistic and free.

"You're beautiful," she breathed, suddenly shocked by the radiance in her mother's face, the years which seemed to have dropped away into the garden somewhere as they had danced and laughed.

"Thank you, Ally. And you just look like me. You are just like me," Maggie replied, and Ally felt her insides constrict with an incongruent mixture of pleasure and fear. The two sat down and held hands, Maggie suddenly seeming lost in reverie.

"I was once a model, Ally," she began, and Ally settled down. It was a story she had heard many times before. She picked up a blade of grass and surreptitiously held it to her lips, trying to make it squeak as James did.

"I had a friend who was a photographer. He took pictures of me on the beach, in a swimming costume, and then close-ups. The local pharmacist used one of the pictures in their window to advertise make-up. I was a mod, and had hair all the way down to my waist. And legs all the way up to meet it. I used to wear big platform heels and in those days we all wore bright colours and prints. It used to look like a rainbow at festivals. That was before all the darkness came along."

Ally nodded and chewed on the blade of grass, having failed to make it squeak. She jumped as she heard footsteps behind her, her skin suddenly shivering into tiny bumps. Ben had joined them. He sat on the grass quietly, next to Maggie, and placed his arm around her.

"Both all right?" he asked gently, and Maggie nodded and leaned her head back on to his chest fondly. Ally watched, her mouth open. How come Ben wasn't annoyed? She couldn't understand the sudden gentleness between them. Maggie closed her eyes and Ben, with his free arm, pulled off his dressing gown and popped it over Ally's shoulders. She suddenly realised she was terribly cold.

"Do you think we should go back inside, now, Mags?" Ben asked, and she smiled at him as he got to his feet and took her hand, pulling her up. Ally wrapped the dressing gown more firmly around her shuddering shoulders and trailed after them as they walked across the lawn, pausing to look back at their new patch of garden. When she turned back, she grinned to herself. Maggie had pulled Ben into an embrace and was dancing with him, his feet moving clumsily across the grass in time with her steps. Her mother was humming again softly, and both parents had their eyes closed, communicating in some language Ally couldn't understand.

"It's time to stop, now, Maggie love," Ben whispered, and the words floated eerily across to where Ally stood. She turned them on their heads, looked at them upside down and then back to front, but they didn't make any sense. Maggie nodded and slumped more heavily against Ben, and the three of them went back inside.

Like dolphins sending sonic messages, she thought to herself, wondering if they were speaking together in their minds, or if the moonlight said everything that needed to be spoken. Maggie paused as they reached the kitchen, and considered her daughter carefully.

"Do you love me?" she asked, and Ally nodded, because at that moment she loved Maggie so hard and with such passion that she would have slain herself at her feet if that's what her mother requested.

"With all my heart," she answered, and at that moment it was true. Maggie reached out and ruffled her hair, her sleeve coated in dew, and then allowed herself to be led back to her bedroom.

Chapter Twelve

Alex had been doing her laundry, sitting in front of the washing machine as it went through its lathery cycle. Staring into the depths of the tumble dryer as it hissed and rolled her clothes into crisp dryness. When she returned to her cubicle, her arms full of sweetly scented garments, Doreen was crying. Alex sat on her bed and watched the older woman as she rocked and dribbled tears over her sleeve and down her front. She looked at her curiously, as the woman sobbed and heaved. Doreen was quite fat, with a moon-like pale face, now blotched and rough with salt water and snot. Alex stared at her, as if somehow Doreen's tears would prevent her from seeing the rudeness; as if she were hidden behind a veil of sorrow which could not be penetrated by a long hard stare.

Doreen cried loudly, with snot-filled snuffles and racking sobs. Alex was unperturbed, and didn't think to comfort her until she had stared for a while and the fact of Doreen's sorrow finally registered itself with her, as if she had been pulled out of a far-off place and brought sharply to the present.

"Doreen, what's wrong?" Alex asked, remembering to be kind. Doreen wailed a little louder, and Alex frowned to herself. She didn't think she had enough room to be kind to someone. It was an effort of will to stand up from her place in the corner of her bed and walk over to the fat heaving shape on the other side of the room.

"He left me. He locked me in the shed and said he'd come back for me, and he put the three of us in the shed but then he didn't come back. We waited and waited and there was a spider, and I told them it would be OK because they were so young but it wasn't ever OK again," Doreen said, her voice suddenly surprisingly lucid and clear amid her sobs, as if the words which emerged were well practised, rehearsed until they were articulate with the maximum of precision. Alex nodded and placed a tentative arm around Doreen's shoulders. The effect was amazing. The bulky woman leaned her dark head of curly hair on to Alex's shoulder, pushing into the bone. Alex nodded again. She understood.

Gardening in the Dark

(He left her. She was so small, so young, and he left her. The scar inside itched and stretched, and she re-found loss itself, which clawed and clawed at her insides until she could take in a ragged shallow breath and feel it pull. He left her, walked out of the door, and she would never recover. She would never love again because he took her trust away.)

Doreen shivered.

"And then it was all going to be fine because we were going to the seaside, but then she said we couldn't go, and she hit my sister over and over again, until there was blood everywhere, wiped on to her pinafore and running into her stockings. Even her petticoat had blood on. Her petticoat that had taken so long to sew. We would sew and sew and it looked lovely, the slip, all white and clean but then it got ruined. Do you know how hard it is to remove blood? They told me to use salt, and then wine, but nothing shifted it and she cried and cried over it all. She cried more for the slip because I'd embroidered on it."

(She was vicious, uncaring. She hadn't wanted Alex. She had looked at the small girl and her face had twisted with hatred, and she had drunk and drunk until she could no longer stand, and still she found the steadiness to hate. That look stayed with Alex, etched into her retina. When she was hurting, when her mind was lost to madness, she cried out to be loved, to be forgiven, though she wasn't entirely sure what she had done wrong.)

"And then it was harder because he was the eldest, and he was such a good looking lad. He used to go off to the garage on a morning and he looked so sharp in his overalls. He was everybody's favourite one, until he ran off with that lass and we never saw him again, and that made it all worse. I used to hide behind the chair and watch him with his sweetheart, he was the one, and he got the meat at dinner-time and he was the one that could come and go as he pleased. They said I should have been a boy, a boy makes the money, a boy gets the dinners and has his laundry done. Us girls were in the shed. The shed."

(He was the favourite. He was wanted, worshipped. He looked down on her and sneered, knowing that she was an outcast in her own home. He looked at her with disgust until Alex was just a thing. That adoration she had felt for him faded, leaving aching loss. Everything to do with them, the three of them, was sepia-tainted, washed in loss and grief.)

"Spiders. A big spider and it ran across her foot and she screamed, and no one came. She wasn't there to let us out. Hours and hours and trying to be warm. Trying to get out."

(She died. She died and was gone, without ever telling Alex that she was sorry, without reaching out one of her delicate tapering hands and asking for love, offering love. She died alone without warning, and there was never again a chance to tell her that she loved her, and ask her to love in return.)

Doreen's cries were lessening, turning into a series of choking sobs that emerged at more quiet, more regular intervals. Alex found a rhythm in them, and wrapped her arms more closely around the woman's ample body. Her chest was drenched in tears, and she looked down at Doreen's head as she nestled against her, her eyes closed. Alex began to hum, a tuneless response to the woman's sorrow, and her own. She rocked Doreen backwards and forwards gently, lifting her hand to stroke her fluffy dark hair. Doreen was like a child, living in some place years ago, trapped in her shed. Alex began to cry too, noiseless tears that ran down on to Doreen's hair, mingling with the woman's own.

"Shush. It will pass. It will pass," Alex said, and then hummed on, her thoughts going backwards and backwards until she was lost, too, in her own reverie.

"It will pass," she promised, even as her mind filled with darkness and her heart constricted in her chest. The tears continued to fall, both women silent now and intent on the rhythm they had created together.

*

Suddenly becoming alert and alive, Alex lifted her head and began to look about her. She noticed things which she had absorbed unthinking through her skin before, now visible and demanding to be seen. Her bed was narrow and institutional, permeated by the memories of bodies of other people who were clinging on to life and trying to rationalise the way their minds had begun to reject it. She looked hard at all elements of the place where she was, and found herself loathing it. What had begun as a safe place, shelter from herself, had started to feel like a prison to her.

However, Alex still managed to find pleasure in unexpected places, and each small thing that could make her smile was so rare it had to be cleaved to and cherished. The first cup of tea in the morning, adding in the sweet milk and stirring the rich liquid, then waiting impatiently until the temperature had reduced enough to allow her to lift it to her lips and dissolve the caked nightly grime of her dreams. The shower in the morning, the feel of the water pummelling her neck and back, coursing over her body still warm and clammy from sleep, imagining it washing her clean both inside and out. The scent of perfume, delicate and steady, striving to be noticed amid the institutional scents of mass-produced dinners and sick minds. The nightly visit from Stuart, who came regularly without censure and brought her things to make her smile, like crisp fresh fruit, books which she was too wired to read, or new music. The look on Stuart's face as he registered her growing happiness with relief, his blue eyes creasing into a smile as he left behind his reservations about her and trusted that she was becoming herself once again.

There were other pockets of joy to be had. The realisation that her mind, which had tilted into a strange angle, was gradually righting itself again – more than righting itself, rather curving upwards and seeking out happiness. Her thoughts had turned from grey and bleak to sunlight. The view from the window in the smoking room, the tree which bent and straightened against the wind, and the grass which looked greener and more lush than she remembered.

Best of all, permission to go outside and walk next to a quiet member of staff, who understood that for half an hour a day she needed to breathe in spring scents and trail her hand through leaves, lie full-length against the grass and imagine its strident points pushing and straining against her skin. The craving to look up at the sky and watch the clouds in tumult, chasing across the blue expanse with the rapidity of her own new thoughts. She loved being outside. She ran like a caged animal, pacing in ever-growing circles around her keepers, making them laugh. Mark, the staff nurse, growing wary and fencing her in when the arcs grew too wide. Katie, the brown-haired laughing assistant choosing to look the other way as Alex raced across the grounds, desperate to burn away some of the excess energy as her legs begged to be flexed and stretched to their maximum.

She felt like a child, but no child she remembered being. Newly born, freshly alive. She noticed things which her eyes had never registered before, like the way someone's mouth could turn down by itself out of habit, causing small lines to form which fixed the expression in place. She noticed the way human beings had only a simple list of things which they needed to survive: food, warmth, attention, conversation, affection. Affection was hard for her fellow residents to come by. Alex distributed it warily, giving smiles and encouragement where she could, making sure it was unseen by the staff in case she somehow unwittingly upset the balance of misery on the ward. She found that she had endless capacity to smile again, as if her previous depression, the pit, had consumed her, but now she was being repaid by an excess of happiness. There was no balance, just a rush of all one thing, and then all the next. She lifted her arms wide to the wind and felt blessed that at least she swung from one to the other in this way. She looked at the residents around her, and many of them seemed to have only sadness. They couldn't look forward to the bubble of joy which nestled comfortably in Alex's middle and promised to make her alert, positive, and full of boundless energy.

Martin, of course, was partially responsible for this. She found herself waking in the mornings after a few fitful hours of sleep, her head racing forwards to times of the day where she could seek some pleasure, and he became the focal point of those thoughts. She wanted to look at him. With her gaze, she wanted to penetrate his skin, swim in the channels of his blood and navigate his bone and sinew. Climb into the recesses of his brain, so similar to her own, and find refuge there. She liked his eyes, with their wisdom and sparkle, and the way he considered things briefly before jumping to an elegant conclusion. His thoughts ran like sand through a timer, and she understood them innately, as if she and

Gardening in the Dark

Martin were part of a single set of cells which had somehow become separated.

They sat together on the floor in the upstairs recreation room. The windows, behind the bars, were pushed open so they could breathe in the air, and they had moved the furniture away to let them sit as closely as possible to the outside, huffing in the fresh scent and shivering under the delicious coolness which swept inside. Alex leaned against the wall and smiled luxuriously. They had created a piece of outside, together. Martin was watching her curiously, his blue eyes considering her, playing over her skin and features. Alex shivered again.

"What is it?" she asked, looking away from his deep gaze. Martin frowned, his face close to hers.

"I don't know you yet. I want to know more. You have fifteen questions. And then, so do I. Be quick though because my head wants to move fast. I want to absorb you like a sponge. You're the first thing I've found that has held my interest." Alex smiled and nodded. She understood.

"Fifteen questions. Do you think you'll know me after that?" she asked. Martin returned her smile.

"It's a start. Along with the smell of you, and the way your hair catches the sunlight even through a barred window in a dark room."

"OK. First one. When did you realise you were ill?"

"I'm not ill. I just do things differently from other people. Most people are like this, to a certain extent. I knew I was unusual because of the arrogance and the energy, first. Thinking I was something different from everyone. It's not true, of course. I'm just the same."

Alex understood the arrogance. Suddenly having the unswerving belief that one was the best at whatever one chose to do. The sneaking suspicion that you may be a goddess, simply an undiscovered one. Keeping the secret close that you were better, different, more sensitive, more alert. More special. Talented and gifted. One day a ballerina, one day a famous professor. Limitless. She smiled and the smile turned into laughter as she stared at Martin, entirely comprehending what he meant.

"Have you travelled anywhere?"

"Everywhere," he replied. Alex wondered if he really had, or if, like her, he had travelled through books, music, other people's minds.

"If you could be anywhere right now, where would you choose?"

"Here. With you. Or outside. With you," he answered, seriously.

"Who are you?"

"The same as you. But male."

They looked up as the door was pushed open, and Mark entered to check on them. His eyes swept over them, noticing the way they sat, and the smiles they wore. He looked disapproving.

"You two OK?" he asked. They both nodded, falling silent for a moment. Once he had left the room, leaving the door partially ajar, Alex resumed talking.

"What is your favourite thing to do?" she asked. Martin passed his hand through his hair as he thought, leaving the dark curls messy.

"I like to write. To read. Growing things. Eating and sleeping and running and learning new things."

"What is the most important thing you have learned so far?"

"To laugh."

Gardening in the Dark

"If you could be somebody different, who would you be? Would you choose to not be mad?"

"No. This is who I am. I want to be me. But more controlled. That was two questions."

"I've lost count. It's your turn," Alex said, mulling over his last answer. Martin stretched comfortably and turned over on to his stomach, studying the weave of Alex's jeans as she sat beside him.

"Who are you?" he asked. Alex put her head to one side.

"I'm Alex," she replied.

"Who is that?"

"Someone who I have become. Independent. Erratic, unpredictable. Unreliable."

"Do you like Alex?"

"Mostly. I made her."

"Where have you been?"

"Down in a pit, and up in the clouds. And sometimes somewhere between the two."

"Where are you now?"

"Flying."

"What do you want?"

"To love. And be loved."

With that, Martin reached out his hand, warm and large and comforting, and placed it over Alex's own. She looked down with detachment at the two intertwined hands. They were both beautiful, completely different.

"What has been the happiest moment of your life?" Martin asked suddenly. Alex chewed on her lip and thought about it. She couldn't come up with one.

"I think it's yet to come."

"And the saddest?"

"Being too young."

"Do you trust yourself?"

"No. Not yet."

"Would you be anything different?"

"I don't know, yet," Alex answered. Martin smiled his comprehension, and Alex looked at him. She felt a sudden rush of warmth that came with the luxury of being able to answer honestly, to be herself without risking alienating the person in front of her. She leaned in to Martin quickly, and kissed him. He sat upright, startled, and then pulled her towards him. They kissed for a long time, exploring each other's mouths, eyes closed and searching inside. They pulled apart guiltily as the door was pushed further ajar and Mark once again appeared in the frame. He shook his head, walking in to the room and standing before them. Alex felt suddenly like a child again, and it made her feel defensive and nervous.

"I think the two of you ought to come downstairs now, and go to your separate rooms," Mark said, his voice stern with no trace of a smile on his lips. Martin stiffened and moved upright until he was face-to-face with Mark. He was taller and more imposing at full height, and Alex relaxed a little. She was not a child, she was not alone. And they had done nothing wrong. She could taste Martin on her lips; sweet and bitter at the same time.

"Why?" Martin asked Mark, his voice neutral and pleasant. Alex smiled a little and looked away. It was a good question. Mark exhaled and frowned again.

Gardening in the Dark

"You're being inappropriate. This is a hospital. You are here to get better, and you should both be focusing more on yourselves right now than on any other person," he answered. Alex suddenly realised her situation again, something which her time with Martin had made recede. Of course.

"We'll come downstairs now, Mark," she said, standing up and pulling the window closed. Martin turned away, frustrated, and looked out at the garden below. Mark nodded and turned on his heel, leaving the room with the door fully open.

"Have you noticed how no one ever gets physically ill, here? It's like they are so consumed by the sorrow or illness in their mind that there is no room for them to suffer in any other way," Martin commented. Alex turned in surprise, wondering at his ability to move forward so quickly from one thought to the next.

"Do you think you could cure bad diseases with depression? Like an inoculation. Inject the grey inside and then people could focus on that instead and their bodies would stop being ill?" she replied, and suddenly the two of them were laughing again. Alex turned to face Martin, grabbing his arm to pull him downstairs. She wanted to absorb his skin. He had become her sustenance on the ward. He nourished her.

The two went to their separate rooms without saying anything further. Alex flung herself on her bed and looked at the ceiling. She couldn't settle. She had energy pulsing through her limbs, and her brain was flowing thoughts along too fast to keep up with. It was draining, but she wasn't tired. She recognised her feelings. She had been here before. It was a great place to be. She jumped slightly as Susan marched into her room, pushing back the blue curtain with a wide sweep, and sat herself down on the bed with a little 'ouf' noise. She turned and studied Alex, who quickly sat up and retreated to the corner of her bed, arms and legs folded against the look on Susan's face.

"I want to talk to you. I have known Martin for a long long time. What do you talk about?" the nurse asked, and Alex took a moment to follow her, used as she was to long preambles which led into more direct questioning. Susan's abrupt interrogation surprised her.

"We talk about everything. Each other, our feelings, who we are and what we want to be," Alex replied, wondering why this was relevant, and why Susan felt that it was important to know. She felt violated, as if Susan had walked in on her and Martin whilst they were making love. Exposed. Susan looked stern and unforgiving. She didn't seem to heed Alex's answer.

"What are your intentions towards him? What do you want from your...friendship?" Susan asked, persistent and disapproving. Alex choked back a laugh, surprised and amused by Susan's words.

"You sound like a Victorian father! We aren't betrothed, we're just together."

"Martin is not a well person. Don't lead him on, give him the wrong impression. When you leave here, and return to your separate worlds, you won't feel the same. It isn't healthy for people here to form relationships. You are here to focus on yourselves, not each other," Susan admonished, her face stern and hard. Alex flinched.

"I don't understand. We're not doing anything wrong. We can support each other. He understands me, and I understand him, and surely that's beneficial?" Alex felt frustrated that Susan couldn't see the logic. The nurse simply stared at her for a moment.

"It's inappropriate," the nurse stated, and turned on her heel, leaving Alex alone again. Alex hid under the sheet, thinking things through. She felt as if the staff at the hospital were looking at her disapprovingly, and yet she had come here to get better, and now she felt better. Meeting Martin had made her feel better. She felt annoyed that she was not able to pursue this kernel of happiness and allow it to blossom. It felt pure and white to her, and she was surprised that it could be regarded as anything vulgar or wrong to other people.

She wandered to the canteen and sat among the other inmates. It was the first time she had ventured in to the room while a meal was being served. She slid into a red plastic seat on one of the round tables and nodded at everyone around her. Some nodded back, others gazed at her curiously, while others still busied their eyes with knives and forks, waiting for their meal. Alex watched as people walked up to the serving hatch and selected their meal. It reeked of school dinners in the canteen, an unpleasant smell of fish, boiled vegetables, and metal containers. Alex shuddered. A woman with short grey hair came and sat next to her, looking at her with open curiosity. Alex smiled briefly and turned her attention back to the line of people selecting their meal. The man behind the hatch was joking and laughing with the residents, speaking a loud monologue of inconsequential humour. Some of the residents came alive with it, responding to his jocularity with eager nods and giggles. Alex smiled.

"Sometimes there is fish. And sometimes there isn't," the woman with grey hair said conversationally. Alex looked across at her and nodded. The woman was tiny, her hands and face elfin and sharp, her big round eyes the only soft thing about her. Her elbows jagged the air at either side of her as if in defence against unseen predators, and her hands shook violently as she picked up her cutlery and began to eat.

"Do you like fish?" Alex asked, and the woman shook her head, no, but her mouth was full of the stuff, pushing it down her throat without chewing, her eyes suddenly focused on the task in hand.

"Hng shur hnggingshur," the woman said, trying to get the words out of her mouth, while keeping the fish in. Alex nodded at her and looked away quickly, just as a small white flake escaped from the rest and landed on the table between them.

"And Alexandra, our newcomer, what will it be for you today?" the gentleman behind the hatch said, shouting across at Alex so loudly that his jovial query made everyone in the room turn and stare at her in the corner. Even the woman beside her stopped chewing, her mouth slightly agape, waiting for Alex to respond.

"I…" Alex began, her face burning deep red. She paused for a moment, conscious of all the eyes awaiting her next move. She stood up quickly, and fled from the room. Once in the safety of her cubicle again, the ward silent, Alex relaxed. She thought about the flake of fish jumping from the woman's mouth. She picked up her mobile phone and looked at it, before dialling a number.

"Stuart? It's me. I need some vodka."

Alex put the phone down after a few minutes more, and lay on her bed, watching the hands on her watch slipping around the dial. She needed to get outside. She needed a way of shedding the heat of the ward, the madness, the cloying supervision and continuous assessment. The ward had stayed the same, wrapped in a shroud of insanity and routine. Alex was changing.

Gardening in the Dark

Chapter Thirteen

It happened so quickly.

> Ally had told a friend.

> Who had told her mother.

> Who had told a teacher.

> Who had told the head.

> Who had told a social worker.

> Who had told a policewoman.

> Who had told Maggie.

> Who had told Ben.

> And then he was gone.

> And the months ticked past.

Maggie swung down and down and down, until it seemed to Ally that she would fall through the floor with her unhappiness. It clung to the curtains, making the room darker. Maggie's sadness was palpable, material. It let off a scent of sour sweat and grey cigarette smoke tinged with the sweetness of leftover wine and spilt spirits. It made Ally's stomach churn with anxiety and nausea, leaving her like a wild animal who can sense an all-consuming fire on the too-orange horizon. She felt constantly alert, and it was tiring. James had taken to disappearing for a few days at a time, nowadays, and this left Ally as the primary carer for her unbalanced mother.

Maggie was crying upstairs, making sniffling noises and howling expletives to herself. Ally was content to tread a wary wide path around the bottom of the stairs, looking up with trepidation, until Maggie called her. The screeched summons made Ally stiffen to attention, and she tasted the salt-metal tang of dread in the back of her throat. She walked up the wooden steps one at a time, slowly, imagining the executioner's block awaiting her arrival at the top.

"Mum," she said, announcing her presence to Maggie quietly lest she should shock her and cause a reaction of some sort that would end up in a purple bruise and the pair of them in tears rather than one.

"Ally, Ally." Maggie was crouched down by the side of her bed, tear-streaked and blotched with misery. She was wearing her usual jumper, a black and white striped monstrosity with stains and cigarette burns across the front.

Ally held back, reluctant to go near her mother when she was in this mood. Her sadness was infectious. If Ally spent too much time with her, she would feel her own pit opening up by their feet, threatening to engulf her. She looked away as Maggie sobbed.

"What is it now?" she asked, her voice more concerned than impatient, but still she felt a certain detachment. Don't get involved. Don't hear the answer, she told herself, and the sentence replayed itself again and again in her mind, a mantra against Maggie's desolation.

"He's gone, and I'm all alone again. He preferred you to me. He preferred you to me," her mother gasped out, and Ally flushed with shame and shock. They hadn't referred to Ben fully since he had left all that time ago. Her face burned.

"Don't be stupid. He was just sick in the head, that's all. It's not about preferences," Ally reassured her, still hovering in the doorway. Maggie turned her face towards her daughter, her nose red and sore, her eyes bloodshot. She looks demonic, Ally thought, as she looked back at her mother. She could feel herself being appraised, as if Maggie was weighing up her various merits to try to establish how Ben could have behaved in that way.

Gardening in the Dark

"Stop it, Mum. Pull yourself together," Ally snapped, wanting to get the interview over with. Maggie sniffed, but there were so many tears coursing down her cheeks, snot pouring from her nose, that Ally doubted if it would make any difference. She walked over to her mother hesitantly and pulled some tissues out of the box on her bedside table.

"Where's your brother? Where's my James?" Maggie said suddenly, and Ally rolled her eyes.

"He's out, somewhere. He's been gone for two days," she said. This set Maggie off on a new wail of anguish.

"He doesn't love me, any more. You both love your father more than you ever loved me. What did I do wrong? All I've done is cooked for you, cleaned, done your washing and brought you up right. It was me that made you do your homework, me that made sure you were dressed and bathed and respectable, and that taught you to be polite," Maggie ranted. Ally gritted her teeth to try to stop her response, but she flared up.

"You never cleaned. We cleaned. We had no clothes because you were too pissed to get out and buy us any. You don't do the laundry, I do. You don't shop for food, I do. I cook, I make sure the house is decent, I do my own damn homework. If you weren't so self-absorbed you'd probably notice that, wouldn't you? At least Ben gave a shit, however that showed itself," she said. Maggie turned her drunken eyes, big pools of self-pity, on her daughter and Ally felt a sudden desire to slap her, hard. She stepped back, out of reach of Maggie's hands, in case her mother felt the same. Maggie suddenly stood up, her red face flushed even further, and walked towards her daughter.

"Come here," she demanded, her voice low and threatening. Ally backed towards the door.

"You bitch. You take my husband, and now you're trying to run this house," she seethed, lumbering towards Ally who came to an abrupt halt as she felt the wooden door behind her. She backed into it, causing it to slam. She was cornered. Maggie raised her arm and started hitting Ally over and over again, in the face and head.

Ally cowered down and fell into a protective ball. She was detached as the blows rained down, wondering how long it would be before James came home or Maggie drank herself into a stupor, so she could get some peace.

"I hate you, I hate you, I hate you," Maggie was screaming, and Ally curled up tighter, protecting the soft bits of her body – her stomach and face – from the blows. Most of them were ineffectual, but she was still aware of the pain. She looked up at the wrong time, and Maggie caught her full in the face.

"Fuck," Ally said, gasping in pain, and scrabbled to get out of the door. It was a tricky operation, because Maggie was blocking it with her bulk, but she scrambled between her mother's legs and pulled the door open hard. Maggie fell with a satisfying thud, and Ally managed to run downstairs. She could taste blood in her mouth, and her head was ringing.

"Fuck," she repeated, running to the bathroom to inspect the damage. She looked messy, already, with a cut on the side of her eye streaming with blood, her nose beginning to pour. She felt annoyed with herself that she hadn't managed to read the signs well enough to get away in time. More than this, she felt angry with herself for not acting on instinct and lashing out at the madwoman upstairs. One day I'll do it, she vowed to herself, taking toilet tissue and wiping her bruised face. One day I'll get my own back.

She sat on the edge of the toilet seat and cried for a moment, furious with herself and furious at her mother. She knew, now, that other families didn't operate like this. And now she would have to cut school, and lie low for a while until the bruises faded, which meant that she would be stuck inside the house. Damn it. She thought about Ben, the lesser of two evils. At least he would have protected her from this. She remembered how he had come home once when Maggie was in the middle of one of her rages. Her mother had Ally pinned up against a door in the hall, her fingernails buried to the quick in Ally's bare arms. Ben had taken stock of the situation and grabbed Maggie, lifting her off the floor by the neck. He had put his finger right into his terrified wife's face, and threatened her if he caught her being violent to the kids again. Ally had giggled, terrified. Ben's being in the house had meant there would be no violence, as if Maggie had been scared enough to control her temper, back then. Now there was no Ben, and Maggie's fits of despondency and anger seemed constant. Ally wiped her eyes and considered her situation. It didn't look good. She had at least two years left of this before she could decently escape. Her grades were falling, and Ally knew that this meant it would be harder to get out and be successful when she finally left home. She needed to study harder. It didn't seem possible in the house, with Maggie like a whirlwind of rage each evening.

Ally had been trying to find ways of dissipating the anger, but Maggie's fury didn't seem logical. Ally was keeping the house immaculate, having spent hour after hour upon Ben's departure clearing away rubbish, washing windows, cleaning the carpets and washing the curtains. She had opened windows and scrubbed walls to get rid of the tar stains on the surfaces. She had been scrubbing away her old life, her old shame. The house looked almost neat and decent enough to invite people round without embarrassment. If only Maggie wasn't there to spoil it, with her piss and vomit and habit of flinging things about, smashing them. Ally sighed. Her life was an endless procession of cleaning and washing, trying to get some order into the chaotic situation Ben had left them in. She was tired; gut-tired, dead-tired.

James crawled in, his pupils looking wide and dark. Ally went to meet him at the door, and he paused before walking in, raising a finger to point at his sister's bruised face. It went unmentioned in the wake of other, bigger news.

"Donna kissed me," he slurred, his face alight with pleasure. Ally grinned at him, but soon stopped as she realised how much it hurt.

"Nice one!" she said, and he smiled again. They both froze as Maggie's footsteps sounded above them.

"What number?" James whispered, his eyes round as saucers in his pale face. Ally grimaced.

"Nine," she replied. James's shoulders slumped. A nine was bad. Nine meant inebriation and fury all rolled into a spitting seething mass of pink flesh and mottled features. A nine was despair leading to rage, leading to violence. The two children stood stock still in the lounge. Ally considered James's face.

"What are you on tonight?" she asked, curious to find out what had made her brother's pupils so large and black. They covered over the colour in his eyes, making him look rather beautiful and sinister at the same time. James grinned again and lifted his hands up, suddenly distracted by the way his fingers moved, and the skin on his arm.

"Acid. It's a biggy," he said, and Ally shook her head, smiling. She hadn't tried acid, yet, but knew that James would at some point hand some over to her. He took pleasure in his drugs, researching each one carefully and trying them out in a controlled space, and then offering them to his sister once he knew they were safe. So far, she had smoked pot (a lot – it was James's favourite and there was always some kicking about in his room), snorted speed (it made the housework infinitely more fun), and dabbed a hesitant finger into a line of cocaine (not as good, though for a few minutes afterwards she had thought she was stunningly beautiful). Acid, though, seemed a little more frightening. James was absorbed in looking at the sofa, his finger tracing the pattern on the suite with childlike reverence.

"It all moves about," he mused, and Ally could tell his brief moment of sentience had passed, as he gave himself up to the chemicals working their way round his brain. She instinctively stood in front of him as their mother made her way down the stairs.

"Where have you been? Where have you been?" Maggie demanded as soon as she saw her son. Ally took a breath and answered for him.

"He's been staying with friends. They had revision to do, Mum," she said, and felt a grateful squeeze above her right elbow. Maggie's eyes darted from one child to the other, weighing things up in her mind.

"Come here," she said to James. Ally felt him stiffen, and she placed a cautionary hand against his chest, reaching behind to hold him back. Ally squared her shoulders, trying to look tough even as more blood began to pour from her nose and down her shirt.

"What do you want, Mum?" she asked quietly. Her voice was beginning to sound odd as it made its way through her swollen lip. Maggie sneered at her.

"I wasn't talking to you, whore. I don't want you anywhere near me," she spat, and Ally took a deep breath. James cowered lower behind his sister, and she could hear his breathing, ragged and afraid, behind her neck. James, usually so strong, had been reduced to a small squab of terror as the acid changed his mind, made him see things that weren't there.

"She's a witch! She's a witch!" he whispered, and Ally had to stifle a smile as she agreed with him. Maggie stared at Ally, her eyes narrowed. She wasn't used to seeing her children displaying solidarity.

"You have to leave him alone, tonight, Mum," Ally said, her voice careful and quiet. Maggie stepped forward.

"Why? Why?" she asked, and James shrank to the ground.

"He's not well."

Maggie walked up to them and shoved Ally out of the way, staring down at her son. James kept his eyes hidden, but Ally realised he had started to cry, his shoulders juddering silently. She felt a pang of love in her stomach for the boy-man cowering on the floor in the face of Maggie's rage.

"Get up, boy," Maggie demanded, but James continued to lie in a heap on the floor, not daring to lift his eyes up to meet her. She reached down and hauled him to his feet until they were standing face-to-face. James was now taller than Maggie, and was probably capable of holding his own, but not tonight.

"How do you dare to waltz into my house, at any time you like, without telling me where you've been?" Maggie said, her voice low and dangerous. Ally tensed her arms and legs in readiness, wondering what was going to happen. James had tears streaming down his cheeks, and she heard him chanting under his breath about Maggie being a witch.

"What are you saying?" she demanded, and Ally closed her eyes as James increased the volume of his mantra, looking right into Maggie's face.

"She's witch, she's a witch, she's a witch," he said, as if it was going to ward off evil. Ally shook her head in despair. Stupid idiot, she thought to herself. Maggie was becoming visibly more and more inflamed, seeming to double in stature even as James shrank. She stared at him, and got him by the arms until he was desperately close to her. She shook him, hard, and James flopped and wriggled in her grasp.

"That's enough, Maggie," Ally said. Maggie pushed James up against the living room door.

"That's ENOUGH, Maggie," Ally repeated, feeling her blood pulsing hard and hot through her arms and legs. Maggie slapped James about the face.

With that, Ally snapped. She launched herself on to her mother's back, beating and kicking and pummelling her until James fell to the floor and crawled to his room. Maggie twisted and turned, trying to get Ally off her, but she was drunk and drugged, and Ally was extremely sober and furious. Ally jumped down and turned her mother round to face her.

"You will never lay a finger on him, or me, ever again. Never. Never. Do you understand?" she said, her voice calm and low. Maggie glared at her, unmoving. Ally raised her hand and slapped Maggie with all her strength across the face. She had to reach upwards to do it, but she had enough anger and venom in her to make it hurt. Maggie's head snapped back, and she raised a forlorn hand to her cheek, where Ally's hand marks lay in perfect symmetry, white against burning red.

Gardening in the Dark

"Do you understand?" she asked again, and Maggie seemed to wither and slump, nodding her head. All fury gone, she looked simply like a broken woman. Ally nodded too.

"Good. Now I'm going to check on James, and you are going to go upstairs and go to bed," she said. Maggie nodded again and turned away, her hand still touching the place on her cheek where Ally had slapped her.

Ally sat down for a moment, her hands shaking and her head reeling. She took a deep breath and then walked to James's door, knocking on it quietly.

"James, love, it's Ally," she said, and she heard a scuffling in the room. She pushed open the door carefully and walked in. Her brother was hiding under his bedclothes, silent and still.

"Will you come out?" she asked. "It's safe now. She's gone."

James poked his head out of the covers, and Ally stifled a smile, thinking how much like a woodland creature he seemed. His pupils were enormous pools of black. He held out a shaking hand to her and she grasped it tightly.

"It's OK, now," she said, and he emerged slowly from the covers.

"She's a witch. She's a witch," he whispered, and Ally nodded.

"I know. I know she is. But it's OK."

She gathered James up in her arms and rocked him backwards and forwards, and he started to hum. Ally relaxed at the familiar sound, something she hadn't heard for years.

"There were spiders running across the walls," James said, and Ally held him tighter.

"Not any more. There aren't any spiders any more," she promised, holding him gently. "Can I leave you for a minute and get you a drink? A cigarette?" she asked, wondering how long it was since James had last eaten or drunk anything. He shook his head and so she continued to hold him, rocking him backwards and forwards.

"Was it my fault?" he asked, his voice young and high. Ally paused, wondering.

"What do you mean?"

"Was it my fault?"

"What? Was what your fault?"

"Your face."

"Oh. That. No. Not at all."

"Was the other thing my fault?"

"Hmmm?"

"Ben. Was that my fault?"

"No. That wasn't your fault either."

"Was it your fault?"

"No," Ally whispered, and her heart grew tight and hard and cold, as she rocked her brother gently to and fro. She felt his grief, heavy and impenetrable.

"We're good people, you and I. One day soon we'll be out of it, be free. You can get a little flat and play guitar and learn to paint and draw. You can set up a dealing racket on the side. I'll get another flat and do jobs, and study more. We could go to university, one day, and be like all the other students. Or we could go abroad somewhere brand new and start again. You could take Donna and I'll have Tiger and none of this will be important any more."

Gardening in the Dark

James's breathing slowed and he nodded. Ally settled him down on to the pillow and covered him with a duvet. His body was relaxed, and he seemed safe. She pushed him on to his side, an instinctive gesture learned with Maggie, and left the room. As she pulled the door shut, she heard him begin to snore, an open friendly childlike noise that made her smile through her bruised cheeks.

Ally went to the kitchen and surveyed it dismally. It was immaculately clean. There was no ironing to do, no laundry. She reached into her jeans pocket, pulled out a tin and rolled herself a joint. Pouring herself a glass of vodka, she gathered an ashtray and sat at the pine table. She smoked and drank quietly, thinking about the evening's events. She wondered where Ben was, and what he was doing; how he could leave them both with Maggie. Although, after the police and the neighbours and everything that had come out, he probably had no choice. She still felt forsaken. Apart from James, no one else on earth knew about Maggie and how she behaved. Ally had been careful for as long as she could remember, trying to cover up for the shambles of her family. She had concealed her bruises and marks, making excuses at school to avoid getting changed in front of the other children. Maggie was normally considerate, in this way at least, careful to kick out and punch only in places that could be hidden away.

Ally rested her hot head in her hands, being careful not to touch the welts and bruises. She was tired. Not tired in a way that sleep could erase, but worn out with grief and fury. She was tired of having to worry about her family, wondering if Maggie was going to lash out; worried that James didn't come home very often. She was tired of going to school most days with something to hide, struggling to make her grades up in the small hours of the morning when the house quietened down. She poured another drink and reignited the joint that had extinguished itself as she sat thinking. The house was silent and darkening, promising Ally some time for herself. She smiled as Tiger jumped up on the bench and pushed his face into her arm, demanding to be stroked. He purred enthusiastically, climbing in to her lap, and she leaned her head on the table for a moment, crouched over him. They were a team, the two of them. She let herself be lulled by his rhythmical purring, her hand playing across his ears and under his chin. He smelled good, of warmth and outside. She pushed her glass away and leaned on her arms.

*

She was dreaming of hammering a nail into a piece of wood. No matter how hard she banged it in, with more and more force, it refused to budge an inch. The wood was too tough. Her hand ached from heaving the hammer up, back, and down, over and over again. She lifted her head, the kitchen covered with darkness.

There was someone banging on the door, frantically, a haphazard rhythm of intense perseverance. Ally jumped up, the bench flying backwards and the remains of her vodka spilling over her jeans.

"Shit."

She wrenched open the door, rubbing her eyes. Mr. Thompson was standing outside, his arm raised for another bout of knocking.

"What is it? What's wrong?" Ally asked, taking in his agitation and the look of concern in his eyes.

"I think your house is on fire. I've called the fire brigade."

Ally stared at him in astonishment, completely nonplussed, and then stepped outside next to him and glanced up. A blue-grey column of smoke was coiling its way up into the expanse of black night sky.

"Oh my God! God. Thank you. Thank you!" she said, and then returned inside, slamming the door.

She had to act quickly. Her first thought was James, lying sleeping in his room. She raced through the kitchen, the lounge, the hall, and ran into his room. The whole house was beginning to fill with acrid smoke.

Gardening in the Dark

"James, Jamie get the fuck up!" she shouted, and saw him curled senseless in the corner of his bed. She pulled the duvet off him and ran to the window, opening it wide. She could hear sirens in the distance and closed her eyes for a second in relief. James sat up, blurry with sleep, and stared at her. Half dragging him off the bed, she propelled him towards the window, thanking Heaven that he was still fully dressed.

"Get out. Get out of the window," she shouted, turning to watch as he scrambled out to safety. As soon as she was sure he was out, she turned her attention to the next most important member of her family.

Tiger was nowhere to be seen. She ran through the lounge, calling him, and caught sight of him cowering under the sideboard. She coaxed him to her, trying to stop the panic from entering her voice and scaring him. Finally, in frustration, she lunged and grabbed him, scratching and spitting, and struggled to open the living room window and throw him out of it.

She put her hand over her mouth as she looked up the stairs. The fire was obviously in Maggie's room, possibly from some discarded cigarette butt. She hesitated for a second, but her thought process made her shudder and she began to run again, taking the wooden stairs two at a time, breathing through her sleeve. The smoke was making her eyes run, and she almost faltered as she saw yellow-orange flames licking at the ceiling above Maggie's door.

She opened the door cautiously, afraid of back draft. The bin in the corner was a charred glowing mass, and flames had just started to crawl up the duvet where Maggie lay unconscious. Ally no longer hesitated, but rushed to the bed and grabbed at Maggie's feet under the duvet. Her head lolled back and Ally mustered all her strength and heaved her off the bed and to the door. She had no way of covering her mouth, now, and she felt the smoke enter her lungs, making them crackle with heat. She half pulled, half fell across the floor with Maggie bumping away behind her, through the door to the top of the stairs, and then propelled both of them down in a heap of arms and legs. Maggie didn't stir as Ally dragged her across the living room floor, hooking her up to the open window and pushing her half out of it. She sagged in relief as strong arms reached for her bundle and dragged Maggie out, then reached in to assist Ally. She was pulled through the window in a choking heap, and then dragged across the patio and down the drive.

The drive way was coated in shimmering blue light, and Ally heard shouts and the rush of running water before she turned to her side and coughed.

"They all OK? Tiger?" she asked, her voice harsh and ragged. Someone cradled her head and assured her that everyone was fine. She let herself fall backwards, down and down into the kind arms.

Gardening in the Dark

Chapter Fourteen

The ward rounds came and went, and Alex's mood was continually elevated. They were calling it 'the switch'. Alex was climbing out of the pit. In fact, she was no longer climbing; she was nowhere near the pit at all. Something had happened, perhaps overnight while she lay sleepless and fidgety, her mind racing, for the first few days of her euphoria, until they began to knock her out for the night.

The switch, apparently, was not some birch rod for her back, but rather a button pressed somewhere inaccessible on the inside of Alex, which suddenly made her happy again. Alex was feeling happiness first in small things, when she opened her eyes and smiled at the wall, then at the delicious tautening of her arms and legs as she stood up and stretched. The room looked brighter. The colours were almost edible, with pale delicate blues and creamy smooth whites. The furniture, the walls, even, looked better. Cleaner. More spacious. She got out of bed in her tartan pyjamas and looked at the window. The sun was streaming in. She hadn't noticed it before, but here it was all of a sudden as if welcoming her back to the world.

"Well good morning!" she said to the window, and the sun seemed to brighten even further in response.

"Good morning!" she said to Doreen, who leaned up on her podgy elbows and watched Alex, a big smile on her face.

"Good morning," to Mark, to Susan, to the cleaner and the person who delivered the medication. To the people who administered it, Lois in the smoking room, Gary as he mooched about by the entrance to the ward, looking hopefully at the lock on the door.

"Good morning," to Martin, who sneaked into her room to give her a hug that lifted her off her feet, making her breathless and delighted. His eyes reflected hers, brimming with confidence and light, sparkling blue orbs that danced with life.

Alex felt glad to be alive. Glad of the rhythmic things her body performed, like breathing with regular ease, and blinking. Swallowing was blissfully automatic. She trusted her body, which had continued to function for so long even while her mind had been busy plotting how to die. It was a fantastic, indomitable machine. Alex looked down at her stomach, suddenly gone small and thin, a concave brown surface. She felt her ribs and was disconcerted to see that they stuck out on either side. She had shrunk, somehow. She wasn't padded any more.

Alex straightened the covers of her bed, placing the pillow neatly at the head, and then drew up the blue waffle blanket and cotton sheets carefully. As she was lifting the mattress, a thick blue oblong coated in some form of plastic film, she raised her head suddenly and frowned. The time she had spent in the ward so far seemed unreal, bizarre. She shook her head and looked about her, suddenly slightly shocked to find herself in a hospital.

How could she have acted in that way? Was it really herself who had been moping and hoping to die? She bit her lip, embarrassed. What had happened, and, more to the point, what the bloody hell was she doing in a nut house? Alex wandered out of her room sheepishly and looked about her with new eyes. She felt very ashamed, suddenly, to wake up as if from some nightmare, and find herself here. What was going on?

It was surreal. She knew what to do with herself; had been there for long enough now to understand that once she was awake, she should repair to the bathroom and wash herself. She hurried past the reception area surreptitiously to find her favourite bathroom. Everything looked the same, and suddenly terribly different. She ran a bath, watching the water swirl in the bottom of the tub, pouring in foam to make bubbles climb up the sides, frothing and hissing. She climbed in happily, luxuriating in the feel of the bubbles popping against her skin, the red-hot water scalding her arms and legs and turning them steaming pink. Standing up, Alex lathered her body until it turned an even deeper red. She smiled to herself, feeling the energy pulsing in her limbs, as her brain played a tune over and over again in her head at top speed. She tried to hum along, but the jingle went faster and faster.

Gardening in the Dark

The door flew open. One of the nurses stood in the entrance, looking at Alex. Alex was completely exposed form head to foot. Her mouth dropped open in shock. She felt a thick blob of bubbles snaking its way down her torso. In a flash, the craziness of the situation made itself felt to her. She was standing in the bath, the door wide open, in a mental hospital. Behind the nurse, a group of people were gathering, looking at Alex, looking at them. Alex spread her arms wide, suddenly, and began to laugh. If they wanted to see here, here she was.

"Is everything OK in here? What are you doing?"

"Sewing."

The nurse frowned and began to pull the door shut. Alex stopped her.

"Excuse me?" she asked politely. The door opened a fraction.

"Do you think I might be able to have a bit of privacy?" she asked. The nurse looked at her again, her lips forming into a smile, and she gave a brief nod.

"I'm sorry to have disturbed you," she said.

After that point, the five-minute checks began to recede. Alex didn't notice at first, but she would find herself sitting alone for longer stretches of time. She could follow a thought process through to the end without being disrupted by a friendly face enquiring after her. She took to having baths as often as possible, revelling in the privacy and the opportunity to be herself without being observed. All the while, the energy that was uncoiling inside her began to increase, unfurling and sending sparks running down her arms and legs, up the nape of her neck until her skin tautened and turned into pinpricks. She wanted to run, she wanted to play. She paced the ward waiting for her time outside, watching the clock which proceeded with infuriating slowness. She hassled the staff at every opportunity, the conversation always the same.

"Can I go for a walk?"

"Maybe later."

"May I go for a walk now?"

"When we have some staff free."

"May I walk now? Can I go outside?"

"When the shift changes."

"When it's quieter."

"When we've had lunch."

She found solace in Martin, the only person on the ward who seemed to be experiencing exactly the same feelings and frustrations as herself. He explained that it was the medication they were taking, that it was designed to send them flying up and up off the scale, before bringing them down to some level of normality; to who they were before the pit happened. They talked about the depressions in detail, Alex marvelling that another human being understood exactly what it was like, having felt it.

Depression. The word sounded like the imprint left on a pillow, left by a lover after you've broken up. Like the marks in the skin after you've been beaten, before the swelling starts. Like a pit which winds and spirals ever downwards, pulling you in with gravitational force. Like the skeleton caving in after the flesh rots and separates. Depression. In itself, removed from meaning, it was a nice word. It had the 'shhh' like silence, almost deep. Like impression, the second part was smooth and hushed. Alex didn't think the word was appropriate. It was too far away from what it represented. It didn't sound black enough. It sounded like a vague grey colour. Martin spoke about his experience, articulating sensations that Alex had only just begun to realise were generic; that were not a part of her natural personality. She listened, enthralled.

"The world becomes black and white," he said. "There is no colour. There is an intense physical pain. Thoughts become confused. I lose the ability to even remember a time when it was not like this. I can see no future when it might go away. My mind keeps repeating 'kill yourself', 'kill yourself', 'kill yourself', 'kill yourself', and I keep seeing visions of car crashes and every other way of suicide that you can imagine. It is all I can do to hang on. It's like being in hell."

"How about being manic?" Alex asked. She had never before realised that the euphoria she felt was not a natural successor to the depressive state, but rather a part of the same illness. She needed to listen, learn, speak more. Manic sounded primal, conjuring images of masculinity and panic. Manic. That, too, sounded something better left behind in favour of stability. Stable ability. Better.

Following ward round, Alex was officially diagnosed as having Bipolar Affective Disorder. Her head reeled with possibility. She could be normal. She could live without fear of darkness crowding in on her life, urging her to destroy everything. It seemed that every element of her – the creativity, the moodiness, the longing to escape everything, the desire to drink – was all tied up in those three words. She sat by the window in the smoking room and looked out at the tree, waving dappled-leaved in her direction. Who was she, without madness? She tried to find a core to herself and failed. She asked Martin.

"Who am I?" She was coming to terms with Lithium, the need to pee and drink, pee and drink, the way things seemed to be calming down. But without her madness, would there be anything else?

"You're you," he said. "Only more so."

Alex nodded, trusting him.

*

"Are you allowed to go out, now, Alex?" Martin asked her one morning, while the two of them were lingering over the breakfast table. Alex nodded. They had been talking, vying for space in the room while all the others, the depressed and under-confident and sullen had withdrawn to their various corners and left them alone, sensing the pulsing energy that emanated from them both. They were lost together, untouchable, impenetrable. Alex was finding it increasingly hard to keep her thoughts in check as they ran and ran by themselves and only Martin seemed to be sharp enough, bright enough to keep up with her.

Her psychiatrist had been damning, saying she was going into a manic state that was as destructive, in itself, as the depression had been. Alex knew the state well, having been there at least three times a year for the past fifteen years. While it ultimately resulted in a huge amount of damage, she longed for it. It was her favourite time, this surge. It was when she became beautiful, articulate, quick and genius-clever, confident and bright. Energy made her capable of realising everything she always wanted to be, pushed her to rack up degrees and qualifications, achieve all the things which marked her out as a successful businesswoman, a high achiever.

Martin had not been so lucky. He was more rash even than her, and had left a failed string of business opportunities behind him, each one going to be the one which made his fortune. Alex learned that he had simply picked himself up when normality returned and shaken his head, vowing not to do it again, but it was irresistible. He spoke at length of the things he had tried, and Alex nodded with him, recognising herself in so much of it. Failed relationships were the funniest. People trudging behind them trying to keep up, losing interest in them, fading as they sparkled.

"Because we're always just that bit better than everyone else!" Martin said, and she understood. At this moment, she was more beautiful, more clever, shinier and brighter than she had ever been.

Martin was even brighter. He was outstripping even her, charming and bristling with energy. He seemed stunningly beautiful. Alex watched him in quick bursts, drinking in his light, stretching into it.

"I'm allowed twenty minutes now. I can go out in the grounds if I want and I'm not supervised any more, but if I stay out longer or go off the grounds, or drink then I'm…grounded," Alex said. She smiled sheepishly and Martin grinned too.

Gardening in the Dark

"Brilliant," he said, congratulating her as if she were not, after all, a thirty-one year old woman who should have been in complete control of her own life, taking responsibility.

"I wonder why they can't tell that we've swung up again, and we're OK now?" Martin asked, his face showing dissatisfaction as he gazed out of the window. "It's autumn now, Alex. We should be running about and kicking up leaves."

"Can you go out?" Alex asked. She wondered if they would be allowed out together. Martin nodded.

"I expect so. I haven't really felt the need, so I haven't asked. But now I've got all this energy and I need to run. I need to run faster than myself," he said, and Alex nodded, in complete agreement. They both sat at the table, legs twitching and huge surges of energy coursing through them. Martin reached out for her hand tentatively and Alex caught it quickly. Their eyes locked and she felt his energy flow like a power surge up her arm. She giggled nervously. He continued to look at her, and Alex wondered if he had felt the same thing.

"We need to run," she said.

"I'll ask." Martin got up and walked rapidly out of the room, leaving Alex to pick up the breakfast dishes.

She couldn't sit still. She stalked from window to window, looking out at the grass beyond, and thinking about what she wanted to do. Climb a tree, run and run until she had no breath left in her body, until she had exhausted herself physically enough to make her mind grow still. 'Run faster than myself' Martin had said, and that was what it was like, an urge to generate speed, go faster and faster until she had caught up with, and then exceeded, her own thoughts.

It felt like a huge rushing burst of energy, joy and excitement over nothing, large pulses of pure white confidence. It felt like taking the best cocaine, drinking the purest vodka, it was like dancing to the most exhilarating music which seemed to run on a loop in her mind. She was clear and sharp like a brisk winter morning, her thoughts crisp and fast and wild. It was a fabulous, beautiful honest feeling of primal wildness. She could sense it in Martin, too. Even the way he spoke had changed, become more rapid and exhilarated, his thoughts spilling out in great rushes, and Alex's own mind revelled in keeping up with them, sometimes running apace and sometimes going even faster. It was good to share it, to sit next to someone who finally understood. It made her more alive than she had ever been, in stark contrast to the dead thing she had been when she was first admitted to the ward.

"Well?" she asked, as her friend returned, a wide smile on his face which made two neat dimples appear in his cheeks.

"It's OK – we can go. We have half an hour. To run. How fast can you run, Alex?" he teased her, reaching out a hand for her to take, pulling her quickly across the room to fetch their coats and be let out. Alex felt a surge of anticipation run through her body, her legs suddenly tingling at the thought of going outside.

"I'll outstrip you anytime, mate," she said, and Martin gave a laugh of derision as he pulled his coat on.

"Riiight," he drawled, and they went to the front door and hovered impatiently until Sarah, one of the nurses on duty, came to sign them out.

"Half an hour, on the grounds, no more. Or you'll be grounded, the pair of you," she warned, but she smiled at the sight of them, like two children clamouring to go out and play. Alex nodded emphatically, and Martin agreed.

"Right you are, Nurse Sarah," he said, sarcastic and charming, and then they were outside the ward door which clicked closed behind them, and walking towards the entrance hall. As soon as they were outside, they turned and grinned at each other, then clasped hands, and then they were running, legs pounding the concrete path, moving with one accord further and further away from the red brick building. Alex felt the wind in her face as they moved faster and faster, sprinting full tilt. She became aware of her breathing, rapid panting that seemed to be expelling the heat of the ward and replacing it with cool, crisp afternoon air. It felt amazing.

Gardening in the Dark

She laughed, and the sound was caught up by the wind they were creating and cast back towards the hospital.

They ran in large loops, all around the grounds, doing lap after lap. Martin was faster than her, but he pulled her hand hard so she stumbled forward, catching up. They ran until Martin's breath emerged in ragged panting shards. Until Alex's head was pounding with newly awakened blood, rushing in her ears like the sea.

Running, racing, tumbling, they fell over each other in a heap of arms and legs. Alex scratched her face on the concrete, leaving a gritty darkened bruise along the side of her cheek. She couldn't feel it, and only realised when Martin raised a tentative hand and touched the place where she had fallen, lifting his fingers away to show her the vivid red blood on the tips. She smiled at him, and he brought his hand in front of his face, looking at the very inside of her.

"It's beautiful," he said, and Alex understood. The red was the red of living, pulsing, breathing, beating energy.

Alex rolled on to her stomach on the grass, and let the blades play through her fingers.

"Imagine if we were the only people in the world," she mused. Martin watched her hands, and reached out to cup them in his own.

"Then we wouldn't be mad. We'd be normal."

"We're not mad. We're unique, special, fascinating and fantastic."

"I think we are."

"Martin, what did you want to be when you were young?"

"Old. You?"

"Everything."

They spoke rapidly, covering any subject that popped into their minds. They spoke about the weather, the sun, their lives (always cautious, even at the height of their talkativeness, to hide certain things) and politics and the world and the future. They spoke about religion, arguing their various points ahead until it turned out they actually concurred about all of it. It came down to energy, of course it must, God and energy were the same things, a bright reusable thing which entered them both and carried them at a tremendous rate through life only to suddenly withdraw at some point. The two of them clambered over the entire face of the earth together. Lying on their backs in the grass, punctuated by laughs and then fighting, rolling over, tackling each other and then falling back on the ground like children, laughing. They forgot about the time, talking and talking and then they were disturbed by Mark turning up, looking serious and a little annoyed.

"Where have you both been? I've been looking for you," he admonished.

"Oh, God. The time. We didn't mean to be late, it was just we got talking and we had all this energy to run out and it's simply beautiful out here and the leaves are turning and it feels that we haven't seen it for so long," Alex said, not pausing for breath as she justified her absence. Martin looked abashed, his usually confident manner turning suddenly meek.

"It was my fault, Mark. I distracted Alex, and she forgot the time. I'm sorry."

Alex paused and stared straight ahead of her. She felt desperately uncomfortable. She looked ahead of her and thought she saw the shadow of her younger self crossing the grass. She turned away quickly and scrambled to her feet, then followed Mark and Martin through the doors, her shoulders drooping as she heard it slam shut, heavy and wooden, behind her.

"It's dinner-time, you will get us all into trouble, not just yourself, and it's not fair on the other residents who might think you are getting preferential treatment," Mark said. He was not smiling. Alex felt mildly ashamed as the two followed obediently behind him, as he walked with quick strides like an angry schoolmaster.

Gardening in the Dark

Martin suddenly changed his gait, stalking ahead in a manner so like Mark that Alex couldn't smother her giggles.

As they paused in the hallway to go their separate ways, Martin turned and winked at her.

"I had fun," he whispered. Alex flushed, her face glowing, the smell of leaves and outside clinging to her like wind and water.

"I'm not sure it's healthy, this Bipolar convention," said Mark. "You're going to be trouble, you two, I can see that. You can't be feeding off each other's mania like that."

Alex ignored him, returning to her room, scrabbling under the bed sheets for her bottle of vodka. She drank deeply, feeling it rough and warm inside. She smiled to herself, thinking about Martin, their conversation. Walking through to the dining room, she grinned as she saw the object of her thoughts walking by her.

"We are both geniuses," he whispered to her as he passed, and she knew it to be true.

Chapter Fifteen

"Fuck off."

Lois was sitting in the smoking room, rocking backwards and forwards, her long hair trailing wildly behind her back, her velvet skirt entangled with leaves and dust. She had been out for a full day and night, coming back to the ward raucous and unmanageable. Alex could see the tension in the eyes of the staff on duty as their charge had re-entered the hospital, glowering and shaking with pent up rage.

"Fuck off!" she screamed again, cornering Gary, arguably the most nervous and gentle of the residents, as he made himself impossibly small in the corner of the room, his eyes darting anywhere but towards Lois, who was looking feral and mad. She was smoking a cigarette brutally, dragging air through the tiny funnel until the end blazed with orange, the ash creeping down the length of it, holding on to its previous form even when it was long since dead. Alex stayed out of reach, sitting in the opposite corner to Gary, cross-legged and hunched away from Lois's pulsing, throbbing insanity. She smoked quickly, wanting to get the nicotine into her body quickly enough that she could escape unseen, leaving Lois to smoulder alone.

Gary whimpered to himself, unsure how to placate his friend. When Lois was being sweet, he responded to her. He was like a pet, constantly seeking out affection and reassurance. He now looked like a puppy that had been beaten into submission, tail down and drooping ears, in the face of Lois's rage. She was angry for the sake of it, angry because it felt good, positive. A release. Gary looked hurt and surprised, and Alex wanted to run to him and gather him up in her arms, and lead him away to stop him from hovering uncertainly like a moth going back and back to a burning flame.

Alex stood up quietly and walked over to Gary, extending her hand. He took it gratefully, and allowed himself to be led from the room. Alex turned back to Lois, who was now glowering in her general direction.

Gardening in the Dark

"Did you write that Jane Austen book?"

"No. That would have been Jane Austen."

"I don't believe you."

"OK."

"Have you slept with my boyfriend?"

"Who is your boyfriend?"

"Craig."

"No."

"I don't believe you. You're a fucking liar."

"OK."

Alex sat down opposite Lois and regarded her openly. She wondered what monsters were running about in the woman's mind, keeping her unsettled and fractious.

"Are you all right, today, Lois love?" she asked. Lois shook her head, tears springing readily to her eyes.

"No. No. Never all right. All wrong. All wrong. I feel...I feel..." she trailed off, her mouth turned down. Alex nodded.

"This passes. It goes away."

"Yes. Did you sleep with Craig? He said you did. He told me."

"I didn't sleep with Craig."

And so the questioning went around and around, until Alex stood up. Lois reached out and grasped her arm quickly. Alex flinched and turned back to her.
"Don't go. Stay here. Stay."

Alex nodded and sat back down, lighting another cigarette. The room was becoming hazy with smoke, thick and acrid when Alex drew a breath. She imagined it clinging to her hair, skin and clothes like a protective sheen that would stop people getting too close. The two women looked up as Martin opened the door and slid inside to join them.

"No seats, buster," Alex said, grinning at him. He nodded and settled on the floor by the window, pulling rolling-tobacco and papers out of his jeans pocket, his eyes moving from Lois to Alex.

"What's new, mad Lois?" he asked, his voice smiling. Lois grinned at him, and then her face shifted to shadow immediately.

"All bad. I feel things. I feel," she answered.

Martin nodded sagely and resumed rolling his cigarette. He winked at Alex as he licked the paper and folded it shut.

"I feel too. I feel a lot," he said, conversationally. Lois was already lost to the thread, rocking backwards and forwards, a tragic Miss Haversham with her flowing skirt and leaves and cobwebs. She looked, Alex thought, typically insane. She stood up suddenly as Gary came back in the room, and glared at him. Alex stood too, instinctively protective of the slight young man with trembling hands.

"It's you! You did it!" Lois shrieked, her eyes blazing and fists pounding the air. Gary flinched back, his mouth forming a perfect round 'o' of pure shock.

"I...I..." he stammered. Martin stood also, pulling Alex back behind him, as she giggled nervously and watched the two people interact. Lois was shrieking now, her voice wild and high, a garbled stream of words that issued, coated in saliva, around Gary. She raised her fist and punched him hard, once, in the face, and he fell to the floor in tears. Martin sprang forward and caught Lois's fist, and the two grappled for a second. She was possessed, her madness giving her a surprising amount of strength.

Gardening in the Dark

"Don't hurt her. Don't hurt her," Alex said, her voice shaking. She ran to look after Gary, who was crying harder, his face coated in sticky bright blood. She cradled him to her as the door flew open and three members of staff ran in. They reached for Lois, pushing Martin out of the way. Two of the nurses held her as she writhed against them, lashing out for their faces, spitting and clawing at them. The third, calm and practised, rolled up the long black sleeve of her top and gave her an injection. She slumped to the floor like a black sack.

"There. There, now," one of the nurses said, leaning down by Lois and stroking her hair. Lois was quiet now, mumbling to herself, her face wet with tears. Alex and Martin sat in the corner, shocked and silent, Alex holding Gary close to her, rocking him as he cried.

"Another day in the office," one of the nurses quipped, winking at Martin and Alex as two of them carried Lois to her bedroom. The third, a younger female, reached out for Gary and led him away to be cleaned up, leaving Alex and Martin staring at each other, wordless.

Martin was the first to split the tension.

"Lovely weather," he said, and with that, they were laughing harder and harder, Alex clutching her side and Martin's giggles reaching out louder into the room, dispelling the heavy atmosphere.

"I need a beer," he said, when their giggles subsided. Alex nodded in sympathy, and pulled him to her cubicle for a sly drink before the ward settled down for the afternoon.

*

Alex's bright mood was continuing. There was more sunshine in the early morning and a better quality to the light. The ward seemed more alive, somehow, as if energy tingled just out of reach in every corner, as if Alex could suddenly reach out and grasp it if her reflexes were sharpened enough.

"It's changed," she said conversationally to Susan, who looked at her kindly and smiled as if she understood, when Alex walked out of her cubicle and took a seat on the floor in the hallway. The nurses were sitting chatting, waiting for the ward residents to begin to stir and start their day.

"Feeling better, now Alex?" she asked in her quiet voice, and Alex grinned and nodded. She wanted to walk. She wanted to go outside into the light and stretch her legs, run, burn up the surfeit of energy she had suddenly noticed pulsing and fizzing beneath her skin.

"May I go outside for a walk?" she asked, a stirring of hope beginning somewhere. Things had changed. Susan smiled.

"Later," she promised, and Alex remained sitting, fidgeting and impatient under this sudden rush of feeling. Her body stretched and sparkled as if she had been slumbering for a terribly long time and had now emerged from some chrysalis ready and eager to begin living.

"If you eat, you can go out," Mark said. Alex looked at him, bemused. She went with him to the kitchen and they made tea and toast, an incongruously normal activity.

"What's brought this change about, Alex?" Mark asked as he took down a plate and some bread, making toast for her, pouring her a cup of coffee with lots of milk and sugar. "You've been like this for weeks!"

Alex shrugged.

"I don't know," she said. "I don't care as long as it stays." She took the plate and looked at it. Mark took her into the dining room, where they sat together in silence as she ate. It felt wonderful after the first bite, and her body seemed to come alive once it realised that she was about to give it more sustenance. She ate cautiously at first, the food seeming unfamiliar in her mouth. She drank the coffee quickly, and felt the warmth and sweetness of it spreading through her. She felt alive.

Gardening in the Dark

"Good," Mark said, as she finished eating. "You've been getting a bit bony." Alex looked down at herself and realised that he was right. She felt her ribs in surprise, as they jutted out beneath her pyjamas. She smiled, suddenly embarrassed.

"Shall we go for a walk? Do you want to go outside and get some air?" Mark asked, and Alex nodded. She could see a tree outside the kitchen window, in the little gap, and it looked burnished bronze and red. Autumn had arrived. Alex had missed a season.

"I'll grab a shower and then can we go?" she asked, and he nodded and led her back to her room. Alex went quickly from her cubicle to the bathroom, gathering up clean clothes and her toiletries. She jumped into the shower, in a great mood, revelling in the regular pulse of the water as it hit her shoulders and neck. The room filled with steam, and Alex traced a smiley face on the mirror, watching her finger as it worked across the glass, marking lines in the condensation. She could see the outline of her lips in the trail her finger had made, and they smiled at her coquettishly. It was going to be a great day. She towelled herself dry roughly, looking as her arms and legs took on a pink hue, glowing with barely concealed energy. Life pumping through her. Nourished, newly discovered life.

In their shared room, Doreen was awake, walking to and fro lining things up and then moving them again. Alex smiled at her as she went in.

"Good morning, Doreen," she said, and the woman paused in what she was doing and looked at Alex in surprise.

"You look different today," Doreen commented, pausing in moving her water jug and studying Alex for a moment. Alex nodded. That would make sense, now she was alive again. She grinned at the older woman, who sat on the bed and clapped her hands in delight.

"Do you want to dance?" Alex asked, and Doreen stood up, giddy with glee, and allowed Alex to take her hand, place an arm around her ample waist, and waltz her around the room. Doreen laughed, her hips and bosom shaking, twirled around in a circle.

"Are you staying here, Alex?" she asked, her voice girlish and plaintive. Alex hesitated, dropping her hands from around Doreen's waist.

"I shouldn't think so, love. Are you?"

Doreen nodded enthusiastically.

"Oh yes. Yes." With that, she went back to her bedside cabinet again, lining up the jug, the box of tissues, the little plastic glass. Alex smiled and shook her head.

It was time for a change. She could smell it on the wind when she tried to wiggle open the window of their bedroom, determined to blow out all the old air and replace it with something as crisp and sharp as her thoughts. Change whispered to her in the drops falling from the shower, telling her to reach up and out until she was as tall as she could be. She could feel change in her limbs as she warmed up ready for a long hard circular run around the grounds. It was in the lyrics of all the songs which she heard on the radio, all too slow to keep track of her arms and legs which were begging to be stretched and used. And her mind, her fast furious and inimitably rebellious, curious mind, was screaming at her to make changes. Not just any changes, but life-affirming, bubble-of-joy, orgasmic huge sweeping changes which rocked the world to its foundations, razed everything to the ground, set fire to all givens and provided newness, hope and possibilities.

There was no gentleness in it. Alex was courting revolutions. The sort of pleasure that can be found when a dripping candle reaches its target. The kind of pain that one gets when making love, the up-thrust of agony. She wanted destruction, but on a huge scale. She wanted world war, absolutes, decimation in the highest degree. She wanted to stand on top of the largest mountain ever known to humanity and scream her truths out to the world, which would listen to her because she was right. She wanted to open herself, yield everything, and offer herself as a sacrifice to anyone who took a moment to stand and accept what she was holding in her two hands. She wanted to spread her arms and grasp water, earth, salt and sun between them. She wanted ecstasies. She wanted to run amok in other people's dreams, hauling them to corporeal fruition.

Gardening in the Dark

She was a goddess. She was Cleopatra incarnate, Venus personified. She was an amalgamation of the best qualities represented by Apollo and Dionysus. She was dancing, naked and ethereal. She was running with the wolves. She was primal energy. When she opened her mouth and exhaled, it was pure Prana that tumbled out. She could breathe on the world and ignite it. She was raw, hard sex. She was every woman; she was both Eve and the apple. She had the power of divinity. She had travelled further than any mortal being. She had reached out her hands and touched each of the corners of the earth, gathering the treasures it held hidden and secret. She came harder, breathed more deeply, fell faster, and climbed higher. She could fly, sometimes. One drop of her deep rich blood could fall and transform the world. She was limitless. Limitless.

She was also going out for a walk with Mark. Her hair was scrambled beneath her hat, and her coat was askew, as she caught up with him near the entrance to the ward.

"I need some paints, Mark. I need paint and paper and brushes and a water jar – any old thing will do – I'm going to paint something while I'm here, to make sure I use the time up properly before it runs away with itself. I want to make something. I'm going to start off with painting the tree that you can see out of the smoking room window. Can we go and look at it now? And then I want to check out the pond because of the fish, and the way the light streaks across their backs. I used to be a good painter. When I was in school I did it and then colours fell away and I started using words instead, but now the words are too quick so maybe I can do the colours instead. Doreen and I danced a waltz, I think I cheer her up sometimes. Gary was in the smoking room with three cigarettes, all lit, in his mouth at once. Is that because he wants to die?"

Alex drew breath and Mark shook his head at her, laughing.

"Try and follow through one thought at a time. We can't all keep up with you and Martin, you know." He smiled. Alex shrugged and bounded out of the door as Mark held it open.

"Do you want to run?" she asked, her face eager. Mark shook his head, no, and sighed.

"You need new ways of burning up that energy," he commented, as Alex walked backwards and forwards, doing eight steps for Mark's every one.

Alex drew near to the nurse again, and considered him with her head to one side.

"This is better, though, isn't it?" she asked, although of course she knew it was, that it had to be. Mark shrugged and looked away.

"It needs managing, Alex. Just like the other."

Alex sloughed off his words before they could land around her. He didn't understand, anyway. She ran to the tree, imagining the end product once she had captured it, caught its colours and movement, and painted the sounds it made when the leaves rustled in the breeze.

*

There was a large black figure, shrouded in a cape like a monk or a monster. It was beckoning to her, and when its hood was turned towards her, there was a big void where the face should have been. She opened her mouth to scream, but no noise came out. It reached out a bony hand to grasp her arm, and shook her over and over again, growing more and more –

"Wake the fuck up, Alex, for God's sake!"

She sat upright, hot and confused, as Martin released her arm. She stared at him in surprise, and opened her mouth, only to have Martin place a warning hand over it. His eyes were gleaming in the dim light of the room.

"Be very very quiet. Do you want to go out and play? I'm terribly bored!"

Gardening in the Dark

Alex nodded, shaking her sleep off and slipping out of the bed. She hesitated as Martin padded over to the door and looked back at her.

"Coast is clear," he reassured her, so she followed him warily, her feet making no sound on the wooden floor, her breath coming in short gasps of excitement. They were going on an adventure.

"Where?" she asked, and Martin shook his head and led Alex down the corridor quietly. She could hear the nurses on the night shift, smothered laughter issuing from the smoking room, the fan loud enough to cover any sound that they could make.

He led her down to the end room on the ward, where Gary was staying. She hesitated, starting to giggle, as Gary pushed his head around the door, nervously chewing on his lower lip and grinning at them both.

"Come in, but be quiet! Bob's asleep," he whispered, gesturing to his snoring room-mate with a stifled laugh. Alex tiptoed in past Martin, who let the door swing shut quietly.

"What's going on?" Alex asked, and Martin just lifted his finger to her lips and gestured towards Gary, who was standing by his window proudly, brandishing a spoon.

"Gary's whittled the block away from his window – he can open it all the way!" Martin said, and Alex shook her head in disbelief.

"We can go out?" she asked, and Gary nodded, looking like a pleased child who had done a particularly good piece of homework.

"Gary, that's amazing! Fantastic!" Alex said, and Martin grinned at her before pulling gently on the window, letting it slide up and up. Alex stood for a moment, letting the full cool night breeze lift the damp hair from the back of her neck, feeling the wind blow across her skin. She breathed in, in delight, before clambering out of the window to drop on the ground with a soft thud beside Martin.

"We're out!" he exclaimed, reaching his arms up above his head, turning around in the silvered darkness. Alex smiled and stretched, the evening rolling out ahead of her in a series of possibilities. Martin turned and gave the thumbs up to Gary, who hovered delightedly by the window for a few moments, revelling in their freedom before pulling it closed again.

"Is he not coming with us?" Alex asked, curiously. She couldn't understand how a young man could work so tirelessly to achieve something, and then not reap the benefits of that achievement.

"No. He gets afraid if he's outside. He likes to know he could but, when it comes down to it, he's not ready for it. He's been doing it for years."

Alex laughed, a little sadly, but then turned her attention to Martin and held out her hand.

"What are we going to do?" she asked, looking into his face which shone with anticipation.

"Everything." He caught hold of her hand and they flew across the grass, behind the hospital to a wooded area by the fishpond. Martin slipped off his jacket and placed it around Alex's shoulders, and they sank to the ground. Like a magician, he pulled out a small bottle of whisky, cigarette papers and tobacco. They rolled a cigarette and sat looking about them, taking it in turns to sip the sweet hot liquid.

For a few moments, the moonlight dissipated and left them sitting in absolute darkness. Alex leaned closer to Martin and traced his features, invisible now, with her fingers. She searched his face and neck, reading his emotions and thoughts through the lines her fingers made. He leaned forward and kissed her, deeply, and they held on to each other tightly. He tasted of whisky and smoke, and something indefinable beneath, sweet and soft. She shivered slightly and he pulled her closer as they drank more. Alex held her hand up in front of her face but could see nothing. And yet, she felt completely safe with him.

When the moon came out, she leaned in to his neck and whispered.

"Let's run."

The two of them stood clumsily and she took his hand, and they pelted around the grounds in a huge lap, pausing by the fishpond to let the surprised carp nibble on their fingertips. They climbed a tree, Alex snagging her pyjamas on a low branch. Martin climbed higher and faster than her, until he was almost out of sight; then he extended a long arm, monkey-like, to pull her up to his vantage point. They sat on a wide branch and surveyed their empire. The grounds stretched out beyond them, and beyond that the town lights were twinkling, with far off sounds of sirens and shouts encroaching on their stolen privacy.

"What shall we do?" Alex asked, looking beyond the grounds wistfully. Martin thought for a minute, swinging his legs backwards and forwards, chewing on a nail.

"I think we should do some gardening," he decided, suddenly starting to laugh, smothering his mouth with his hand which poked out of the over-long sleeve of his jumper. Alex turned to face him, her mouth open, suddenly reminded of something. She stared at him with her head on one side, considering his suggestion.

"Imagine if we could transform it all, how surprised they would be," she mused, picturing the reaction of the inmates in the hospital, the sudden joy of being surprised by something positive.

"We could put it all outside Doreen's window, so when she wakes up and draws the curtains, all she'll see is colour," Alex suggested. Martin suddenly smiled; a growing grin which stretched his beautiful face almost in two.

"Perfect," he agreed, and the two linked hands and slithered down the tree as if with one mind, running swiftly and silently until they came to an abrupt halt, breathless below Alex and

Doreen's bedroom window. Alex turned and surveyed the area of land which Doreen looked out on each day. The earth was drab and bare; a brown patch.

"What shall we do? Where shall we start?" she asked, as Martin surveyed the scene. He was suddenly omnipotent, and she was aware of their power when they touched hands and shared a vision, however small.

"There are pots and plants and things around the front," he whispered, and Alex nodded. They turned again and went to retrieve the things which would build Doreen a garden. They worked in silence, somehow communicating without words, using the moonlight to illuminate their path as they moved backwards and forwards across the grass. Now and then the two caught each other's gaze and smiled, and the silvered light reflected in Martin's face, making him seem ghostly and otherworldly. They worked in unison, sharing tasks with vigour which Alex couldn't remember feeling for months, perhaps years.

Alex arranged pots around Doreen's window, as Martin found a stick and began to dig with it, creating a row of even holes to place plants in. Together, they ran to the front of the hospital grounds and sourced large sweeping cordylines and small rounded hebes, hostas, euonymus and lavender. They took the plants with care, making sure each would not be missed among the others. They carried them to their new garden and placed them in to the holes, Alex preparing each one for Martin to carefully press down. They worked for over two hours, until the moonlight was sinking back beneath a cloud and a pale glow on the horizon behind the hospital building signalled the slow beginning of a new day. Alex and Martin stood back from their handiwork, and shared a sudden feeling of exuberance as they realised how much they had achieved. Linking arms, the two jogged backwards to view their work more fully.

"Wow," Alex whispered. Doreen's patch of earth was transformed, a cacophony of greens and yellows, with each colour vying for space amid pots and planters. Martin had placed a series of stones through the mass of vegetation, which looked like an invitation to follow a trail around in a wide arc through the centre of the new garden. He turned to Alex, his face alight, and the two of them walked on the new path through the plants, admiring their work.

"This is amazing," Martin said, suddenly feeling limitless, understanding that the two of them could be magnificent, however small their task.

"We've finished," she said, feeling a rush of impatience, and Martin nodded.

"So what now?" he asked, and traced Alex's chin and cheek with a grimy finger. His hands smelled of earth, a rich brown scent that made her shiver.

She leaned forward and kissed him fully on the lips with an intensity that made him almost stumble backwards.

"Ahh," he murmured, breaking into a smile. "That."

The sun came up slowly, and the two were one and a part of everything. They made love, rolling and breathing in the dirt and leaves, feeling the energy which they had between them combine and lift them. They fell apart afterwards, each lying on the grass, fingers entwined, and finished the whisky, smoking a last cigarette in front of the new patch of garden.

Gary was almost upon them, breathless and scared.

"It's time," he whispered, and they stood up and shook themselves down and the three of them ran back to his window, climbed up noiselessly and slipped back into their rooms just as the ward began to stir with the sound of staff arriving and breakfast things being clattered in the kitchen. As Alex left Martin, he cornered her suddenly, his eyes intense and serious.

"Alex, will you promise me something?"

"What is it?"

"Will you start taking Lithium?"

Alex studied his eyes, Martin who seemed to know her so well, who saw straight into the heart of her. She thought about losing the high, this amazing sensation of being everything, capable of achieving anything. She bit her lip. She thought about the possibility of a future with this man, who had changed her life and made her smile again.

"I will. If you will," she said. Martin looked away for a second, and then held her gaze tightly.

"Deal. I promise."

"I promise."

As Alex showered that morning and slipped back to her cubicle, she smiled to herself. Lithium would not be so bad, if they could hold on to whatever it was they had created together. Without it, they would always be gardening in the dark. Alex imagined a different life, the first stirrings of a hopeful future. It featured Martin.

Gardening in the Dark

Chapter Sixteen

Ben had been gone for what felt like an eternity, month after month spilling away until the gap left by his departure had sealed over. Leaving behind a house that seemed too big some of the time, until Maggie was in one of her moods and she filled every corner with glowering and noise. Ally sought out her corners in the rooms away from James and her mother, crawling in to nooks and crannies and curling into sleep. She loved sleeping, now that Ben was no longer there to wake her up. She could drift off and sleep was thoughtless.

And yet, she missed him. She found herself as the months passed thinking about him more and more. He hadn't been in contact with them all for some time, unless you counted the phone calls with Maggie, hushed and then suddenly screaming. Ally deliberately didn't listen, didn't want to think of her father calling the house and being intercepted by Maggie to talk about money and bills, when actually Ally wanted to grasp the phone and cry down it, asking why she had been left here, deserted with two people who didn't seem to like her very much.

Ally was getting dressed, shrugging into clothes that felt crisp with cold, pulling on trousers and a jumper hurriedly, as if the speed would lend some heat and her frenzied movements would impart warmth into the stiff fabrics. It was autumn, and the windowpane had huffed cold all over the glass, obscuring the garden and field beyond with haze. She was going into town; she was going to catch the train with her friend and shop.

Except it wasn't exactly shopping. It was free shopping, furtive and deft handling of items into wide coat pockets, inserted up sleeves and down tops, until their coats bulged suspiciously and they left, exhilarated and laughing nervously, to impart their new goods into carrier bags. Ally's friend Sarah had been coaching her a little, while they stood behind the shed at school and smoked half-cigarettes, talking about the best things to steal. Make-up was ideal. Small and discreet vials and tubes that could be pushed up into your sleeve quicker than a security guard could blink. Books were harder, being cumbersome and somewhat inflexible, but they were the things which Ally liked the best. She had been going into town more regularly with Sarah, starting off slow and scared and then building up gradually until she had perfected the art of stealing. She felt proud of the skill. It took courage and determination, a strong nerve and a nonchalant air which was helped in part by her angelic appearance. Ally was blessed with an innocent face, wide eyes and a laughing mouth, and hair which was too long and drab to be considered fashionable. She dressed carefully for their sprees, selecting demure jumpers and immaculately pressed jeans. Most of her new wardrobe had been selected in haste and stolen by donning items under her existing clothes, in department store changing rooms. She had begun to dress well, having found this new skill. She no longer needed to ask Maggie for money. In fact, money seemed to be rather irrelevant to shopping overall.

Ally liked Sarah. Her friend was wise and knowledgeable about matters which Ally had not even considered before their friendship had started. Sarah was coarse and common with a vicious sense of humour and a love of mischief. Sarah had taken to Ally once she had discovered that she liked drinking and smoking, and that James could give her access to whatever drugs he was dabbling in that week. Ally had already begun to perfect the art of pilfering. She had practised on Maggie (an easy target, who usually had her eyes closed anyway) with cigarettes and money, and then progressed to James, who was also becoming easier to dupe these days as he was going through an experimental phase with drugs and also spent a lot of his time with his eyes closed lying prostrate somewhere, semi-unconscious. Ally had palmed dope from him the first time, having spied on him to see how he prepared it for smoking. She had taught herself to roll a joint and shared her first one with Sarah, pretending she was an old hand, a drug veteran. Sarah had been impressed. In return for cigarettes and pot, Sarah had taught Ally the basics of shoplifting. Sarah also looked much older than Ally, which meant she was able to walk confidently into an off-licence and purchase alcohol without being asked for ID. It was a good friendship, based on mutual miscreant behaviour and the thrill of the illicit. Ally had kissed Sarah a few times, and Sarah had kissed back. Sarah was soft and squishy, and her skin was pale and freckled. Her hips had protruding bits that felt colder than the rest of her. She was cold and rounded. They talked about boys (there was a

Gardening in the Dark

guy called Bob who lived a few doors down from Ally, and Sarah had wanted an introduction).

Sarah had had sex. A lot. And she had started her period, which Ally was rather in awe of and somewhat jealous about. Sarah had breasts that were pendulous and full, whereas Ally seemed to persist in remaining stick-thin and willowy, growing up instead of out. She had no hips to speak of, and her breasts remained stubbornly small and irrelevant. While Sarah flourished with the rush of teenage hormones that lent her body an adult ripe quality, Ally was developing acne and sprouting tufty hair in odd places.

But Ally sometimes puzzled Sarah who didn't read books. She couldn't understand why Ally chose to steal them, as they didn't perform any function of beautification but rather weighed them down when they dragged their booty back from the train and up the winding hill back to their village. She urged Ally to focus on more fruitful thefts such as scent, bras, and make-up. Ally thought about Sarah as she made her way out of the house, stepping over Maggie who was lying face down on the living room floor.

Sarah was blonde. She had a sheet of thick hair that she wore around her shoulders defiantly. Regardless of the weather, or how active and debauched Sarah had been, her hair lay obediently like a faithful glossy collie, straight and perfect. It gave her an angelic quality which made security guards look the other way in shops, conscious of her beauty, aware of something within themselves which was unseemly in their response to the teenager. Sarah wore jeans that were deliberately frayed across the bottom, trainers that peeped out and looked terribly cool beneath. She favoured tight jumpers which stretched over her full chest, and carefully applied make-up that brought out her peachy good looks and accentuated her sharp cheekbones and full mouth.

Ally walked quickly down the road to Sarah's house, pausing to rake her fingers through her hair which was getting tangled in the breeze. She felt a thrill of excitement in her stomach as she approached Sarah's ramshackle house, thinking ahead of the shoplifting to be done, illicit cigarettes and a quick drink on the train. She approached the front door and looked at the peeling paint, and stepped over the broken pots littering the front path. Sarah seemed to have an endless supply of brothers, all older, all blond and freckled, tall and gangly, with the same snubbed nose and large eyes. Ally was never sure which was which. They all looked the same – unkempt and light-hearted, with rakish smiles and sardonic gaits.

As she knocked on the door, Sarah was immediately there, pushing Ally back out on to the path.

"Morning. You're on time. We can get the ten o'clock train and be there for half past. I've got my big coat on, look, and I've sewn a secret pocket inside. Sebastian and Nicholas are going to a music festival and Mum is annoyed. I've got some cigarettes and I pinched a lighter off Marcus. Have you seen Bob? He called me the other night. I think he likes me. Can you arrange for us to meet up again? Have you got any dope?" Sarah walked just ahead, turning around and asking Ally questions without pausing for an answer.

"How are you?" Ally asked, wishing it were Sarah, rather than herself, that asked the question. Sarah ignored her and continued her monologue, tripping on an uneven paving slab as she walked and reaching back to grasp Ally's arm for support, pulling her along.

They made their way to the train platform and stood, bored, watching the passengers on the other side of the track milling about.

"Do you know if you put a penny on the track, Ally, it gets all squashed to twice its size?" Sarah asked inconsequentially. Ally nodded.

"James does that sometimes. He gave me one. It's cool," she answered. She thought of James, and wondered what he was doing that morning. She had stolen some pot; a half-joint left lying on his bedside table. Sarah smiled.

"Your brother is well fit, Ally. Do you think he would go out with me?"

Ally shuddered and shrugged, looking away. She didn't like the thought of Sarah and James together.

Gardening in the Dark

"He has a girlfriend. He likes brunettes," she said dismissively. Sarah looked at her, unperturbed.

"I'd like to meet him properly at some point. He's never out in the pub or anything is he? What does he do?"

Ally shrugged and watched a gaggle of passengers disembarking from a train which had come from the city.

"Dunno," she said, and tried to change the subject. James was out of bounds, just as Maggie and Ben and the house and her domestic life were all completely off-limits to this persistent blonde. Ally felt a twinge of jealousy as she compared her friend's house and family with her own.

Reaching the town centre, Ally and Sarah got off the train and looked about them, both seizing each other's hands with the portent of the day stretching out before them full of possibilities and potential. Sarah pulled Ally along quickly, dragging her into a perfume shop first of all, where she wandered about innocently, asking to try this scent and that, while her hands were busy and discreet beneath the counter.

"It's Maggie's birthday, next week," Ally mentioned to her friend, suddenly thinking that she ought to steal something worthwhile to give to her mother. Sarah smiled.

"Get her some perfume, then," she said. "What scent does she like?"

Ally smiled to herself, biting her tongue to stop the words 'wine and fags' from slipping out. Maggie only ever seemed to smell of wine and cigarettes. Ally pondered for a moment and then wondered how much dexterity it would take to steal Maggie some Chanel. A big bottle.

"Distract the woman, then," Ally said quietly, and Sarah moved forward and asked to try another scent. Ally moved quickly, sniffing at different bottles, and then pocketing a large cellophaned box of perfume. She felt her heart race and her face begin to flush, so she joined Sarah for a second and caught her elbow, smiling at the saleswoman.

"I need the bathroom, Sar," she said, nodding apologetically at the white-coated woman, and guiding Sarah away.

"Did you get it?" Sarah asked, her eyes shining and triumphant as they exited the shop. Ally nodded, laughing with relief as they made their way across a courtyard and settled on the steps of a monument.

"Let me see?" her friend asked, and Ally produced the cellophane packet with a flourish.

"Wow. That has to be our biggest steal yet!" Sarah breathed, fingering the delicate package, running her hand over the embossed Chanel logo. Ally felt a thrill of elation.

"It's beautiful. Maggie will be crazy over it," Alex said, and the two giggled and planned their next venture. Sarah wanted to go to a chemist and try for make-up, as it was easier to pocket the slim packages. Ally didn't mind what they did.

"We could try Woolworths," Sarah suggested. "They have everything there, and the security isn't very tight." Alex agreed, and the two set off arm in arm, laughing at the woman from the perfume shop, flushed and breathless with victory.

The two wandered into a few more shops, Sarah huffing with boredom as Ally pocketed a couple of books from WHSmith and paused outside to lovingly sniff the pages and read their backs. She was looking forward to getting some time to herself, curling up in one of her spaces at home and burying herself in the leaves of the novels. Sarah was impatient to move on, and they walked to Woolworths. The shop was inviting, with red lettering and a commotion of people inside, milling from aisle to aisle, picking up games, setting off toys and listening to singles. The shop was warm inside, so crammed with people that the large windows were cloudy with condensation. Other people's breath obscuring the daylight.

Gardening in the Dark

"Perfect," Sarah said in satisfaction. It was so crowded they could roam from one place to the next without fear of attention or discovery.

"Here we go. What do you want? I need a new eyeliner, and I could do with some jewellery. What are you going to try for? Do you want to go separately or together?" she asked. Ally shrugged.

"Separate. Less obvious, that way," she decided, and the two wandered in, and parted company once they were fully through the sliding doors. Ally roamed aimlessly, looking at the bright colours on the shelves, wondering what she would steal. She looked longingly at the chocolate on display: gold packages with ribbon, rich sumptuous colours and mouth-watering images of truffles and pralines. She trailed her hand along the shelves. She didn't know what to get. The books were cheap, made of wafery paper that bent and creased as soon as they were read. Ally preferred the bookshops, places where each book seemed to be crafted with love instead of mass-produced for a greedy public.

Make-up? But Ally didn't care so much for that, and anyway she had taken to stealing Maggie's, who had an amazing array of lurid colours from the sixties and seventies, and had enough to cover both of their faces for the foreseeable future. She didn't favour jewellery, and didn't need anything else. She thought of the perfume nestled in her bag, and smiled. And the novels; two crisp and fresh paperbacks. She had no more desires in the world, than these two things.

Sarah appeared beside her.

"What are you getting? I'm doing well!" she hissed, and Ally smiled and shrugged.

"I can't find anything," she said, without regret. Sarah waved a hand about her.

"How can you not? It's a gold mine! A treasure trove!" she exclaimed. Her face suddenly twisted into a frown.

"Are you bottling it?" she asked, and Ally discerned a note of mistrust in her friend's voice.

"Of course not. I just don't know what to choose, that's all," she said. Her voice was hard and defensive.

"Well, I'm going to carry on. It's perfect for it," Sarah sneered, and walked away again leaving Ally lost and forlorn, being swayed as other shoppers made their way past her. Ally wandered to the front counters and looked at the displays. She liked the toiletries in their little packages; whites, creams and greens. They all seemed to be garnished with leaf images. She picked up a small box of bath salts and lifted the lid to sniff them. Her nose was assaulted by a cloying smell of jasmine. Old lady smells. It reminded her of her grandmother, long gone. Her grandmother used to wear perfume, layer after layer of it, until a sickly miasma of jasmine and rose surrounded her.

Sarah was suddenly beside her, her hand shaking slightly as she steered Ally towards the door.

"We need to go. Now," she hissed, and Ally allowed herself to be propelled out of the automatic door and back on to the pavement.

"What?" she started to ask, and as she did so the word froze in her throat, was stopped from issuing, and she felt a hand seize her shoulder. Her legs seemed to give way under her, her stomach lurching and roiling in dread. She turned to look at Sarah, who was struggling under the grasp of a uniformed security guard. Sarah's face was white; pale enough to rival the colour of her hair, as if she had been suddenly coated in a thin veneer of chalk dust. Talc, Ally thought. And did people really put their hand on your shoulder, just the same as what you saw in Grange Hill or other programmes, when they caught thieves?

"Back inside, please, young lady." The stiff hand that grasped Ally's shoulders had a voice, gruff and northern. There was no smile in the voice at all. Ally turned, mouth open, and stared at her captor. He was middle-aged and quite hairy. She craned her head and searched for Sarah, who was behind her, being propelled forward by a man who looked similar to Ally's own.

"Fuck," Sarah mouthed at her, and Ally bit back a giggle even as her stomach lurched again and threatened to make her sick, sick over the pavement and her shoes. She pulled herself upright, willing the feeling and blood to go back into her legs which seemed to become very wobbly as if the bones had just melted away into jelly.

"Oh dear," Ally said. She turned and looked at the man who was holding her as they marched back through the automatic doors and through the shop. People stared at them, mothers with children pointing smugly. Ally felt her face burn hot and bright and she kept her eyes cast down. She looked at people's shoes. She passed some white trainers, a pair of Dr. Martens boots with white laces, and some sandals which seemed slightly inappropriate for the time of year. Then she was hustled through a plain white door at the back of the shop, and she found herself with Sarah, being told to sit at a long wooden table, facing her very stern captor.

Ally looked about her, and her legs carried on trembling even as she fought down a desire to laugh out loud. The office was cramped and cluttered, with bags and files pushed on to the shelf space higgledy-piggledy, looking as if they were ready to fall down at any moment. There was a small window to the left, but it was almost obscured by a brown-edged plant and more files and folders. The naked bulb which swung above their heads shed a wan puddle of light on the brown table, tingeing the skin of the man opposite them and giving him an eerie sallow appearance. He was fat. Ally lifted her gaze to him and found that he was staring at her, a frown on his face and his eyes intent.

"I don't think it's legal for you to keep us here. It's not right," Sarah stated firmly, and Ally kicked her under the table and put her hands over her face. The man shifted his bulk and sighed sarcastically.

"I'm sure you can make your complaint to the police, dear. They are on their way and will only be a few minutes," he responded. Ally spoke from beneath her fingers.

"I'm so sorry. I'm sorry that we have put you in this position," she said, and her voice was tremulous and wobbly, as if it were her jelly-legs that had spoken rather than her. The man tutted and shook his head.

"You're not the first," he answered, and Ally braved a look at his face through her hands. He seemed to be smiling a little, and appeared a bit bored. Ally felt her face with her fingers. Her cheeks were burning hot, and she imagined them blazing with so much redness that she lit up the room, battling for supremacy with the pale circle of light from the swinging bulb.

"What happens now, sir?" Ally asked politely. Her voice was a little more reliable this time. The man shrugged and looked away.

"They'll take you down to the station. Ask you questions. Might throw you in to jail, might not. It all depends, you see?" he answered. Ally nodded at him. Beneath the table, she fumbled in her bag for the packet of Chanel and fingered it cautiously. She slipped it out of the compartment and pushed it up her sleeve, and then eased it out on to her lap.

"Have you been doing this job for long?" she asked, making her voice interested. The man kicked back into his seat and folded his arms behind his head.

"Far too long. Since before you were born, I shouldn't wonder. We didn't have cameras or anything in the old days. It was much harder. We never had any evidence either, it was always more difficult to prosecute. You know, all sorts of people steal from this shop. People of all ages, all backgrounds." The man warmed to his theme and Ally nodded intelligently, as she placed the perfume quietly on the floor beneath her feet. She leaned forward and coughed loudly, coughed until tears were streaming down her face. As the man paused and looked at her, half-rising from his feet, Ally kicked the Chanel away from her, through the back of her seat and into a pile of plastic bags. She couldn't check its progress. She stopped coughing. Sarah looked at her, puzzled. Her face was scornful.

"Sorry about that. I think it's the situation," she said. The man nodded sympathetically.

"You'll cop it when you get home, a nice young girl like you. Your mother will be devastated," he said, trying to be sympathetic. Ally choked again, this time with derision, but kept her face mournful. The security guard stood up and walked to the door.

"Stay here," he said. "I'll get you some water."

He left the room, and Ally picked her beloved paperbacks from her bag and ran to the window, stashing them carefully between two folders which were spilling their contents out. Sarah sat, immobile for a second, and then opened her bag rapidly and followed suit, stuffing handfuls of make-up into any available space which could conceal them. Ally started to giggle. She looked over at Sarah and watched her, then stayed her hand suddenly.

"Keep the thing that they caught you with. That's all we can do," she warned, and Sarah nodded, suddenly comprehending. She reached behind her and pulled out a small black eyeliner. In silence, she placed it back in to her bag. They sat back, breathless and flushed, as the man returned with a small plastic cup of water.

"Perfect," Ally said. "Thank you. I am sorry to put you to this trouble."

"Don't you worry young lady. You're not the first, and you won't be the last, I'll be bound."

Ally sipped the water gratefully, steeling her eyes so that they wouldn't stray to the beloved packet of Chanel. She mourned its loss quietly. It had been beautiful, and someone else would gain the benefit of it. She sighed. Sarah sat beside her, sparkling, and Ally felt a sense of satisfaction that for once it had been she, not her friend, who had shown some resourcefulness.

The three looked up as the door was pushed open, and a uniformed policeman entered the room. Ally's eyes widened in fear. She stood up and grasped Sarah's hand, and the two of them walked through the full length of the shop again and reached the automatic door. Ally turned and sought out her security guard, who was wandering closely behind them.

"I am sorry to put you to inconvenience," she said, and the man smiled and actually patted her on the arm.

"Good luck, lass," he said. Ally grinned back ruefully and turned away. The policeman gestured them into the back seat of the waiting Panda, and Ally and Sarah slipped into the seat and breathed out as the doors were closed behind them.

"Careful with your story. You only took the one thing," Ally whispered, and Sarah nodded behind her bag. The policeman got in to the car and pulled away.

"Bloody youngsters," he muttered under his breath, and Ally smiled to herself. She imagined how much more annoyed he was going to be, when he found that they were going to the station for the sake of a single eyeliner. She felt lighter and less concerned, knowing that the worst that could happen was that she herself would walk free, and Sarah might get a telling-off and a mild warning. She grasped Sarah's hand in the back seat and squeezed it. Sarah squeezed back. Ally promised herself there and then that this particular hobby was probably best left behind. She would read more, from now on. And she should probably get a job.

Gardening in the Dark

Chapter Seventeen

The evening had passed slowly, moving away in staccato jumps as Ally and James had navigated around Maggie. Maggie had been in a strange mood, and neither James nor Ally could understand her. She was shaking and white, the sprinkle of freckles across her fat cheeks and turned up nose showing up too dark against a colourless face. James had stayed in his room for the most part, and Maggie had cried softly to herself, weeping in front of the television in her bedroom. Ally had hovered about in a state of anxiety, trying to fathom the reason for her mother's odd behaviour. She walked upstairs and down, pausing and waiting outside the bedrooms of the two people she was inexorably bound to, feeling peripheral and insecure.

Maggie was being different. Instead of reaching for a glass and working her way through a bottle of spirits, slowly degrading in front of them, she had stayed upright, suddenly getting up from the floor and undertaking a task like cleaning the sink, or doing the ironing, but her hands were unsteady and she burnt a small red stripe across her wrist when she moved her arm across the plate of the iron. Ally looked on warily, afraid of catching her mother's attention but aware that she needed monitoring in some way.

"Are you OK?" she asked Maggie carefully, looking at the floor to avoid igniting some hidden wrath that felt as if it were bubbling beneath the surface, boiling-water and magma and plates shifting to make the ground unsteady. Maggie had nodded too quickly, raising her pale face to Ally's own and giving her a twisted grimacing smile.

"I will be. I will be," she had said, and Ally noticed that Maggie didn't slur her words, but rather had a tremulous quality in her voice, as if she had not eaten for weeks and it had made her quavering and weak. Ally had nodded and accepted it, but still watched silently from corners of the living room, the kitchen, and Maggie's bedroom.

"Can I pour you a drink?" she asked, thinking that perhaps this was what would make Maggie feel better. Maggie had looked up, an ironic grin suddenly creasing her mouth again.

"Not tonight, love," she had replied, and Ally had nodded again, confusion furrowing her brow beneath her heavy fringe.

Not tonight? The bottle was a part of their family, formed the fourth party in their bizarre collective. Ally walked into the kitchen and looked at the side. The bottle was there, innocent-looking and half-full, but it hadn't been touched. Ally reached out a finger and traced the pattern on the side of the label. There was white wine, and vodka and tonic water, but Maggie was fussing over the ironing board and shaking instead of drinking anything.

And still, James kept away. Ally paused outside his bedroom door and listened, and she could hear the vague thrumming of his tape player, a hiss and bump that marked out the repeated playing of one of his favourite songs. She sighed to herself and waited patiently in the hall, ready to busy herself should James exit his room, but hoping that he would at least come out, visit the bathroom, do anything so that Ally could search his face and communicate her fears. However, his door stayed resolutely shut, and Ally turned away at last, moving back to find Maggie and continue to watch her.

Ally had become a little lost since Ben's departure. There was no longer anything to look forward to, and life had become more desolate than she could remember it being before. She had had a tumultuous time, trying to quietly defend herself from James and Maggie, learning to keep away when the tension grew sharp in the room, and emerge again once Maggie's explosions had been disgorged and completed.

Ally was left to herself most of the time. James didn't speak to her, in fact hadn't even looked at her face since before Ben left. Ally felt a twist of loss when she thought of her brother, who seemed to have grown taller and more self-assured in the space left by the departure of the patriarch. Ally herself seemed to have done the opposite; she felt shrunken and bedraggled. James commanded all the space when he walked into a room. His voice had deepened,

Gardening in the Dark

he had developed something resembling a fashionable goatee on his face, and his shoulders seemed to have expanded. He looked like a man, now, and Ally was a little afraid of him. He didn't even punch her any more, as if she were completely beneath contempt, not worth even a negative acknowledgement. Ally missed him on some level, and smarted under his scorn. She felt lonely, sometimes. Ben's departure had caused her to withdraw into herself, and step back from the various friendships she had made at school. Her clothes had become more unfashionable than ever before, and at fourteen these things felt critical. Maggie continued to alternate between rage and self-pity, the first always directed at Ally now, which increased James's contempt for his sister. James was now beyond reproach, sitting in his bedroom smoking pot until the scent, like green pond-water full of algae, billowed out under his door and made the hallway smell like a forest.

Ally was concentrating on school, the endless homework which she undertook with a sense of pride, watching her grades get higher and higher even as her hair went uncut and her trousers grew shorter. She tackled English quickly and easily, slipping into the covers of a book and residing in it wholly, turning pages and drinking in the words until she reached the last page and looked up, blinking with some sort of sorrow, to be finding herself back in her life. She spent hours upstairs in the spare room, reading her way from one end of Maggie's dusty collection to the other. She was indiscriminate in her choices, devouring Jeffrey Archer and Dickens, Stephen King and Isaac Asimov with the same reverent appetite. She had read Maggie's Mills and Boon collection, snickering to herself in the half-light of dusk in her room, mocking the simple language and ridiculous phrases which marked out the fickle relationships of the main characters. She had come to love Jane Austen, becoming the main characters in their crinolines, twisting her parasol at some picnic with Mr. Darcy or horse riding with Emma. Books had become Ally's alternate world, inaccessible to those of her friends who were still playing with dolls. Ally would sneak into James's room and steal his cigarettes, or pull on the end of a joint which James had grown tired of, then climb into the cupboard with Jane Austen and lose herself for a few hours until the book fell from her hand, completed. Through Jilly Cooper and Pam Ayres, Virginia Woolf and Henry James, Ally was beginning to see that there was a world beyond their house, where people were somewhat more stable, less likely to fall in a crumpled heap for reasons which couldn't be explained. Ally had started to link her life in with the characters in the books. She started her period with Jane Austen. She started smoking with Shakespeare. The Brontës had guided her through her first kiss, a strange and distasteful fumble at the back of the school hall. She felt less alone, accessing their two-dimensional worlds, than she did when she walked through her real life.

That evening, Ally had walked through the living room and wandered to the kitchen, taking a few moments to straighten it up. She wiped the pine table carefully, Tiger winding around her heels, and washed up. As darkness fell outside, she watched the window above the sink gradually shift focus, so that the view of the garden receded and she was left staring at an illuminated reflection of herself. Ally was not fond of the reflection. Her hair was growing long and unwieldy, and the fringe had become too long also, so that she had to raise her nose in the air to see properly. It gave her a haughty air, which contrasted with the sleeves of her jumper, which ended about three inches prematurely, revealing her skinny white wrists. Ally had pondered the changes in her body, noting the breasts which had begun to form, hair sprouting in odd places, and kept them guarded and hidden from Maggie, who never really seemed to see Ally anyway. Ally watched her companions at school as they embraced the changes, shouting about menstruation like excitable children, lavishly flaunting their newly acquired breasts, much to the confusion of the boys in their class, who seemed to stay statically young.

Women are scary, Ally thought to herself, picturing a wild Maggie in her dressing gown, arms flailing and pendulous breasts bobbing unsupported beneath. Checking for the whereabouts of Maggie and James, Ally quickly poured a stiff drink, adeptly mixing tonic and vodka, and then swallowed it in three draughts. She felt the warmth spread down her neck, out along her shuddering arms and into her head. It felt like a hug. She smiled to herself, revelling in the rebellion of it. Even if Maggie was not allowing herself to drink that evening, Ally put no such rules upon herself. She reached down to the second shelf beneath the kitchen cupboard and pocketed a packet of cigarettes. Maggie never seemed to keep track, purchasing them in bulk and buying more before they ever ran out.

Gardening in the Dark

It kept James and Ally fully satisfied; able to hand them out as currency at school, or enjoy the the luxury of owning a complete packet of twenty by themselves.

Ally walked back into the living room and looked at her mother, who was struggling to fold one of James's shirts, holding it lovingly against her body as she tussled with the arms, still creased and steaming. Maggie glanced up as Ally entered the room, and her face looked suddenly haunted. She had been crying again.

"I'm sorry I've been such a bad mother to you, Alexandra," Maggie said, her nose releasing a long thin strip of transparent snot. Ally looked at her in revulsion. She felt suddenly afraid for the shirt, that it would become spattered and need to be laundered again. Maggie's quick burst of activity would not last long enough for another laundry cycle.

"Never mind," she said, finding it difficult to hold her mother's gaze, watching the shirt as it waved beneath the snot. The comment was meaningless, borne of Maggie's self-pity rather than constituting any genuine regret about Ally and her life. Maggie was developing into a nothingness, a blobby pale mass of tears and self-pity. She sat down heavily on the sofa, releasing the shirt and focusing on her hands, which shook uncontrollably.

"Do you love me?" Maggie asked, her voice suddenly babyish and unsure, which lent her face a macabre expression. Maggie was too vile to play at being a child, Ally thought. She considered the question, for some reason actually giving it credence as something worth responding to.

"Sometimes I do," she replied. That was probably the most honest answer, though not the one her mother was seeking. Sometimes Ally could stand back from their surreal family, study the three of them with detachment, and feel sorry for Maggie. This pity sometimes led to a feeling akin to love. The real love, the craving to be cared about, to be acknowledged by Maggie, had faded after Ben's departure. Ally no longer needed to be loved, as if the part of her that had thrived under her father's attention had shrivelled and died, withering away without sustenance until it could no longer be revived.

Maggie shuddered, and Ally suddenly sensed her sadness. She shook her head abruptly to remove it again. She wanted no one else's grief; she could generate her own easily enough if she was that way inclined. Ally looked down at herself and imagined her heart, which had once been open and needy, slowly clamming up, shutting down. Heartless. Maggie sat in front of her, desperate to receive some kindness, and Ally couldn't bring herself to offer it.

"I love you," Maggie said thoughtfully. Ally shrugged.

"Do you?" she asked, her voice suddenly bored. She searched inside herself and found she didn't really care.

"Sometimes," Maggie concluded, and suddenly they smiled at each other, as if they had reached across mile after mile of wasteland and found some humour. It pulled them together for a moment. Maggie reached out her trembling arms and Ally found herself drawn into them. She closed her eyes, and the two rocked together. Maggie was humming a song, a tuneless flat drone which reminded Ally of being very small, before everything turned to shit. She liked it.

"I've stopped drinking, Ally-Pally," Maggie commented suddenly, her voice quavering with the momentous confession. Ally tensed up and pulled back, brought to the present, and frowned.

"OK," she said, not committing to approval or belief. As if she actually cared.

"That's good. Well done," she added. The words fell hollowly and pushed their two spaces apart again. Maggie without drink was not Maggie. Ally stopped herself giving a snort of derision, and avoided her mother's gaze. The chasm between them deepened, and Ally suddenly sensed Maggie's yearning for a drink, the thing which numbed her mind and obliterated memory. She felt it as she understood hunger, a gnawing desperate need.

"Why stop? It makes no difference any more," Ally said suddenly. She had felt a sense of futility wash over her, cold and brutal. Maggie looked at her and frowned. They stared at each other for a moment in silence, as Maggie processed the comment.

Gardening in the Dark

"I have no idea," she said, and Ally could read the confusion in her face, and understood it. The two of them had nothing to lose, it seemed. Ally had stood up and walked to the kitchen, grabbing the bottles of vodka and tonic, and two glasses. Why would Maggie go through the misery of self-denial, when she had nothing else in her life worth cleaving to? Ally poured two measures out adeptly, and held hers up to the light. Maggie watched her, her greedy eyes transfixed by the glass. Ally paused for a moment and moved the glass from side to side, trying not to smile in disdain as Maggie focused on it like a huntress. It was tragically pathetic, and Ally felt her lip curl against her will as she handed the glass to her mother. Maggie drank it swiftly, and almost immediately the colour returned to her cheeks and her hands stopped shaking.

"Better," she said, more satisfied but already eyeing up the bottle of spirits, which was over half-full. Ally shrugged and drank. It made no difference to anything, anyway.

Following the drink, there was peace in the house again. Maggie resumed her routine of getting thoroughly drunk, passing out on the sofa and snoring away to herself. James exited his room in the early hours of the morning, having been busy for hours doing unknown adult things. He passed by Maggie in disdain, barely looking at her as he went to the kitchen and foraged for food. He kicked out at Ally's chair as he passed, ignoring her, and Ally had shrugged into her glass of vodka and smiled to herself. She liked these moments of quiet, when the night obscured outside, ensuring the telephone wouldn't ring, and the television hummed to itself with white noise in the corner. Tiger jumped on her lap and started making a bed for himself, and Ally checked the amount of drink left in her glass and reached for her book. She was reading Philip Larkin, on the recommendation of her English teacher, a dour elderly woman with a harsh grey bob. Ally was not entirely convinced by poetry. It took a few lines for her to immerse herself in it, become it, and then the verse would be over and she was back to herself again. She preferred to traverse the long winding corridors and turns of fiction, the thicker the book the better, because it afforded her longer reprieves.

Philip Larkin, to her mind, was a miserable old git. Afraid of death, he wrote with some terror about getting old. And he seemed to complain about everything. One thing he did do well was swear. Ally felt a thrill of surprise when he said 'fuck', the harsh short word shouting at her from the page. She liked it.

James was rustling away in the kitchen, a pig seeking out truffles. He had obviously found something of interest because he took a moment to sit on the bench. Ally could hear his feet scuffing and the bench sliding across the tiles as he sat. She paused, her head on one side, and pictured him. He would be wasted, with bloodshot eyes and lolling head, cramming food into his mouth like a machine. Ally looked at the back of her book and searched through the index of first lines with languid interest.

'They fuck you up, your mum and dad' she read, and giggled suddenly. How would Philip Larkin, bespectacled and grey in his cheap linen suit, know that? He was closer to death than birth. Surely the leftover damage by one's parents couldn't stay with you for so long? Ally sighed and turned to the page, quickly devouring the words. They were funny and irreverent, peppered with Larkin's trademark cynicism and acerbic humour. 'And they were fucked up in their turn' she read, and suddenly paused to consider Maggie, lying across the length of the sofa, her blotched face turned to Ally, her eyes closed and flickering. Was Maggie fucked up by her parents? Ally wondered. She vaguely remembered her grandparents, creased and smelling of cigarette smoke and old stew. What harm could those old withered people have perpetrated, to create the damaged mass of flesh that lay on the sofa now? Ally couldn't imagine it. Maggie spoke sometimes of her past; drunken ramblings involving beatings and shouting. To Ally, it sounded like every other childhood, but better than her own. She suddenly sensed life as a perpetual cycle of mistakes, each parent swinging from one extreme to another in order not to revisit the same problems they had themselves experienced.

"They fuck you up," Ally commented aloud, and looked at Maggie again. Draining her glass suddenly, Ally leaned forward and poured another, aware that the vodka was nearly finished. Her body lurched a little as she moved, as if it were heavier than she had anticipated. She giggled a little and slumped back in her chair.

Gardening in the Dark

"They fuck you up," she stated, again, the 'f' of the word sounding too long, slurring into the 'uck'. Maggie stirred and moaned to herself. Ally watched her. Maggie looked old even in repose, her hair matted and streaked with grey. Her face could not relax its lines even as she slept. Ally suddenly wished that Maggie could be clean, wash her hair and clothes, and look more normal. She pulled the packet of cigarettes out of her pocket and took off the cellophane carefully, looking around for a lighter as she opened them. She pulled out a cigarette and sniffed it appreciatively. Unlit cigarettes smelled of nuts and grass. And she had a whole packet to get through, and Maggie was heavily asleep. She lit the end and pulled on it, watching the flame flicker and die, as the cigarette started to burn. The first mouthful always shocked her body, and Ally could feel her throat and chest constrict against the hot smoke. She leaned over and moved an ashtray closer, and settled back again into her chair. She had a drink, a book, a fag, an unconscious parent and an absent brother. In life, sometimes, the pleasures could be small but momentous. She smiled to herself, copying Maggie's way of holding the cigarette, with the glass in the same hand, feeling a childish pleasure in pretending to be grown-up.

James left his room again and walked through the lounge, checking on his mother to make sure she was asleep before picking up the vodka bottle, swirling it in his hand and then taking a deep draught from the neck. Ally watched him, eyes narrowed in defence in case he would lift his own eyes and meet her gaze, but he didn't. He coughed on the raw spirit, and then fumbled at Maggie's side for her cigarettes, pulling out three or four from the packet. Ally watched, stifling a giggle as James navigated clumsily around Maggie's outstretched arm which had fallen almost to the floor as she slept. Maggie's arm was pale and clear of blemishes, the skin looking soft with blue veins protruding from her wrists like lines on a map. This was a game they had played many times, sneaking in and out of rooms in time with Maggie's breath, in order to ensure she continued to sleep. Groping in the dark for her drink or wallet, timing each step like art thieves entering a gallery. They were both adept at prowling and sneaking, their eyes cat-like and wide in the dark. The mass of Maggie would be the focal point, and her belongings secondary. Creeping around an outstretched arm or twitching leg, jumping and freezing if Maggie were to roll over or mutter in her sleep. It always made Ally laugh, a hysterical trembling of giggles which threatened to overcome her until tears ran down her face and she was in danger of making so much noise her mother would wake up. James's movements were clumsy, and he lacked the lithe certainty that his body had owned before puberty. It was a comical sight, and Ally had to bite her lip as James walked unsteadily back to his bedroom.

Ally opened Larkin again and let her eyes rove over the pages. She was thinking of other things, not registering the black lines which danced beneath her vacant gaze. The vodka had warmed her brain, and made her limbs feel relaxed and luxurious. She put the book down and reached her arms up, stretching. Standing up unsteadily, Ally wandered around the room. It always managed to look dirty, even after she and James had cleaned it. The brown carpet was threadbare where their feet had worn paths over the years. The entire room stank of stale cigarette smoke and years of dust. It was a room which looked better in the evenings, when the partially concealed corners shrank back from the pale halo cast by the lamps. Ally walked over to the window and drew the heavy curtain across, jumping a little as Tiger emerged from behind one of the folds, looking sleepy and warm. She reached down and fondled the back of his neck, and the cat arched his back and flexed his paws against the carpet, purring. Walking over to the sofa, Ally leaned gently behind Maggie's prostrate body and tugged the curtains across the wide blank window. She saw herself reflected in the glass briefly, and paused before fully closing the curtain. She had grown tall at some point, her face and hair looking suspiciously like Maggie's, before Maggie had changed.

"I'm grown-up," Ally whispered in a conspiratorial tone to Maggie's sleeping bulk. "You don't hit me any more," she added, smiling in satisfaction. Somewhere in the time between Ben's departure and Maggie's downfall, Ally had become too self-assured to be beaten. She couldn't remember when it had happened, but she felt safer these days. Even James had suddenly become wary of Ally, understanding that she was a woman and the old rules no longer applied.

Ally stared down at her mother, studying her openly. She felt a mixture of revulsion and pity as she watched the creased face. She reached out a hand and smoothed the hair from Maggie's forehead. It felt damp and clammy, and Ally wiped her palm on her jeans after the gesture. Maggie's breathing was snuffly and shallow like a small creature. It made Ally's stomach lift a little with the sweetness of it, before she caught herself and drew away.

Fetching a blanket from her bedroom, Ally carefully covered her mother with it. Maggie's head was at a funny angle, and Ally put her arm beneath it carefully and adjusted her neck, placing a cushion under it. She looked peaceful, the snuffly-creature noises making Ally feel tired. Maggie started snoring gently, and Ally smiled down at her. Driven by some impulse, she leaned down and kissed Maggie's head suddenly. Maggie's eyes flickered open for a moment, and she reached up and caught Ally's hand with her own before Ally could pull away.

"You're a good girl, Ally," Maggie muttered, her words thick and damp. Ally looked down at her and smiled. That was a first, for her mother. Ally wondered if she had ever said those words before.

"I try," she said. "Go back to sleep. Everything is OK." With that, Maggie's unfocused eyes closed again and her hand fell limp on to the blanket. Ally moved about the room methodically, picking up the cushions and replacing them on the chair, then padded through to the kitchen and poured a glass of water which she settled by Maggie's side.

"Goodnight," she whispered, turning the lamp out and retreating to her bedroom. Her mother seemed small and childlike in sleep, and Ally realised she was no longer afraid of her. She climbed into bed quickly, the covers feeling almost damp with cold, and pulled them up to her neck. Curling into a ball, she felt the heaviness of sleep overtake her body before it reached her mind. She thought of James in his room, locked behind a closed door and dreaming, and wondered briefly where Ben might be and what sort of life he was making for himself. She slept fitfully, alternating between being hot and cold, the sheets tangling around her limbs like creepers.

A few hours into the night, Ally was startled awake. She had been dreaming of something which lay just beyond her memory; dark shapes and harpies, long grey hair tangling in her hands, and a low eerie wailing like a banshee. She shivered to herself, letting her eyes adjust to the darkness to seek some reassurance from within her room. Familiar shapes came into view: her wardrobe, white and girlish, seemed to glow in the darkness; the sofa, half-burnt and still letting off an acrid scent; her clothes piled neatly on the floor in readiness for the morning. All was well. She slept again.

Morning came with a quietude which puzzled Ally. She climbed out of bed carefully, unravelling the twisted sheets from her damp body. The sun was pouring through the curtains, hurting her eyes as she drew the material apart to let the light fully in. The house was too quiet. James would still be asleep, his body working to eliminate the drugs he had pushed into it. Maggie was probably upstairs, retreating to her room when the sunlight began its slow tortuous hauling into a new day. Ally jumped as Tiger pushed his way into her room, winding around her legs. He needed something to eat.

Making her way through the living room, Ally was surprised to see her mother still lying asleep on the sofa. Tiger meowled imperiously, and she walked with him through to the kitchen, opening a tin of cat food and putting it in his bowl without bothering to wash the relics of his previous meal from it. He never seemed to mind. He ate noisily, purring and champing his way through the meal, while Ally sat beside him for a moment and stroked his back mindlessly.

Wandering back to the living room, Ally drew the curtains again and let the light in. She glanced at Maggie as she leaned over her. Her face looked odd. She had a greyish tinge to her skin, and Ally frowned and leaned forward, pushing her index finger into Maggie's cheek. It felt hard and cold, and didn't give the way a fat cheek normally should.

"Oh," Ally said, bending down and studying her mother. There was heavy silence where breathing noises should have been. Ally reached out cautiously and moved Maggie's head to one side, and drew back as she saw a foamy substance, pink and damp, issuing from Maggie's half-open mouth. The head rolled easily, as it had so many times when Maggie was drunk, but it was lifeless.

Ally walked through to the hallway and knocked on James's bedroom door. She stood back patiently, imagining him dragging himself out of sleep. She put her hands in her pockets and cocked her head to one side, hearing the sound of her brother swearing and stumbling, pulling his trousers on one leg after another, and appearing at the door, furious and bedraggled.

"Whaddyawant?" he demanded, scowling at Ally. She bit her lip and considered the question.

"Come here," Ally said, and something in her voice made James respond to her, look at her. He followed her without further question into the living room, and Ally gestured at Maggie, the foamy flecks on her face. She stood back and allowed James to move towards her, and then suddenly draw back in comprehension.

"Oh," he said, looking to Ally, confused and afraid. He had a deep line down one side of his face where he had been lying on something. Ally looked at it. James reached out and poked Maggie's cheek experimentally, and then recoiled because the skin didn't move as he expected. He shuddered suddenly, a violent shake which made the hair on his scalp stand to attention.

"Dead?" he said, deferring to Ally's knowledge; Ally who had performed the same surprised ritual moments before.

"Yes," Ally said, her voice steady.

"Oh." James sat down suddenly. Ally sank down beside her brother and together they stared at Maggie. Maggie had assumed some interest in death, her skin unusual and mildly shocking. Tiger ambled between them and tried to jump on the sofa, to greet Maggie, and Ally instinctively held him back. James turned to his side and vomited on the floor.

"Poor Maggie," Ally said quietly, staring at her mother's body and – for a second – imagining a different life for her. James shrugged and wiped his eyes, looking suddenly terribly young. He started to cry, and Ally turned and frowned at him; at her brother who had no feelings. His sobs were whimpering and childish, and they turned Ally's stomach, as if forcing her to acknowledge a part of her that had been shut down.

"Shut up, James," she said, and James again deferred to her, smothering his sobs and dashing at his face to remove the tears. Ally stood up briskly and went to her room to get dressed, leaving her brother staring and rocking on the living room floor. She dressed quickly, selecting smarter clothes than she normally would for a weekend. Tiger followed her curiously. Ally brushed her hair, straightened the bedclothes still warm from her body, and pulled on her shoes.

She walked back through the living room and worked quickly, filling a bowl with water and bleach and clearing up the pool of vomit next to James. She picked up the vodka bottle which now lay on its side, taking it through to the kitchen with the glasses. She carefully washed up. She stashed the bottle in the bin, then went to the drawer and retrieved Maggie's purse, pulling it open and taking all the notes and change. She returned to the living room and picked up Philip Larkin, who was lying on his side by the armchair. She pocketed the remaining packets of cigarettes, and turned about the kitchen looking for other treasures. Finding none, she pulled on her jacket quickly and stepped out of the house, pausing to pick Tiger up and kiss his soft head.

"London," she told him, before pulling the door shut, locking it, and dropping the keys back through the letterbox. Tiger watched her as she made her way down the drive, but she didn't turn back. He waited for a while, to see if she would return, then turned and slipped back into the house.

Chapter Eighteen

Owen opened the door fully and stood back to let Alex enter. She stepped into the hallway with confidence. She had been looking forward to this moment since the nurse told her she had another meeting scheduled. She was looking forward to sitting in the little room with Owen, the most normal person she had encountered since the entire surreal experience in the hospital had begun. She walked up the stairs quickly, and sank into the chair without being asked, waiting for Owen to also sit down.

She took some deep breaths, letting the knots in her stomach uncoil and her face relax, as if allowing herself to show her true feelings and personality in a place where she wouldn't be censured for it, or observed; where notes wouldn't be taken and she was free to feel and articulate without being afraid of being watched and judged.

"Alex," Owen said, tucking one leg beneath another, lounging in the chair perilously. Alex looked sharply to see if he would fall over, but his long body defied gravity. He was wearing a bright orange shirt and the same style of ripped scruffy jeans and white trainers, looking for all the world like some student who had sauntered into the room unbidden and was playing at counselling. Alex smiled at him.

"Hi," she said.

"Good day at the office?"

"Marvellous. I'm loving it." Alex gave a sardonic smile.

"Where are you at this afternoon?"

"Here. Happy to be here. Feeling safer."

"Good. And are you pissed right now?"

"Nope. Saving it for later. On rations."

"Good. Let's talk, then. Where have you been since I last saw you?"

Alex paused. She thought of the time that had elapsed since she first met Owen. It was to be catalogued more in terms of mood than temporally, as her position had elevated in a wide arc until she could no longer see how low she had been before. How could she catalogue the events of the past week? The way the light had moved as she made love, on the damp grass, to Martin. How she had asked Stuart to smuggle alcohol in and they had drunk it together, sighing in pleasure as the warmth coursed through her blood. How she had been frightened, how nightmares had plagued her, how in a few days she had gone from being lost to being someone labelled and partially understood. How she felt as if there was unending hope, now, where before there had been merely darkness and loneliness. Her life spread before her like a deck of cards, and she was holding all the aces.

"I'm in the nut house, still. Diagnosed as Bipolar. Bipolar."

"I don't know much about that. What is it?"

"Manic depression. A mood disorder. Something that makes everything make sense."

"How do you feel about that?"

"Relieved. Grateful. Normal."

"Is it all positive?"

Alex looked at Owen, and a host of memories suddenly rushed into her brain, clouding her euphoria temporarily. A woman sprawled across a bed, lying in her own vomit. The look on a young boy's face, shocked and disgusted. The feeling of hiding, instead of running into the wind. The knowledge that a young girl was too grown-up. Shame. Embarrassment. Desperate sadness. The feelings crowded in on her, shouting and babbling, a cacophony of misery and fear. She gasped out loud, and Owen watched her curiously, his kind face tilted to one side in enquiry.

"What is it?"

"Nothing."

"It was a very big nothing."

"I know a bit about Bipolar."

"Your Bipolar, or someone else's?"

"Not mine. None of this is mine."

"Do you want to talk about it?"

"No." And then, as an afterthought, "Thank you."

Owen smiled and nodded, looking ahead to find a new topic of conversation.

"How did our plan for the week hold up?"

"Plan?" So much had happened. What was the plan?

"To drink. To survive."

"I'm still here. I'm very here indeed. Stuart brought some vodka in and I've been drinking it, then he brings me some more every day. It's made everything bearable. I'm still here."

"So."

"So it's just for now. It's just until things calm down."

"Have they not calmed down? You seem very different this week."

"No. They haven't calmed down, they've just changed. I'm not an alcoholic."

"Of course you're not. Most people in nut houses get their mate to smuggle booze in for them. It's standard practice," Owen said, and Alex felt a flush of anger.

"What do you know about standard practice in a mental hospital? How do you know what it's like?" she flared. Her head was racing too fast to follow a single strain of conversation, as she worked to push down memories and struggled to find a point to cling to. Owen was simply too stupid to understand. She took a breath and opened her mouth, desperate to talk but unable to catch one of the lines of thought that were running in all directions. She moved her leg up and down on the seat, and twisted her hands first one way and then the other.

"Alex? Are you sure you want to do this today?" Owen asked, his good humour resilient against her temper. Alex shifted in her seat and breathed deeply. She felt a sudden pang of guilt.

"Of course. I'm sorry. I didn't mean to snap. Everything's too slow. And I'm too fast. I'm taking Lithium. It's a mood stabiliser. To stop the new mania. But it takes time to work, and it hasn't started yet," she acknowledged, and Owen nodded.

"The alcohol doesn't seem terribly important to me, today. How about you?" he asked, and Alex nodded quickly. Of course it wasn't important. It was a temporary thing. She could get drugs to stop her drinking if the vodka ran out. She could go to an off-licence later, when she had been released. The things that couldn't be salvaged were the dark spaces in her mind that were crowded with memories, taking up space that should have been used for something positive. Perhaps, in fact, this was why she was mad, Alex thought to herself.

"Talk to me. Don't think about it, don't censor everything. Let it all out," Owen suggested, and Alex nodded. It seemed like a good idea.

"I want to tell you a story. I need to talk about my past. I need to tell you about a woman called Maggie and a man called Ben, and a boy called James who was all broken up inside, and then an Ally who thought it was all her fault, and now an Alex who still thinks it was."

Owen nodded and leaned into her, encouraging her with the tilt of his head.

"When I was fifteen I ran away from home. Except, by that point, there wasn't really a home to run from. My mother had just died, and I left my older brother to pick up the pieces.

"I never spoke to him again. I don't know what happened to him, really. There was a newspaper article, he's been on the Internet. He must have qualified as a doctor, because he wins awards for mental health breakthroughs and things. I think he's married.

"I never spoke to my father again, either. I lived in London and I worked in a bar, and then a hotel, and then I went to university and got degree after degree. I have always known madness, pushing me up and down like a pendulum. When I've been euphoric, I've achieved everything. I have certificates and diplomas in every subject under the sun. Degrees and courses and certificates. I'm qualified in so many different things. And then when I've been depressed, all I have ever thought about is wanting to die.

"And that sums me up," Alex concluded, but sat back and looked dissatisfied, aware of all the gaps in her small story, the weight pressing beneath each word. Owen shook his head, nonplussed, seeking for a way in. He looked at her, suddenly, and spread his hands wide. Alex looked away. She felt a tide of emotion working its way up through her body; her head was reeling. It was their last meeting before she was discharged. She felt frightened, but also full of a quiet, steady resolve. Everything had changed, even as she was the same, her life would be the same when she emerged from hiding into the wide open. She was going to step back into the world she had chosen to escape from. She was afraid.

"What is it, Alex?" Owen asked, his eyes concerned. Alex took a deep breath and shook her head, biting her lips. His kindness suddenly made her want to cry; not just shed tears but to explode in grief, weep all over the chair, the floor; throw herself down and release it all into the cushions on the chairs, the threadbare rug, the rough denim of his jeans.

"Let it go. Talk to me," Owen said, seeming to understand. Alex looked at him, tears now flowing freely.

"I want to be free. I want to make choices. I want to be different to what I am. I hate myself. I hate living under a legacy that feels like it's mine by birthright. I hate my mother for what she has bequeathed to me. I hate living in a path she has already forged, walking forwards into inevitability every day. I hate myself for courting failure, for destroying myself on purpose. I hate the way I give in, instantly, to the pit and let myself fall over and over again, how even when I'm high I choose to self-destruct. I want to be something different. I want to be someone else. I want to beat all the demons and be proud and like myself and hold my head up and be healed, and look to the future and see new roads ahead of me instead of old, trammelled ones. I want to do something different. I hate my past. I hate Ally. I hate my father. I hate everything they left with me, everything I carry. I can't support that girl on my shoulders any more. I need to be rid of it," Alex said, her words a garbled mass of jumbled emotions.

Owen looked at her, and Alex noticed that his eyes were damp, just as hers were.

"You can. Alex. You can be rid of it," he said. Alex looked up again and took in a deep breath, as Owen handed her some tissues.

"You can be anything you want to be," he remarked, and smiled at her.

"Is there anything that is purely yours, for pleasure? That you can do regardless of your mood?"

Alex considered the question, and a sudden smile split her dour features.

"Gardening. I love gardening. I like to take a patch of earth and grow something beautiful in it. I like the smell of the earth when it rains, the feel of the leaves, the dew scent and the creatures. I like to watch the worms twist and tunnel in a piece of damp rich earth. I like to make compost, watching the vegetables and fruit rot down into something peaty and rich. I like to eat things I've grown, tasting the handiwork, knowing it's pure and safe and clean. I like to plant row upon row of flowers – delphiniums, chrysanthemums, daffodils, sweet peas, snowdrops – and watch them thrive.

"Things need to be nurtured. Gardening allows me to do that, safely. I can take care of them, and watch them grow. Things grow quickly when they're fed, watered, given proper attention and care. Plants like the warm aroma of breath when someone takes the time to talk to them. They can reach up for the sun and stretch. Gardening is my thing," she concluded. Owen laughed as he saw her eyes sparkling; the way she had temporarily lost her problems as she warmed to her subject.

"Did you know that many people think that the soil releases a form of energy, called Prana? It's life force. It sustains and lifts the mood. It makes people feel healthy and happy, and the solidarity that you can gain from freshly turned earth, the feeling of animal belonging, is invaluable. You can breathe Prana in. You can smell it. It smells brown and warm and rich."

"You look as if you've had a healthy dose of Prana this week, then?" Owen asked, laughing. Alex blushed as she remembered lying with Martin, the two of them working in silence in the hard earth to create a new patch of beauty in the hospital grounds.

"I guess I have." She laughed, and held her tongue.

"Is there anything else that makes you feel like that?"

"I'm not sure. There are different feelings, all good. Like taking in laundry that's been blowing on the line, and inhaling the sweet clean smell of it. Biting into a crisp apple, and letting the sweetness play over your tongue."

Alex paused, and considered.

"I like the sound of the rain when it beats on the windows, and you're safe inside somewhere and you can listen to it. And the feeling of travelling too fast in the car. The sensation you get when you've just snorted a load of coke, and it's starting to work through your body. And drinking, the blessed relief of pouring it in, and waiting for that warmth to spread."

"I think some of those likes are better than others," Owen said, his lips twitching in an effort not to laugh. "What else gets you?"

"Running. Running until I can't catch my breath. And dancing to loud music, when no one can see me. Having hours stretching ahead that I can fill in any way I choose."

"Anything else?"

"Forgetting," Alex suddenly said, and the word was final and different, loaded with a meaning that she needed Owen to decipher even as she hoped that he wouldn't. He seized the word and turned it before her, and she could almost make out its sharp edges and silhouette as he considered it.

"Let's stay with that."

"Mmmm," Alex said. She had a feeling that this was something she had to do. "Can I talk to you about anything? Not just about drinks diaries and the various merits of vodka over wine, and how rotten my liver might be getting, and the true definitions of an alcoholic?" she asked. Owen grinned.

"It would be a welcome diversion for me. You've just summed up my entire working day, give or take a bit of piss and vomit," he quipped. Alex sat upright, her face suddenly intent.

"I trust you. I'm not sure why."

"Thank you. What would you like to talk about?"

Alex drew a breath and hesitated. She had already told him so much, and felt lighter as a result.

Gardening in the Dark

"I want to tell you about Ally," she began. Owen nodded.

Alex began to tell him a story.

She spoke of her earliest memories, and how the family of four arched and twisted this way and that in some parody of familial bliss. How she felt lonely every time she thought of her mother; and how she could not, would not ever recover, it seemed, from Ben and what he had done. How she had wanted desperately for James to love her; to forgive her for what she felt was her betrayal. How being in hospital, at this point, felt like the culmination of so much confusion that Alex couldn't work her way through the tattered ends.

When she had finished, the two sat, having shared tears, and stared at each other. The time had run on and on. Owen wiped his face and smiled, watching her.

"Do we need a new plan?" he asked suddenly, and Alex laughed, remembering the various times he had said that to her over the past few months. She shook herself upright and dried her eyes.

"I think we need a new plan. Will you help me?" she asked.

"Of course. We can work through it all, together. We can separate it out into its component parts, so we can rebuild Alex away from Ally, away from Maggie, away from Ben. We can work out what Alex is without madness. What the Alex will be when you come to terms with the fact that you are living in a middle ground instead of swinging like a pendulum. We can pick it apart, and then put together the real Alex. How does that sound? I'll be here, with you."

Alex lifted her shoulders, squared up in the chair, as the penny started to drop. Of course.

"It's all my choice, right?" she asked, and it wasn't a rhetorical question. Owen nodded.

"Completely," he responded. Alex looked at the clock on the little table. Her time was almost up.

"OK. Let's start here. One week without drinking?" she asked. Owen nodded.

"One week," he agreed. "And then we need to carry on with your story."

Alex stood up and wiped her face with her sleeve. She was ready.

"Bring it on," she said, feeling something stirring in her, an old resolve that she hadn't felt since she was very young. Owen grinned and held his hand out and she took it hard, shaking it with a new determination. She thanked Owen as she walked through the door, and as she went down the stairs and out, she saw things differently. It was all her choice, and Alex had been too far, come through too much, to let herself fall again.

Gardening in the Dark

Chapter Nineteen

And it is with a deep breath, a breath that fills lungs of stuffy air and replaces them with promise, that she walks down the concrete path away from the red building for the last time. Stuart is waiting for her, somewhere behind those trees that have changed from summer to autumn colours. Her face is pale, her arms and legs a little too thin, but her mind is robust and full with pinks and yellows.

She has said her quiet goodbyes, thanking those members of staff who have stayed with her throughout, lifting her up, bringing her back down; helping her to learn about a middle ground. A road travelled by many others before her. While she cannot feel sorrow about leaving, she is not sad to have come. She has learned an infinite number of things.

She walks purposefully, her head held up high. She is walking away. She turns for a last long look at the red brick building, and thinks she can catch glimpses of ghosts in each window. She sees Doreen, looking longingly out at the grass, studying the way her garden below the window moves in the slight breeze. Doreen picks out peonies and conifers, the light greens, oranges and plush reds vying for attention.

Alex looks to the smoking room window, and sees Lois rocking, and imagines the mumbled monologue streaming from her lips. She catches sight of the bedraggled hair and black velvet of her sleeve, and smiles to herself. She thinks of Gary, sitting in the corner of the same room, multiple cigarettes hanging from his mouth, thinking of his mother and perhaps grinning to himself about some of the adventures they had shared. She imagines the numerous women in their various cubicles, straightening their sheets and gazing at walls which offer up pictures only they can see, of lost loves and tragedies and memories.

She sees the ghosts of a thousand people walking the grounds, trudging up and down beside their temporary guardians, eagerly looking down the path to find relatives and friends. She imagines them whispering and pointing, walking to and fro, a thousand different outfits from different generations. Alex shudders suddenly and turns to a window on the first floor, her eyes searching out a figure which owns as much prominence in her mind as her own thoughts.

He is there, a shy smile on his face, watching her walk away. He lifts a hand in a gesture of farewell, the slope of his shoulders showing some sort of hope as she catches his eye. He looks beautiful, and lost, and Alex imagines he is reflecting herself back to her. She looks at the twist of humour in his smile as he grins. She thinks of the taste of his lips on hers; a tang of Lithium, a wisp of cigarette smoke, the last bitter traces of vodka on his breath. She breathes him in from where she stands, filling her lungs with the scent of lemony soapy freshness that seems to exude from his skin. He is untainted by the ghosts, the smells, and the routine of the hospital. He walks freely through the bars on the windows, traces his way along corridors that can not restrict his mind. He will be out, soon, following this path that she is about to walk.

She will wait for him, here, on the outside. She loves him.

*

On the way back home, Alex stops off at a church. She sits outside the building, feeling the rough-hewn stones behind her back for a while. She feels new. She walks to a gravestone at the end of a long line of plots. It is overgrown with wild flowers, and has begun to lean a little as if it is settling into itself. Plain and grey, it reminds Alex of Maggie. Wild geraniums twist and weave along the stone, crowning it with splashes of pink. A holly is springing up from the side, prickly and beautiful at the same time. Alex looks down at the stone and imagines her mother lying beneath, looking up, stirred and awoken by the rush of love emanating from the surface of her resting place.

"I'm sorry you didn't have the choices that I have found," she says under her breath. "I'm sorry I lost you before I grew strong enough to help you change. I'm angry with you, but I forgive you. I'm sorry I didn't know you well enough to allow us to be friends. I'm sorry it took me thirty years to understand. I love you."

Gardening in the Dark

Alex pauses, taking in huge breaths of fresh air and looking about her with new eyes, eyes that are suddenly rid of the clouds which have misted them for so long. She suddenly knows what clarity is. She turns around and walks back through the churchyard, looking at the path. The road in front of her seems suddenly perfectly clear. She strides forward with a new purpose.

Somewhere in the past, a young girl with bruised arms, and eyes shadowed from crying, looks up. She is sitting in the corner of her bedroom, rocking backwards and forwards holding her knees. Beyond the myriad of voices in her head that threaten her with losing strength, with fading and wanting to fall into oblivion, something new seems to catch hold. She hears a louder voice, like her own but strong and sure. It is kind.

"Hang on in there. I'm coming to get you," the voice says. Ally looks up into the middle distance, and seems to understand.

*

Alexandra was running. She was gliding across fields, along paths; her heart was pounding in her chest as if it were running too, faster and faster. Her breath came in gasps, shallow and too quick, not pulling enough air in to sustain her legs, her arms, moving like pistons, propelling her forwards. She was almost horizontal, the noise in her head pushing her forward, dragging her body with it, trying to keep up with the thoughts that raced through her mind, the images, the memories which jostled and pushed for attention, in flight. She couldn't run hard, fast enough to escape herself. She thought, If I push myself just a bit harder, go faster, faster, I will outrun me. She ran in a circle, understanding that she would pass memories of herself, and then ran in a straight line, through the field, on to the pavement, past people who turned to stare. This felt like insanity, but liberating and incredible. She was desperately alive. The rhythm of it coursed through her blood. Her whole being was reduced to the beat of her heels on the path. She *was* flight. She was life embodied, the corporeal amazing beauteous thrill of existence. She was electricity and light, she was sustenance and energy. She was everything. She felt the world enter her, rape her, and remain behind, inside her. She was all. She ran so fast that her feet left the ground at points. She was a wild animal. She was blood and sex and rage. She was pure energy, measurable in joules. She was Alex plus.

Everyone has to stop running.

Spent, exhausted, powered out, she stopped running. Her body returned upright, her chest expanding and contracting, her lungs greedily soaking in air as rapidly as they could. Her body caught up. Her mind turned, acknowledged it, and then ran on. She stood in the centre of the street, her arms lifted to the stars, and screamed a raw, guttural outpouring of emotion. She called out, and the world answered back. She turned on her heel, her legs weightless beneath her, and returned the way she had run, oblivious to the glances and whispers of those around her.

She came to a halt, and looked about her. Colours were both bright and dull. The air was both fresh and tainted. She married black and white together, and found something better than grey.

Somewhere Martin would be sitting and watching the clock, waiting for the time when he would walk down the concrete path and out of the wrought-iron gates. They would do it together. They had learned how to run, but also to walk. They would find the road less travelled.